'You don't know me but…

'You don't know me but…

Eric Lund

Eric Lund Publishing
2018

First Printing: 2018

ISBN 978-0-9964656-2-5

Eric Lund Publishing
P.O. Box 345
Greenville, CA. 95947

Dedication

To my father Richard James Lund, 1915 – 2006

Allowed to pick our fathers I would have chosen mine.
   role model toughness, but you need toughness to survive
His principles and values were the best.
He understood people. This didn't block empathy, it enhanced it.
And his being fully human gave life feeling and meaning.
                    always beneath everything was love
   Hoping this book makes you proud Dad.

Table of Contents

Acknowledgements

I would like to thank family and friends whose help provided me with the time to complete this book.

Aunt Mary

Uncle Leon

Uncle David & Charmaine

Yvonne & Bob Camen

Thaumaturgical

My son Roland's musical taste bothers me. Not so much that its bad, which, unfortunately it is, as the type of bad. It all slides to the saccharine. Whether it's what I'd call soft rock, country, or pop (though whatever the supposed genre, it never goes beyond pop as far as I can judge), it's the sort of music that, when I was young, I quickly labeled 'fake'. Maybe it's his age. He's only 14. Maybe in the future he'll be glad he had these preferences, as I have no doubt these acts will be reconstituted, playing in Las Vegas until they expire. Shows featuring their own hits, hits of the era, hits from associated eras before and after. Paeans of evocative nostalgic: remember the music of your youth, artificial efforts to begin with, which your poor taste allowed to become signifiers, squeezed now for all they're worth. The musicians, punished though paid, for inflicting this fluff, forced to play the same song 10,000 times. Why can't he listen to groups that are fueled by youth – edgy, hip; bands that will quarrel and break up; then ten years later, having run through the money, reunite for a tour?

I know that good taste doesn't vouchsafe that those with it will be trustworthy, intelligent, or loving. Some of the nicest and best people I've ever known had kitschy taste. And how variable is taste? We know couples who adore antique furniture, derive a rich feeling not only from family pieces but pieces they've gone out and bought; and other couples, their equals in intelligence, who regard the idea of filling a house's interior with antiques as a prelude to depression. One view isn't right and the other wrong. Another example I can think of is what does a person's favorite color really mean? I know there are periodic efforts to break that down into universal indicators but I've never found them convincing. Or I react to a movie as riveting and my wife derives nothing from it.

You might think I'd be grateful my son isn't into heavy metal, hip hop, or punk; impatiently awaiting the day that he's old enough to brand himself with nihilistic tattoos without our permission. And it's true I probably don't have to worry about the designer amphetamines he'll imbibe in order to trance dance all night to machine-drum-pounding repetitiveness. But I'm truly perplexed. Where did Roland's peculiar taste, or lack of taste, come from? Not from Vicki certainly. And not from me. It's funny, I think I was braced for anything, any sort of rebellion, but not a child with oddly bad taste. I know you could twist this around and say this is all you left your child to challenge you with. But that's a cliché that doesn't apply here. Besides being lame is not an assertion.

I expected: 'Hey Dad the world has moved on. Your music is so stale. Want to hear something that's today? Check this out.' Then, after I tried but failed to get it, he would shake his head and smile, as I had done with my parents. I was primed for that eventuality. I know we have limited capacities. We can only take so much - then we're filled up. We're deeply imprinted with our idea of music that moves and means something – emotionally – to us. Anything that differs from what we treasure we'll find discordant. When Roland was an infant I wondered if I would be able to meet the challenge, stretch, perceive new modes that struck me at first as alien but that he tuned into, found vital, and capturing his zeitgeist. Would I prove too rigid, demand adherence to the structures I grew up with and understood? But there's no challenge to treacle.

He's young but what is striking about the soloists and groups he likes is their emphasis, and I would say self-consciousness, about performance. That what they're doing is an 'act'. Far from covering this up – they make it overt, as if the physical actions were as important as the songs. It's in line with all these shows on TV (which Roland enthusiastically watches) that have aspiring amateurs auditioning to impress judges and viewers that they possess the ability to make it as a professional. The soloists and groups Roland likes have this same transparent openness to the fact that it's all a performance. You might say well isn't that the case - isn't that being honest? Weren't the earlier attempts to come across as genuine more of a fake, since in fact every time someone performs for others it is a performance? Whether played live, or recorded, it's all planned, rehearsed over and over. True, yet to me there's a big difference between real and fake. This embrace of professional delivery is a defeat, an easy retreat from the higher aspirations once held, when I was young, for rock and popular song as powerful because real & truthful. I don't accept that it can't be authentic because it's all rehearsed. Stage actors rehearse and memorize their movements and lines, yet when the play opens and there's contact with an audience, if its good it comes alive.

I have nothing but respect for performing artists: musicians, singers, dancers, actors. The hours of work, the hard discipline, to raise their native ability to reach levels of excellence - virtues we should all admire and reward. But to recognize and support their achievement is one thing. To confuse it with creative art, the living inspiriting form, is a mistake. They further the work of others, but what a writer, painter, sculptor, or composer does in creating something new, is not a difference of degree, but of kind. It's the difference between creation and use. I'm afraid my son is one of those, and they may be the majority, who not only can't tell the difference, but to whom making such a distinction is splitting hairs. To me there's an association of confusing creation with performance and entertainment with art. As if it's all equal and interchangeable. This is a boy who was exposed to cultural quality. But to him nimble performance, checking off a list of gestures with a polish of slickness, is quite admirable.

I feel compelled to volunteer, though you might find this irrelevant, that Roland is an only child. We never planned it that way. It's just how life unspooled. We found his baby period all-consuming. We thought this would change but then his toddler period turned out to be equally all-consuming. The same with all the changes that were thrown at us during Elementary and Middle School. Now he's in the midst of adolescence and we feel like it's too late. Neither of us has the energy or inclination to start all over again. (We both come from normal size families.) Anyway what effect would a baby sibling have on him now? None. I can imagine what you're thinking. This fellow and his wife are cliché type A parents. Over-indulgent, obsessively involved; emphasizing/magnifying early achievement; the pressure of high expectations mixed with excessive praise and reward. Parental interference sure to make the child spoiled and neurotic. I can't even argue this estimate is wrong - sometimes I feel it captures the pattern we fell into. So when I ask myself where the rebellion is, I am also asking myself would his identity and tastes have been sharpened if he had been forced to establish himself against brothers and sisters? Competing but also learning to share. At this point though I'd settle for a few close friends. Like a lot of only children

Roland seems more comfortable relating to adults as equals then to kids his own age. Though he is friendly - just shy and awkward.

I have some gender related worries which Vicki doesn't share. Is he too soft? Has he grown up too sensitive, weak in a way that isn't appropriate for a boy? This is another issue I never contemplated having to worry about. Even though, to be honest, I was repulsed by the idea of giving boys dolls to play with, I'm unreservedly supportive of gender equality in the workplace and at home. I'm all for the goal of men eventually sharing the housework 50:50. My worry has more to do with modern life eroding what is natural and healthy.

I was always ready to encourage any sport that caught his fancy, but he never showed an interest in anything athletic. Splashing about in the pool doesn't count. He always seemed turned off by group sports, as if they were stupid activities only indulged in by the foolish who didn't appreciate the risk of getting hurt. Its possible all this was just a rationalization for being less coordinated than many of the boys his age. To be honest it also struck me as laziness, a copping out, but at a certain point I gave up trying to prod him. I told myself to respect his individuality. He always preferred video games and in them, if I'm allowed to say this, the male competitiveness did come out. Of course it's a kind of a loner recreation, removed from the outdoors, and real exercise. What was I supposed to do? I wouldn't bring this up except now, every once in a while, he will crumble in a way that seems surprisingly vulnerable and weak - more appropriate for someone half his age. It's kind of alarming, to both Vicki and me. Doubts plague us whenever we read about overly protective parents. We're apprehensive about his whiny behavior but what do we do at this late date? It's not just the emotional meltdowns, his aims and interests also seem squishy. But that could be normal for his age. All of it could be normal for the modern urban male. Maybe I, as a father, have to recalibrate and accept an evolving norm. After all he's turned out okay. Despite the occasional tantrum and whining he's not really depressed or disturbed. We were spared having to deal with the real problems some parents are dealt – attention deficit or autism. He's relatively happy and stable, and if most American teenagers don't appreciate their luck, in their affluent advantages, I actually think Roland does.

All this is a much too long preliminary to get to when Roland asked me about LP's, 'back in the day'. I was surprised, and pleased. Not simply because I'd have a chance to slip in sharp remarks comparing my music to his syrup, prods to possibly widen his horizons, but also because this might be one area where I'd have a shot at impressing him. The old stereo system was something I knew. Of course when he was little I got to play Mr. Answer Man all the time. Lately, to my chagrin, when I've started to pitch in and help him with his homework, halfway in, I find myself unsure, trying to remember facts and solutions I used to know. I tell myself I'm just rusty - if I could brush up, properly prepare, things would start coming together. Yes I may be kidding myself. Roland grows impatient but he knows I want to help. He may also sense that I miss the role I once played and the way he used to look up at me.

I never considered myself an audiophile. However I did know several guys who by any standard would have qualified. I'm not just crudely throwing out 'guys' here - all the ones I knew really were guys. And they all possessed this intimidating certainty.

They'd start speaking of 'acoustic' spaces, treble and base ranges, asking you if you couldn't hear the differences, and you were compelled to defer to them. (As most of us do now with wine experts or gourmets. We can't detect these fine distinctions - but we believe/trust they can. Specialists able to perceive things we can't. Persuasively. People who were probably born with an exceptional sense, which encouraged them to develop and refine it further.) Often the audiophiles would play the same piece of music, either rock or classical, to demonstrate which speakers handled a particular aspect of sound better. I would find myself nodding my head, though I wasn't sure I really discerned the differences they did. I say this even though I think I have a pretty good ear. But I was proud of the system I ended up assembling. I held out for an Acoustic Research turntable, even though you couldn't stack on it (the audiophiles told me only Philistines stacked). A Shure stylus. A Harmon Kardon receiver that was way too powerful for any space I was likely to inhabit. And two Infinity speakers able to cope with the receiver. I tried to impress girls with the system, but to be honest, they were always more interested in checking out what was in my record collection.

To set the spirit of the age I told Roland how the album covers played a commensurately larger role in our experience of the music. Frequently, maybe absent-mindedly, we'd study the front, or back, of these covers as we listened. And whereas his generation cherry picks only appealing songs to store and play on their mobile devices, the only guys I knew who did something similar owned reel-to-reel tape recorders. Which seemed a lot of bother. Most of us tended to play whole 'sides', even suffer through songs that weren't our favorites, in order to get to numbers that were. Otherwise you were constantly bouncing up and down. And it wasn't easy to land the needle precisely at the start of a track. Vinyl not only warps, it scratches, and if you kept doing this you ran the risk of damaging the record and the needle. And maybe one couldn't absorb the artist or group for who they were if you didn't endure the weaker tracks along with the stronger.

As it was presumed pertinent to why particular equipment excelled over other equipment, in the course of following the audiophiles' arguments, I acquired a fairly detailed knowledge of the underlying technology, with all its rationales. When Roland was real young his ability to put models together was remarkable. I'm a little abashed to think of it now, but back then it was a great source of (exaggerated) pride and encouragement, as he pretty quickly conquered every challenge. Only later did it dawn on me that this sort of intelligence was a narrow one, and I regretted going as overboard as I had. Though in the long run I'm not sure it would have mattered. Anyway knowing his proclivity to puzzle out the mechanics, I tried to give him a complete breakdown on the old stereo equipment. Hoping to impress of course. I started back with Edison, designing instruments sensitive enough to register the quiverings of sound: engraving spiral markings on a turning wax cylinder. Eventually producing a 'record' of this captured sound. Then he invented the phonograph to play these records. A needle to register the vibrations, the modulations, in the grooves of the circulating disc. Sending them to the 'pickup' in its cartridge. The pickup as the transducer that converted the mechanical waverings into electric signals. Then an amplifier would build the force back up, and it would get translated back – through the speakers - in a version of the original.

This had all been an analog process. But I told Roland I had no problem with the new digital method, with sound broken down to bits (bytes?) of knowledge, sent in that form, and decoded by a modern player. I prefer the laser light reading-without-touching over a needle and the damage it wears. I should note that several of the audiophiles I've mentioned strongly dissent. They have endless reasons why digital is inferior, and go on at length about all the essential elements getting lopped off in the process. Swearing of course that they can hear it. With my more mortal hearing I'm dubious. To me it seems an attachment to the past. Can't an emotional attachment to an old familiar process, when a new one comes along to replace it, influence what a person (what they imagine they detect), a flaw that isn't really there? Granting that sometimes, for commercial reasons, something inferior is inserted to replace something superior. But here the audiophiles were so invested, so knowledgeable, about the intricacies of the old system, it's not surprising that they'd have trouble letting go. Maybe they can hear a difference between analog and digital. But it's like the wine connoisseur able to tell you what side of what mountain the grapes were grown on. Impressive, but not really relevant, if we're honest. Because I've always bowed to their superior perception I occasionally wonder if they aren't right. I'm surprised they're still able to get components, yet it seems a doomed resistance. At some point all the music available will only be available in digital form, no CDs or records, and then what will they do? They should probably invest their energy in seeing how digital could be improved, how its capture could be more complete - enhanced.

Anyway as I was describing the action of the old record-player to Roland I imagined traversing the grooves, seeing them as you would if you were in a low flying, fast moving helicopter, like some of those scenic travelogues on TV. I happened to imagine passing over steep Southwestern canyon walls. Below an unseen river coursed, or had coursed in the geological past. The varying roughness on the sides of the canyon walls were the Braille oscillations the needle needed to vibrate and thereby register the profile of the music. Such rich complexity. I thought of what the needle was doing, and for some reason the term 'the magic needle' popped into my head. I didn't say it out loud, I continued my discourse to Roland on the marvels of the old technology. But at that precise moment I ceased to believe in any of it the way I had believed in it. I realized later this was the consummation of all the subconscious doubt that I had had building up on accepted explanations for how physical processes work. Though it took a while for the all the ramifications to settle in, to figure out what I now thought, my pulling away from accepting belief was tripped at that precise moment.

Modern presumption about the laws of nature of course are that they have always been what they are, from the beginning, though we incrementally learn what they are, like a paleontologist carefully scraping and brushing levels at the side of a gorge. Discovering one fossil piece at a time, slowly putting a specimen together, figuring out its family, what branch it belongs to, and its time frame. So modern humanity assumes the laws of our world have always been as they are, and could never have been violated (plus there's nothing to do the violating).

In the history of civilizations there have always been individuals with a rational bent, stressing the logical and provable, even if the prevalence of what we might call the modern scientific view has only held sway for a few centuries. Entertain this idea: if the laws and matter of the world aren't as we think, i.e. fixed and solid, with everything always as we find it now, but flexible, a reprogrammable construct. The only constant might be that people, of every time and place, always accepted the concreteness of their reality. A version the elect subscribed to, but it also had to be accepted by the masses. If different people had different worlds, if it was that subjective, who would catch on? Each would have the appearance of substantiality. Each would have its own expected consistency. Only when you had something as dramatic as the Aztecs or Incas encountering the Spanish would one world have to give way to another. That might be rare. I began to peel away from the modern belief that there was only one world and it has always been as it is. From my experience I would recommend keying on *appearance* as a way to get disenthralled.

We think of the history of discovery as: 'We don't know.' We don't know. 'We don't know.' eventually followed by: 'We found out!' We found out!' We found out!' The belief is that we will discover facts about the phenomenal world as we progress but the world isn't changing, we're simply learning what we didn't know. What if that's all wrong? What if it's all been arranged? And a more apt description would be a magician on stage, correcting gauging what the audience expects, what will engage them, what they will miss, and what will convince them? We're that audience. What if the evidentiary objects our scientists analyze so carefully and come to momentous judgments on are fake stage props the Magician has manufactured? No, this is not screed for Intelligent Design or any religious doctrine. And I am not off my rocker. (I know it's just my word.)

I am neither ignorant of, nor an enemy of science. I appreciate all the knowledge humanity's gathered through science and technology, and the advances these gains have afforded. As I've tried to explain, specifically around stereo equipment, it's not because I don't know the principles underlying the technology. I do know them. Further I admire their brilliance. I know the theories and the mechanical explanations for how things function. They're very good: thorough, precise, integrated and comprehensive. And they work! I just don't buy that they are the ultimate answer any more. They are surface answers, misleading surface answers. Necessarily plausible and believable, allowing the performance to be taken at face value. I think it's a con though. I'm now convinced that everything we see has been deftly conjured and created thaumaturgically. That is by miracle magic. It's important that you understand what I'm saying. Since what I sense comes by way of intuition I have to plead with you to engage your own intuition in order to follow. Things coordinate with each other, they have a certain equality; but just because they have distribution and order doesn't mean they have real substance.

Let me reiterate, its not for example that I doubt if one researched current acoustic knowledge, and the mechanical engineering step-by-step explanation, that you wouldn't find a detailed description of how the equipment is able to map sound. You definitely would. What I am saying is that all of this is mustered after the phenomenon. And I go beyond that to assert this is true of everything. Whatever the needed manifestation is, its entry – placement - comes first. Then the various plausible 'hows' get fabricated. Since the objective is to trick, convince us, they are made to fit in with everything else. This is possible because all that we take as concrete is more like projected images than anything substantial. It's just that in a world of nothing but images or holograms, that's good enough. The product gives a convincing impression of solidity because there's nothing around with real substance to compare it to. So what I'm asking you to do with your intuition is go beyond the appearance of the demonstration, with all its 'age', 'consistent' and 'logical' aspects to *feel* the presence of empty illusion. To tune into that quality of the manufactured, the fake.

It was after this breakthrough (though I have to laugh, knowing you will see it as a breakdown) that I gradually began confirming to myself what I no longer held - or bought. All the so-called reasonable and obvious explanations for phenomena. Excellent as they all are. The ground must have been prepared beforehand beneath my conscious awareness. Doubt about 'scientifically' proven certainties must have been building for some time, a spreading skepticism, a growing suspicion that the cover story was too pat. All the neat little answers and formulas – presented like a finished jigsaw puzzle, still had a made up quality. An aspect more like a model, or 'virtual simulation', than the separate completed world it was trying to pass itself off as. Yes I know there are mental disorders, like the capgras delusion, where the afflicted come to disbelieve their world, imagine that imposters have substituted for all the people they knew - but they will not be tricked. But follow this distinction – that what I'm asserting concerns only the material, not being or beings. Since I don't consider being a physical quality or substance I'll turn things around and ask you is it impossible to imagine real beings marooned in what is in essence a virtual reality? I've affirmed all the proffered explanations work. (In their narrow little spheres.) The rationales are ingenuous and the puzzle pieces fit. I've even admitted they have my awed admiration. Their seamlessness is what makes the contention that it's all false so difficult. But doubts had eroded my acquiescence, and when, after not thinking about record players for years, I was engaged in explaining to Roland how the 'magic needle' did its job, it happened that I snapped out of the hypnotic state.

I need to reassure you again that mine is not some pathetic reaction or rejection of modernity and humanity's accumulation of knowledge. I'm thankful for our conditions, and I include in this the apparent solidity. That when I step on the ground my foot doesn't pass through it. Or modern innovations, like the exponential growth in the capacity of computer chips. I just see it all as part of the production, as something added (and to my mind, as I will explain, in a hurried improvised fashion) to accomplish a necessary task, allow scheduled developments in human life.

I've been fascinated by the discoveries in science my whole life; the wonderful logic and competence of the scientific method. I write this as someone who was totally convinced of the airtight rationality of testing every hypothesis; the conditional nature of every theory; testing done by separate parties to check results. Roland inherited his disposition from me, albeit his curiosity and imagination are narrower, more task directed. I was the kid who pestered his parents to get him a telescope. Then a chemistry set. Finally a microscope. I was the one who read National Geographic from cover to cover as soon as it arrived. I devoured books on animals, geography, geology, astronomy, and anatomy. Unlike some of my classmates, I loved Biology class. I got straight A's in the sciences. It was solely by chance that I ended up as a (small) businessman. None of Vicki's brothers wanted to run the family business, and it was too obviously a golden opportunity to let it pass.

No one can get an outside perspective because we're all inside the production. We can't peek behind the curtain because the curtain is everything we observe. But let's say we could. We wouldn't spy a wizard of Oz, an ordinary fellow manipulating gadgets to give a magnified impression of great power and control, in order to create intimidated awe in his subjects. No I'm suggesting the opposite, with an opposite response as the goal. A Wizard of All if you like, with unlimited power, using his ability to conceal the power and control, even to conceal his existence - and role. Indeed to hide the nature of the operation. That there is an operation.

Now I couldn't blame you if at this juncture you were to pull back, and say that's enough. Suspecting either I was some kind of nut, sure his fantasy was reality, or that my game was really all a set-up as a proselytizer for some religious view. If the latter the figure of the magician would be a mere stand-in for God, in a kind of fundamentalist context. For whatever my word is still worth let me assure you that I'm not mad, nor am I out to recruit you for a religious affiliation I've been hiding.

The way I see the modern West, people – and thought – divide into two principal groups. One I would call materialistic. Led by people who would call themselves rational and scientific and secular. They are convinced that the only things that exist are what we can prove through physical tests. So materialists dismiss all that is called 'spiritual' as imaginary; as coming from superstition built on neediness. Only the material is verifiable, only the verifiable is real. To them the brain (and the body) aren't necessary instruments in this world. We are a brain. End of story.

While materialists regard the spiritual with condescension, and think of themselves as exemplifying the rational and scientific, they ignore two curious gigantic holes. The first is why is there anything? There should be nothing. The second concerns the very peculiar nature of this universe, which every physicist worth his salt knows doesn't make sense. Why should it be slanted towards cohesion? Why the fortuitous temperatures; distribution of matter; the molecular inclination towards elements and chemical combinations; motion and rest? The equilibrium and stability in the macro and micro systems. For example why doesn't the electron either fly away or collapse in? What are the odds that the elements and conditions of our universe could establish themselves this way randomly? If you're honest you know the answer is as close to zero as its possible to get.

So then we have a second group, which you will have guessed I include myself in, which are made up of people open to explanations that go beyond the physical. Maybe we don't believe our ancestors, for all they didn't know, were complete idiots. They dealt with life and death, maybe in a grittier way then we do. Belief in the soul and a next life come from as far back as we can go, and from every part of the globe. This on its own wouldn't be enough but for many of us it resonates with our own sense of what the essence of life is. The fact that we can't prove the spiritual in a materialistic test, to those who demand evidence that is material, is not our problem. The idea of being transcendent, survivable, would entail not being material. This won't persuade the materialistic, who dismiss such arguments as sophistry - and absurd. What really hampers the spiritual though isn't the sniping by skeptics, even in our modern scientific age, but ancient doctrines that come in and claim you must bow to their particular (often archaic) precepts.

However in the East there is a completely different perspective, which provides an alternative to the Magician, for those of you still worried that I'm using him as a stalking horse. I should be clear it's not the belief of the ordinary people, rather the belief of the highest initiates of the Hindu and Buddhist traditions, who have been dealing with consciousness not for centuries, but millennia. They hold that the soul comes first. The world, its matter and energy, is an illusion that the soul projects. If allowed we might extrapolate that in place of one First Cause(r) you could have a collective projection from the collective unconsciousness. An analogy is the dream. Inside a dream we don't usually know it's a dream no matter how strange it gets. It isn't until we awaken that we realize it was a world we had created. Eastern wisdom may not have the whole answer, or answers, but it fills a gap the West lacks. The participation of the living in Creation. With your permission I'll go on using the Magician figure, now that we're agreed it's not to be taken literally, simply because its easier for me to write, and you to imagine, a single mover, rather than a looping collective projection. (Though I do believe, for efficiency's sake, that a collective consciousness could unify into a single actor.)

As I drew away from acceptance of the normal view of the world as solid and heavy I began to see it more as appearance and a construct. When I look back at the evolution of my thought, though the tipping point occurred when I was explaining to Roland the details of the record-needle-pick up system, most of the groundwork that prepared my disbelief came from my long interest in astronomy. I should add, in case you don't know, that modern astronomy ties in with and relies on modern physics.

When I first announced my interest in astronomy, long before my parents bought me a telescope, my father legitimately wanted to test if this was a genuine interest or an idle passing fad. Prudently therefore he took me to a used bookstore to buy my first book on the subject. This in hindsight I see as a great break. Because the book I got, which was quite good in many respects, was an outdated textbook. (It was post-Hubble, so the writers did know the universe was expanding.) Because it was passé it allowed me to see how presumed conceptions – big conceptions – voiced with authority and reason, could, in a relatively short amount of time get tossed aside as completely wrong.

The predominant view at the time of publication, and obviously subscribed to by the compilers of the book, was 'steady state'. It held that the universe had existed for an infinite amount of time in the past, and would go on for an infinite amount of time in the future. Even the amount of matter that existed had probably always been the same. This view of the universe in some respects could be traced back to Aristotle. Probably only because of Hubble's surprising observation of galaxies traveling away from us, their distance and speed linked, did the 'Big Bang' theory merit mention. But only as a very far out fringe idea. (The term, Big Bang, was actually coined by a detractor, Hoyle, one of the proponents of steady state. It was an attempt to ridicule this theory as obviously absurd on its face.) This made a deep impression on me. Something so basic to humanity's comprehension of the cosmos that surrounds us, getting turned upside down in what was really just a few short years.

It's important that I not mislead you. I didn't see through the facade, intellectually grasp what I now think is going on. No, for a long time it was only a vague sense of a process removed from our direct view and that feeling of witnessing a performance. It had a decided slant, so presumably a purpose. Think about how we see things. We assume things have to be as they are, and function on their own. When we're occasionally impressed, discovering something remarkably beautiful and intricate, we again assume it's always been like this; we simply hadn't penetrated all the way. If I hope to explain what the 'magic needle' moment tapped I need to emphasize the feeling that preceded and pushed me to that culmination. Before anything conscious, the feeling – a sort of suspicion - arose that it was all a performance. A sense that behind everything going on in our world; with all its chaos, multiplicity, competing interests; some things – or everything - was rigged. Conceding that every specific part would contain its own rational back story, there was still a being fed what we expected, with events too pat. So before the 'magic needle' pushed me awake and I broke through, I had been having this drifting along intuition that the show was false. Not just specific phenomena but their origination also. I know how this sounds, but I believe now that that intuition was correct.

Long before I caught on to what my responses signified, or were leading to, I would read about the latest discovery, and it would make me smile, with a distinct 'that's very clever' nod of appreciation. In other words without being conscious of it I was reacting as I would to the execution of an ingenious stunt, a successful trick. Why was I reacting that way? Think of the ultimate astronomical/physics questions and the answers we hold as true today. Help yourself to an 'incompleteness' theorem and for dessert have an 'uncertainty' principle. What centers the galaxies? Ah, it's black holes. Couldn't see them before? Well of course not. They're black holes! Endlessly collapsing points of negation, sucking everything in, including light. (The mathematical formulation was back there under all those stacks of papers on relativity.) Stops questions. The Magician has no trouble producing intricate interactive parts and causes, and making them universal. Complete with all the math & experimental details anyone could ask for. Whatever innovation is discovered is also instantly placed in the past so it looks like it was there forever.

Occasionally the Magician takes obscure theories that have been discarded, lying around abandoned, that happen to suit whatever his current purpose might be. Recall that Max Plank, the inventor of quantum, only came up with it as a temporary place-holder, to allow him to complete his radiation law. Quanta, a packet of energy, statistically estimated, was simply a bridge until it could be replaced by some real answer. Plank never thought, 'quanta, hey that's it!' But our hypothetical Magician scrounging around, came across it, and thought "Yeah, why not?"

Or take the famous story about Paul Dirac, the eccentric physicist. Always held up as an example of pure mathematics showing the way, on his own he figured out the existence of antimatter a year before it was discovered. How brilliant! But I no longer believe that was the sequence. It's true Dirac was playing with different formulas, and in the process he came across the possibility that there could be a thing such as antimatter. But what really happened I believe was that it appeared useful to the Magician, so it was adopted and implemented. It might be more accurate to say Paul Dirac helped create antimatter, rather then saying he discovered it.

New discoveries are coming all the time. What explains the body of the universe, hanging together in galaxy clusters and super clusters? Ah, it's dark matter. Can't see it? Well of course you can't. It's *dark* – it doesn't react with anything we know, we don't presently know what it is. Stick around, surely the answer will both astound and convince. You won't be able to resist applauding. What else? Yes dark matter is only 23% of the universe. Now that might not impress until you realize everything we react with and know is only 4%.

In 1998 we stumble upon what constitutes the rest, the governing 73% majority of the universe: *dark* energy. What I love about dark energy, besides of course it's being undetectable, is that, because it's a quality of space, its density level never changes. (Anyone who remembers 'C-field' from the steady state theory, award yourself a gold star.) If we took an area of space that in a given time doubled in size, you'd expect, whatever the negative pressure or positive energy was, that it's going to be diluted – probably end up being half of what it was. Or say if you're a contrarian, you'd expect it to double, along with the volume. No, the density level stays exactly the same. How neat is that? Like everything else it tends to make sense if you start with the belief that it *must* make sense.

Readers who've stayed with me this far might be curious what of these iconoclastic musings will I share with my son Roland? If I'm honest the answer is none. My modest hopes for him are based on the sort of intelligence he's displayed his whole life. You may reflect if you like on the absolute confidence I have that he will never run across this essay, even though its written by his father - available to anyone online. He doesn't read anything he wasn't assigned to write a report on. Let alone think – reflect on - philosophy, the meaning of life or ethics; or challenging what is accepted. His mind is directed towards practical science or technology. Possibly engineering. I hope his grades will get him into MIT or Cal Tech. I'm certainly not saying that there aren't kids at these institutions capable of juggling philosophy or free ranging thought experiments along with their studies. I am saying that my son is not one of them. Like most people he finds it more comfortable to memorize rather than to question.

None of this stems from any fear that he might cross me off if he believed I'd gone nuts. You have to trust me on this. He'd likely have a predictable reaction of: well Dad's foolish speculations finally led him into science fiction. Roland was always intended to end in the rational/science/materialist camp. I know he'll always love his old Dad no matter what nutty ideas his old Dad happens to embrace.

While most likely he'd dismiss my thoughts out of hand, my fear is planting anything that might shake his drive - his studies and career. Anything that even subconsciously might undermine his certainty. I want him to be successful. Yes in a conventional way. He needs that to be to be happy. To marry a nice gal, probably as deficient in imagination as he is. If I had another kid, and this kid was different, I can honestly imagine enjoying sharing my thoughts no matter the reaction. A kid like Roland needs confidence. All his life he has relied on there being order and answers in whatever task he was set on. He was good in mathematics, up to a certain point. Same with chemistry, same with physics. He depends on following set procedures. 'Group think' is not something he worries about. On the other hand not being with his group might cause panic.

Admission

I think from the outside I would appear fairly successful, confident, maybe proud. Drives an expensive car. Owns a nice house in a nice neighborhood. I think I could get away with saying dresses well. Has a good job of course. One that affords a lot of travel. The fact that I don't actually enjoy traveling, and really dread the longer international flights, doesn't affect the image. (I'm actually more of a homebody: gardening, attempting recipes. Even the restaurants I frequent fall within a pretty close radius of home.)

The point of this memoir is to profile a complex I suffered from - a psychological block. I'm hoping to describe how it manifested, how it grew, and eventually, very late in the day, how I opened my eyes, recognized the pit I'd fallen into, and my attempt to deal with it and recover. At its greatest magnitude I couldn't admit I was wrong. It pretty much poisoned all my personal relations. This condition stretched over many years believe it or not, and even though it was transparent to me, was very comprehensive. It didn't matter if it was something trivial, where a simple 'excuse me' would have sufficed. Or a transgression so grave that any normal person would have instinctively - automatically felt compelled to offer an apology. All were blocked. You should understand that in this condition I couldn't see that I was reacting peculiarly. Though I would never have been so brazen as to say 'I don't make mistakes', as each incident occurred I managed to find a way to shoot it down as not my fault. Any intelligent person should have detected the pattern. But the truth is I didn't.

After I did recognize it, and was beginning to pull free, a picture representing the condition gradually formed in my mind. Strangely enough it was of a dam. I was the dam. A giant construction with massive walls. It was probably because a dam, having a job to do, holds back a great volume, and is stuck in place. There could be no concessions, because any admitted mistake constituted a crack in the wall. Any crack could spread – imperiling the whole structure. So they couldn't be allowed. And the crazy logic went if you didn't acknowledge their existence they wouldn't exist. Pathologies don't need to be rational.

When I say the problem was an inability to admit mistakes you must understand it wasn't conscious. If I had ever caught on to the pattern, that would have been a back door way of seeing it. Therefore the first denial, in recognition, had to be to myself. Again it wasn't that I actually considered myself infallible. If someone, in earnest, had said, 'Gosh Richard, you just don't make mistakes.' I would have said 'What are you talking about? Don't be absurd. I make mistakes all the time.' But what happened was that at any miscue there was a reflexive rejection that deflected it away from being my fault. Some excuse and/or scapegoat was pounced on. That's how it went. Dismissing occurrences one by one. If something was undeniably the result of something I'd done then it all shifted into the category of 'things happen' - that's life. Why make such a big deal out of it? Suck it up people. So it was dismissed in that way – diluted as part of the world – part of life – or as inconsequential.

An even worse avoidance tactic was turning on the party that had suffered the mistake, suspecting that they had deliberately set things up so they could play the innocent victim. I hate to even think about it, but I did this a lot. I also developed this semi paranoid attitude that the world was full of losers who had taken on the role of accusers and levelers, and they were forever scouting about for anyone who dared to stand above the crowd. Naturally my aloofness and self-confidence drew the poisoned darts of these envious inferiors. As weak as this rationalization may seem to you, perception can be obligingly pliable. I assiduously avoided looking at myself for the explanation. No, anything uncomfortable came from the misunderstandings of the small-minded and envious.

I believe my experience is valuable, not as an insight into some exotic mental condition, but as a tale of what loosening your hold on honest self-examination can forfeit. Because I believe, not counting the saints among us, that this inclination is universal. Not that I think it likely any of you reading this will have a 100% block the way I did. But you may have, or could develop a portion of it, which can still have a damaging effect.

As a model of admission, both to address what I did, and who I might have hurt, I imitated the virtual letter derived from AA and therapy. It's not virtual in the sense that you don't write it out. It's essential that you do write it out. Exactly as if you were going to send it, to whomever you're trying to reach. As if they're really going to receive and read it. And judge you. It's virtual in the sense that in some cases it can't be sent. When you can send it of course you do, but it was also designed to ameliorate the haunting relations where communication for various reasons is impossible. Either bringing it up would only make matters worse, or you've lost contact, or they are deceased. In all cases for it to work you have to be completely honest, you can't hold back.

After my father's untimely death Mom went into a tailspin. She started drinking. Apparently at some point she had made a promise to herself that she wouldn't start until the family had had dinner. I guess she thought that way it would be controlled, day's duties completed. As a family we had always had fairly late dinners: 7:00 or 7:30, 8:00, or even later. All of a sudden, in her rush to have dinner done with and get on to the booze, dinnertime kept moving forward. Until it was 5:00 or even 4:30. We weren't hungry, but that didn't matter. And she'd get sloshed every night in her room. If you knocked on the door she'd appear with this melancholic, often tear-streaked bloated face, usually unable to muster a sensible response, just something to get rid of you. The next day when I'd cautiously bring up the drinking she'd tell me some story about combating a horrible headache.

If you're thinking a church-going family should have a network of support in place, I can assure you we did. Our minister was a lovely guy. We all called him 'Wolfie'. And his calling was legit, he had real spirituality. More - he was a family friend. And in the aftermath he could not have been more solicitous and empathetic, to all of us, especially Mom. I believe it was the familiarity that undercut his ability to reach her. I think she saw him as a friend, as 'Wolfie', rather than someone speaking with the authority of the church - Jesus - and a more transcendental perspective. So he appeared to her as just another well-meaning friend who couldn't understand her grief, and didn't know more than she did. That's why his consolation and counsel weren't allowed to work.

It was her sister, my Aunt Bev, who saved her. She's as strong as Mom is weak. More typical of their family actually than Mom is. Being overbearing she badgered Mom until at last she admitted she had a problem. Then the question was well what are you going to do about it? She guided her toward AA. At first I resented Bev's intrusions. Yes we were dysfunctional, who could deny it, but it was our business. Sure Mom was depressed, but didn't she have every right to be? And I thought of AA as kind of hokey. A gimmicky association for the down and outers, the not-too-bright, and the hopeless. Basically winos. I was dismissive without knowing anything.

When I think of Aunt Bev taking charge, it calls to mind how often in life it's the abrasive person who doesn't care if they're seen as annoying - or imposing – who makes the difference. Pushy individuals who by their unrelenting wills correct things. That minority who don't overly respect decorum, and are willing to go against the grain. Whether it's challenging a powerful person, or an organization, forcing them to change an unsatisfactory response into a satisfactory one. Or, as in this case, shaking up a loved one to come to their senses. They don't care about 'making a scene'. They know what's important, and they know how people work. They'll plant themselves in a 'gatekeeper's' face until they receive a concession. Those uncomfortable with going against convention – and that's most of us – allow the status quo to go along unchallenged, even when it annoys, and we don't think its right. We shrink from sticking out. We won't pay the price. Aunt Bev wasn't intimidated by anything, and she didn't suffer from self-doubt. She was no-nonsense, sure things were as she saw them. If she saw something wrong crossing an official or disturbing some routine were of no account. So she zeroed in on stopping her sister's self-destruction. As I said she saved Mom's life.

I'd gotten my learner's permit by this time, and on night's when Bev couldn't make it, I'd drive Mom to the meetings. For me it was the opening of a crucial window into the real world. I'd led a fairly sheltered life up until Dad's illness. These AA gatherings were an introduction to adults and psychology. The people were embarrassingly honest about themselves and their lives. Any type of person can fall prey to addiction. Yes you need to be selfish – but aren't we all selfish? And alcohol is simply one of many traps. At AA you'd witness lives and personalities that covered the spectrum. All the dramatic travails: the collapses, climbs, self-deceptions and relapses. That magnetic insidious lotus of a respite, a bit of happiness, alluringly close. Yet scary – the consequences. What was at stake were people's very lives. I should add that the successes were tangible, and inspirational in a real way. A basic, hard won way. Setting the best example, because the message was: I'm no different from you, so that means you can do it too.

Ordinary people can be surprisingly perceptive and articulate in an environment that is friendly and encouraging. I think the older playwrights were aware of that and gave themselves a wider imaginative dialogue for characters, whereas modern scriptwriters pinch into terse clichés what they think that type would say. Sometimes less educated people are the most surprising in the leaps they make. If you go beneath popular phrases and study exactly what is meant, then how their speech is cut and rearranged, you find the average person, especially during emotional divestments, can be surprisingly original and expressive. And usually their listeners do understand what they're trying to get across. Often it was like folk poetry.

I am fully aware that it's easy to mock the outward forms of therapy. Pick apart points in the underlying doctrine. Inflate the procedures so you can ridicule the beliefs, and the conformity to them by the participants. Such scorn is only destructive. After all who is really being targeted? Those seeking help. People who have confessed a weakness, many with a hyper vulnerability to the opinions of others. Until you, or someone you love, is possessed by a condition that controls them, I don't think you appreciate the risk. Let that occur, when you, or someone you love, finds themselves in a hollow, unable to climb to the ridge, all your efforts ending in a rolling back to the lowest depression, and you'll cease all fussiness about any structure that can facilitate escape. Yes probably it is elementary. Should it be designed to only help the cognoscente? When you're desperate all you care about is does it work? Will it help me get out – will it save me? I regard Freud as the worst sort of imperious fraud. Yet I've known several people who benefited from classical Freudian analysis: the talking therapy. As absurd as I find the man, the method, and its rationales, for some reason it was right for them. Maybe it was the roles played by each. Or talking about themselves to a qualified professional. It fulfilled their expectations of what understanding and help would look like. A ritual that fit them. Rather like lesser religions we regard with suspicion, if we're honest we have to grant that no matter how dubious their origin and precepts, they seem to suit and comfort their believers.

Personally I still think of AA as far superior to anything else I know of. I like everything about it. The higher power can be anything you gravitate to. To me it has the genuine Christian spirit. Earned. And I happen to believe in its precepts. It's wholly unpretentious – with a democratic levelness. Problems will arise in any group made up of human beings. I'm not denying that. But I love the fact that it originated from the bottom. From sufferers, people with addiction; who found a way, in peer helping peer, to be honest and sober. It wasn't a theoretically propounded approach foisted from above by note-taking doctors.

You want to know the key to success? It's fellow AA members. Don't try to con them. They've been there. Long before you. Your excuses - lies - will be seen, nakedly, as lies. As will your self-deception - sad and pathetic. On the other side when they shower a person with sympathy and understanding, it means something. It's the compassion of shared experience. They too journeyed the spiraling cycles of hell and despondency. It's their recognition, guidance and support, that are crucial to you overcoming your addiction.

Whatever latent tendencies I might have had – the inclination to deflect away any responsibility jelled into a full-blown complex during the period of my marriage. Even if the marriage wasn't the first tip-off (there had been some grumblings before at work that I 'wasn't a team player'), it was certainly the cause that moved my default setting to denial.

I believe it arose from the role I found myself playing opposite Karen, my wife. Whatever the truth at the time I told myself I was doing it for her good. That she needed to play off a strong authority figure. I know that sounds bad. But think of it more in the sense of an athlete needing a coach to reach their peak performance. That's the spirit in which I saw it. The coach has to be relied on. You have to let him be the decision maker. His decisions can't be questioned, that undermines authority and allows doubt, which will leak the determination needed to achieve the goal. You don't want to erode that trust. While that attitude eventually hardened in every part of my life, I think it started in this relationship with Karen.

Contrary to popular belief I think most of the life altering decisions we make, speaking of the ones that turn out great disasters, don't occur when we're rushed, or oppressed, or don't have time to reflect. I think they happen in periods of tranquility, when we're lulled by some idyll to dispense with the hard discrimination we employ in our rat race striving. We're lured to try something new, expand our horizons maybe in the spirit of appreciating and enjoying life more. I was in such a mood when I fell for Karen. How could this sweet young thing, even with her transparent coyness, pose a threat to me?

Before our marriage I could never understand the guys you see on local news, or read about in the newspaper, who go berserk, shooting ex-wives or girlfriends, half the time killing themselves. I regarded them as some sort of deranged cyborgs. Different from the rest of real humanity. Thank God I never sank that low. But I no longer regard them as a different species. I understand now how attachment and dependence can grow, and how, when the relationship is ripped apart - though no doubt justly - it can produce a hateful vengeance. My attitude now is 'by the grace of God'. My insight is that the process starts with the insecure controlling husband, or boyfriend. The insecurity and the controlling go hand in hand. Therefore the man is culpable from the beginning. But the couple are entangled in something more powerful than they are. You can say its power and not love but I don't believe that's true. I think it's a twisted mix of both. That other person has become the most important person in the world to them. Not just the time and emotional investment. Or keeping up appearances. No one knows you like they do. Their defection seems like a judgment you can't survive because it constitutes a rejection of the better image of yourself you need to preserve, by the person that knows you best. It's a rejection of the whole of you. It's complete. Who could accept that? You're compelled to tell yourself she's perversely wrong. And disloyal. You work yourself into a fury over this. The story you tell yourself centers around her ungrateful betrayal; and while in that state, because you feel she's robbed you of your true self and future, you feel justified in any retaliation.

In the beginning it was inconceivable that anything Karen did, stay or go, could ever really affect me. I liked her. How could one not be interested, she was lively and pretty. She seemed eager to learn about the finer things. She acted like she was impressed by my opinions, flattered by my attention. And maybe in the beginning she really was. Then later she might have started to doubt my judgment, without letting me notice. Towards the end she was clearly indifferent. I'm convinced there was honesty, belief and goodwill at the start. From both of us. Such are the turns and tests of life. If our trials were brief excursions we could all pass with flying colors. Anyway over time she started to mean a lot more to me, and though I didn't entirely catch on to the seriousness of her disenchantment and rebellion, during this same period my feelings started to mean less and less to her.

I was eleven years older than Karen. I think this did play a part in the relationship and the role I assumed, but I don't think the age difference itself caused our problems. A lot of marriages that last and are happy, have differences, whether of age, taste, personality, which play a significant part in why the relationship works. There's a balancing. Things are kept interesting and alive. Reactions aren't shared and predictable. It adds intrigue, you keep getting surprised – pleasantly surprised. Both have to practice tolerance and accommodation. Learn to accept that you will differ. I think it's fair to say that often an older spouse will be more indulgent of the younger. Realizing some lessons take experience, and some behavior – some tastes - are linked to age. Instead of being irritated you find it engaging. (Of course I should confess this is not how I behaved.) The younger spouse in turn may forgive the rigidity of the elder's responses. Accepting that disappointments in life tend to create a protective exterior for a vulnerable core. So both sides bend towards the other, in offsetting, complementary ways.

And if we're honest, we should admit that early in a serious romance part of the intoxicating rapture comes from witnessing the power you wield over another. I don't mean in a bad manipulative sense. But beholding someone who wants to please you, who wants you to be happy, and is animated to that end. As a friend pointed out, this can easily lead to the delusion that after marriage changing that other person (of course always to 'improve' them, for their own benefit) will be a relatively easy matter.

Karen's curiosity evaporated quickly. Interest should beget interest. Not with her. A cursory knowledge more than sufficed. I should say the exception here was the visual arts, where she truly had a gift. In that sphere I always followed her instincts, which were remarkable. Everywhere else though her profound lack of interest and ambition were dispiriting. An appalling symbiosis of complacency and boredom. I'm sure she blamed me for her discontent. She seemed to always be holding herself back in reserve, waiting for me to prove something. But I couldn't – I didn't know what it was I was supposed to prove. This doesn't bring out the best in one let me tell you. More like the worst. So a matching wariness grew. If a person refuses to initiate, doesn't seem interested in anything, they're bound to find their situation stifling – though the fault is really theirs. Unhappiness while keeping a critical eye on the other became our home state. There was no way of mistaking that. But placing the fault diverged, each of us blaming the other.

In the end she fled. I don't think there is a more apt word for it. Not even a note. Of course I would have pounced on its logic and picked it apart. But she ran like you would from a tyrant. Full of self-justification I have no doubt. I didn't pursue her, I felt by her act of abandonment I ended up the party wronged. Tarred in a way. It was a devastating blow, though I tried to tell myself it wasn't. The worst part was that to overcome my emotions and doubts I kept reassuring myself that she was certain to come back, tail between her legs. And I imagined how I would lord it over her then, lambasting everything she'd done, beforehand and with the discourtesy of her departure. My imagined scenarios were disgraceful and pathetic. And of course she never came back.

Although I couldn't see it at the time she was smart in not returning. I was committed to convincing myself that I had been very unlucky to marry her, while she'd been very fortunate. She was a nobody who knew nothing. Now, in a dastardly display of ingratitude, she had thrown away her opportunity. Heavy into self-justification I couldn't admit how much her leaving hurt me. That was the reason I think I needed to believe this laughably biased version of our relationship. I couldn't acknowledge that I had treated her shabbily.

If I couldn't own up to it now though this whole exercise will be for naught. I was arrogant, my normal mode was patronizing. Controlling. I could be cold. I believed I was acting this way for her own long term development, but that's a rationalization. Still I believe a person can act like a pig and not necessarily be a pig. Certainly not be condemned to be one forever.

Thankfully humans are made of such material as allows for transformation and redemption. And a hard blow can force even the most stubborn among us re-examine how we've behaved.

There's something else I want to throw in here, though I'm not terribly confident that I can isolate it. The age old question of why a particular person has your number? Why them and not someone else? Is she, or him, in some hidden way an opposite – or the 'other'? Are they in some mysterious way a composite rearrangement of qualities you possess; or do they have qualities, or an arrangement of qualities, you lack, and that's the magnet? Why do they know your type? Could the fact that both Karen and I have mothers whom we love, but are embarrassed by, have something to do with the chemistry, when it existed?

I have known women, before and after this period, who in any objective evaluation would be granted the advantage in intelligence, taste, and beauty. Yet they never had this primal hold on me. Their vulnerabilities, while affecting, for whatever reason didn't touch me as deeply. And the thought of marriage never popped into my head. Whereas with Karen, this frivolous young woman, there seemed no reason not to get married. It's the oddest thing in the world. It didn't stem from her employing her wiles on me. I saw through her cute act from the beginning (of course later it ceased entirely). Maybe you get married, or committed, because you're in a phase – a turning point in your life, when you need something more stable. So you invest your hopes in a relationship during that time, in a person present on the scene, magnify them, and dream of future completion. You've made them key to your happiness. If that were the case then basically it would be a time in your life, a need, overpowering judgment; not intrinsic qualities you found in this other person. And maybe by sharing this unique time – when you were capable of such hopes and beliefs – adds to the attachment and identification. You made your bet, took the leap, so it will seem your chances of happiness ride on this gamble, this commitment, turning out right.

Don't we imagine that in a majority of arranged marriages, in traditional societies, no matter how they start, in the end the partners will find themselves loving each other? Even if it's a little different than our Western idea of two people seeking love picking someone they like for the venture. I don't know how far or strong the bond is; but sharing a life, a home, children; watching the children change and mature; depending on each other, growing old together: some form of love is likely to establish itself and deepen. Unless there was some unacceptable defect: cruelty or absence of normal feeling. Then again how much can I not see because of Western expectations? Romantic love is not something every society believes in or holds out for. Maybe the spouse is your assignment, like someone you work with. You both do your part in this 'life job'. If love occurs it's simply dumb luck. Still, from our perspective, we can't understand why smitten love wouldn't be the ultimate aspiration. Doesn't the greatest fulfillment and happiness come from finding someone who inspires your love, whose very presence is joy, who reassures you in turn that you are the most important thing to them, that sharing their life with you is their greatest desire? Of course in these other societies the emphasis is often not on the individual, but others, the extended family, and your duty to them.

While I was married to Karen I was unfaithful once. It was during a particularly bitter period. If I remember correctly it had started with our ongoing disagreement about having kids. Me pushing for it, not delaying any longer. I didn't understand what we were waiting for, while she kept saying she didn't feel ready. With the advantage of distance I can see now it wasn't the prospect of children, the question was did she really want to have them with me. But I was clueless at the time, and thought it just another example of her inability to resolve problems, or make a major decision about anything serious.

In no way am I excusing my behavior. If you're married to someone who wants children but is working her way to figuring out she doesn't want them with you, you should get a divorce. Then move on. I could have stopped acting like a heel. Then her attitude might have changed. I'm not a moral relativist. What I did was wrong. And I'm not blind to the consequences. I know a couple of guys who eventually wrecked good marriages. One marriage has continued but it's a shell of what it was. On the other hand I know rules aren't absolute because people – and their relationships – vary so much.

And there are always exceptions. Susan would be the embodiment of 'exception'. She so obviously makes her own rules – and everyone, including her husband Phil, accepts that she has that right. Almost a right by nature. By an innate superiority. I should add that from the beginning she thought my marriage to Karen was some kind of very bad joke. She was the only one of my old friends who never even pretended to welcome Karen. Quite the opposite of Phil, who was Mr. Courtly, very solicitous and indulgent. Susan viewed Karen as an interloper, a creature out of place; a grasping fraud preordained to die a vulgarian. She never stopped chiding me for my lapse in judgment. And to others she referred to Karen as "Richard's tawdry mall-rat", who must be missing her junk food and bar cruising. It was a cruel caricature. And honestly unfair. Karen did have potential. I wasn't imagining that. Unfortunately she had the bad luck of drawing me as her mentor, the old school coach who went about everything in a counter-productive manner. But someone with a similar goal, who employed an encouraging friendly approach, and was patient with small steps, could have succeeded. I still believe that to this day.

I don't think I would have tolerated that response from anyone but Susan. What's weird is that before writing this down I have never acknowledged to myself that I did accept it. Without reacting, almost as if from Susan it was to be expected. I know it'll seem odd to say this about someone who has never been 'faithful' to her husband, but incredible honesty is one of Susan's sterling traits. Stare anyone straight in the eyes, with an I-have-nothing-to-hide stance. (In my experience it's precisely such scarily out-front people who give short shrift to rules.)

There are women, who in the power of their sexual attraction and I would say glamour, emanate at the same time as their allure a warning. A kind of watch out – danger! Not so Susan. Her self-confidence could be intimidating, but it wasn't of the 'I'll devour you' type. You might be a passing fancy but she only targeted men she respected and cared for. Interestingly she never has affairs with strangers, or near strangers. Only men she knew well. As the object of her ardor your self-esteem would grow, and that was fine with her. Even desirable. There was no ulterior motive, no love-hate mix. She wasn't notching you onto a list. She wasn't about conquering men, though I imagine with her charisma and natural superiority, she often did. But it wasn't intentional, and we all knew the score. Again the breathtaking honesty.

Anyway to get away from me Karen had fabricated some reason to visit her sister for a couple of weeks.

We had been invited to this party and I decided to go by myself. They were all happy to see me again. Sorry to hear the marriage was going through a rough patch. I did feel a little lost. When all of a sudden I saw Susan coming directly at me. I don't know if it was vulnerability, availability, or what. Of course I knew she had always considered my marriage lunacy. At that juncture it did appear to have been a mistake. Still Susan's approach was rather brazenly overt. An 'I want you'. And my first reaction, I must confess, was the glow of being selected. If a man feels flattered, and how can he not, is that really wicked?

I need to add here, though it can't help but make me look even worse, that she had a body that went with that confidence. I was going to say athletic, but I think that gives the wrong impression. Lithe, graceful and gorgeous, but always assured. You did catch on, that though you were approved and necessary, you were not the central focus of whatever was going on, which was her concentration on the enjoyment of the sexual experience. You were somewhat incidental. While a little deflating at the time, in hindsight I think of it as a singular chance to observe a person pursuing, and achieving rapturous ecstasy, free of any regard about impressing you. Of course with real love the other person is paramount, and the spiral is around each other, building together. This was a lower form, but I wouldn't call it mere lust. I'm sure Susan wanted me to enjoy the moment, and assumed I was. So it was this weird mix: thrill, guilt and disenchantment. I thought afterwards I understood better why she had married Phil. He was this neutral foil, perfect for the life she had charted, someone who could only be grateful and tolerant because his selection was so unlikely. Don't misconstrue this as a complaint. I didn't love her. I loved my little 'mall rat', my little Eliza Doolittle. But

I admired Susan. Still do. She is exceptional and there's no use in denying it.

Dear Phil:

Hope all is well with you and Susan. I don't know how much of what I have to disclose will be news. I hope none of it. But some time ago Susan and I had a meaningless fling. I will regret if this surprises or hurts your feelings. From the outside you two seem to have an understanding, an open marriage so to say, even if it's one-sided. And if this is an imposed condition, much against your will, then truly I am sorry. How does one bring up such a subject?

So in principle I believe what I did was wrong and I want to apologize. (Until, and unless, you advise me that you regard carnal relations as a separate business. Though I too believe love isn't about physical beauty and sensual pleasure.)

I'll never forget how kind and patient you were towards Karen. I could have learned a lot by following your example. But I'm a fool. Please accept an apology from someone who turned out not to be as strong as he thought he was. I'm very far from where I'd like to be. All in all, allow me to say, I still think of you as a very fortunate man. Tolerant. A good example. All the best.

Your weak friend,
Richard

I am not sliding over the question of hypocrisy. What if I had discovered that Karen had slept with somebody? I would have gone ballistic. There would have been torrents of raging righteous indignation, guilt-tripping, fury, denunciation and disgust. I know I would have exploited it for all that it was worth – condemning her character, etc. And truly I have no idea if I could have forgiven her. So yes, total hypocrisy.

Yet what if I were married to Susan? Would I come around to the arrangement? I'd know going in what the deal was. Could I accept, adjust to, her endless infidelities? You'd have to ask yourself, to have this extraordinary woman will I permit her dalliances not to bother me? I imagine a lot of European men wouldn't think twice about it. I've read about infidelity causing men, prompted by feelings of guilt I guess, to become kinder, more sensitive. With me it was the opposite. As if I had to justify my bad conduct by judging Karen to be failing - I got colder, and harder on her.

The best friend I've ever had from work was Paul Takayama. He was such a nice guy. As was his wife Terri, and their two adorable girls. They never judged Karen, but after she left they were probably the most supportive people I knew. In a very low-key way. They never distanced themselves as most couples do when you return to being single. I would bring dates over, not just to show the Takayamas I was back on my feet, but so they could see I dated intelligent women, and the women could see I valued family life.

At the time Paul and I were the only professed Democrats at Lenz Holliston. I won't pretend that even at LH there wasn't – isn't – a problem with 'deadwood'. Old guys, some of whom may have had ideas, and ability, in the beginning of their careers. Maybe some talent in schmoozing clients on the wealth management side. Others never had any brains or talent, except to make connections, secure a position, and survive by fiercely defending it against any perceived threats. Over the years I've seen a few female game players; a few suspect 'affirmative action' hires; and the occasional young flimflam fake, bowling people over for a short time pretending they have a unique connection to the new. But by and large the deadwood was and is older white males, whose single talent is burrowing deeper into their position so you can't blast them out with dynamite. And like tumor cells they seem to recognize and network with each other. They are always an obstacle to getting anything done. And in difficult times they can pose a threat. I refused to waste my time flattering them or trying to convince them of anything since their only criteria is 'how will this impact me?' But I could afford to do this because I had protection from very senior executives who knew when it all shook out we'd still need to have a few sharp productive people to keep the enterprise afloat. (Paul was protected because of his contacts in Japan and his fluency in that language.)

International investments, while never a majority of our business, had always been significant. And we've had major successes. For instance as the date for Hong Kong's transfer back to Chinese authority in 1997 approached, a lot of people got cold feet. We cleaned up with what I'd term fire sale bargains. If you start with no illusions you can cope with the real situation and the possibilities that are there. There's something wrong with you if along the way you don't learn that most people only care about their ethnic group. So the Han Chinese only care about Han Chinese – they're the 'Middle Kingdom' and the rest of us are extras. (Though I'm not sure the Japanese are any better in their parochialism.) And you need to know that the Chinese mindset finds any dissent threatening. At LH we knew their MO: stipulate joint ventures so over time they could steal all the technology and eventually squeeze all non-Chinese out. Don't kid yourself that any personal tie you might establish will effect this program. There are still mutually beneficial deals to be struck and the lure of a vast market one day (post Communist Party) that may eventually open. In full honesty I should add that I was more taken aback by the conduct of the Brits. Dealing with them you learn the hard way how imperative it is to nail down every detail in a contract. A bunch of slithering weasels. Leave the smallest option unclear and not spelled out, and these guys feel no compunction in exploiting it to wiggle free. You can understand why, outside their Commonwealth, they are viewed as hypocrites hiding behind the pretentious façade of rectitude.

Lenz Holliston has come in for its share of sniping. A lot of it due to our Chinese success. Snickering about 'sweat shops under a different name', etc. I want you to know that I've never been ashamed to work at LH. On the contrary I'm quite proud. We've always been conservative in the old original sense – i.e. holding standards. No involvement with apartheid South Africa, the Shah's Iran, or Mobutu's Congo. We have steered clear of Arab oil trusts, arms makers & dealers, tobacco or the pharmaceutical industry. All of which were easy ways to rake in profits. No one makes a big deal about it, it's simply understood. If others are willing to take money with blood on it, that's their affair. It's not what we do. We earn profits enough, we don't need super profits from murder or fraud. There is an upside to prudence and ethics. Notice the last banking and stock fiasco never touched us. Whenever a speculative swell occurs the fantasy is sold as an altogether brand new innovation. Check to see if there's anything real about the source. Can you see how it makes money? Scrutinize the monitors. If they're making money hinged to the level of commerce then don't trust their assessments. A warning should go off in your head if you see - as the accountants with Enron, or the credit rating agencies with the mortgage credit derivatives - an incentive to cash in on mushrooming commissions. There's great pressure on every individual analyst, their jobs in jeopardy, because their bosses want to ride the greed wave.

I need to digress somewhat here in order to provide a more complete context and background. In no way am I arguing that being right on the merits excuses personal behavior that is repugnant. These are two distinct areas. Being right as far as correctly reading the lay of the land carries no weight when it comes to turning on a friend in a wholly despicable way. Nevertheless it's important to me that you at least grant that I was right on the meat of the two disagreements that brought on the falling out with Paul.

The first case wasn't anything international but troublemaking from our stupid lawyers who can't even do the job they're paid to do. Lawyers are one group that might actually make economists look useful. I've always had a bad tendency in a certain antagonistic mood of making cruel remarks towards whomever I perceived as opposing me. Cutting down assessments. I blame my parents for allowing this to become a habit without trying to curb it. They thought it was cute. My personality. Every kid is prone to blurt out untactful observations. I was their first child and I think they misread it as my particular personality slant. Besides amusing them, they assumed this was my function, an in-house Ezekiel, broad-siding everyone with scathing indictments, and acerbic evaluations. Not surprisingly, since it was permitted, I began to assume this was my talent - and role. It's natural over time to develop a propensity to search for impressive zingers to show off your dexterity. I regret it now. My parents tolerance and encouragement of this trait was unfortunate, not least for they way it later combined with my inability to admit mistakes in closing the door forever on people I'd driven away.

Contrary to our normal policy LH had become deeply involved - stock involved - with a manufacturer located in New Jersey, not really controlled by his board. For my sins I was tabbed as our point man. Whatever you've heard about new management styles, after my acquaintance with this CEO, and my fairly extensive familiarity in real estate, allow me to inform you that intimidating bullies are not an extinct species. They still exist, and unfortunately generating fear in your subordinates does get results. This guy was right out of central casting for a rageaholic: dark rings under his eyes; the purposefully subdued voice and exhausted posture, in lulls before the explosions. His need to dress down underlings in the most humiliating manner possible, to make small flubs out to be stupid and consequential crimes. I despised this fellow, but I could never get him to turn on me so I'd have an excuse for turning the assignment over to someone else. In one of those weird twists because I was the only one on the scene indifferent to all his acting out the perpetrator gravitated towards me. In fact he actually seemed to like me. I was stuck. It was a big moneymaker for us.

His company got into trouble for ripping off a competitor. Not a close call. They hadn't even bothered to do reverse engineering. The CEO wanted our advice on whether to fight or settle. Our lawyers, because they didn't like the attitude of the competitor's lawyers, recommended not negotiating but fighting. Not as a bluff or tactic mind you, but to go through the whole long process of discovery and trial. Why they picked Paul as their ally in this lunatic campaign I have no idea. Maybe because he's a trusting soul, easy to persuade. Incredibly Paul and the lawyers carried the day. (I knew it didn't matter as the gargoyle would follow my advice and when I told him the smart thing to do was to settle he settled.)

It wasn't simply bitterness at losing, when I knew how stupid their contention was. It was Paul's interference in a subject he knew nothing about. I was so mad I refused to shake his hand afterwards. Then there was my sharp tongue. A group of us were milling about after the conference. I knew he was listening when someone, possibly to make trouble prodded me to give my summary, and I responded, "Well I suppose the upside is that as soon as Paul goes back on his meds he'll see he was wrong." If there had been even a stir of embarrassed laughter it might have provided a little cover. And it might not have seemed as vicious as it was. In the event there was dead silence. So it was plain that I had gone too far.

The second case concerned the wisdom of investing in Russia post Soviet Union, as they supposedly transitioned to a market economy. Paul led the group that pushed for this as a 'once in a lifetime' opportunity. Sow goodwill now (I thought if I heard the citation of Armand Hammer one more time I was going to scream). Russia - richest in natural resources, with an educated population – will remember who stood by them during a difficult time – blah blah blah.

There is a belief in America that while our thinking is simplistic far from being a problem this is actually an asset. While more sophisticated Europeans play Hamlet, fretting over every complication, America, with its eye on the goal, is direct and acts in time in a practical manner. We get results. Never mind Iran, Congo, Vietnam, Chile, Afghanistan or Iraq. Along with mindlessness on policy we also have no apparent memory of our failures or of the figures responsible for the failures. I can give you two prime examples that touch Russia and drive me crazy.

Under Gorbachev, when the USSR and then Russia was transforming itself into a new order, the director of the CIA was Robert Gates. His number one job was to keep his eye on the country that had been our prime adversary during the cold war. To keep his budget and that of the military at the alarmist height they had reached he missed everything. If this isn't failure then nothing is. Yet it wasn't too surprising. I believe he got his appointment because during Iran-Contra, when any thinking person knew Gates was up to his ears in the fiasco, he not only protected himself with a dumb act but he protected the elder Bush. What lay in store for Gates? Becoming Secretary of Defense and then hailed universally as a 'wise man' of Washington.

At the beginning of the Russian transformation I liked the approach George Soros recommended; that the IMF feed money into the system from the bottom: give pensioners $7 or $8 a month. That would have worked, and the Russians would have had something to feel grateful about. But here come Jeffrey Sachs and his fellow Harvard economists, people who know nothing, but are convinced they've studied and know everything, fresh from a supposed triumph in Poland, they advise 'shock therapy'. Sell off all the assets to whomever. No transition in turning the country around from a controlled economy to their divine free market. Can you imagine fools trying such an experiment here in America, land of gun psychotics, with our violent nature and paranoia? There'd be blood in the streets up to your knees. Poor Russia. It all ended with apparatchiks becoming oligarchs, monopolies, gangsters, a falling standard of living; even life expectancy plummeting. Of course to be fair if we're simplistic, what in the world are Russians? Given a choice between a man who will go down in history as truly great, who was honest and hard working, or a crooked sack of vodka, followed by a nationalistic murderous strongman, the Russian majority is all behind the drunk and the strongman. (Gorbachev did make the tactical mistake of bringing up the issue of alcoholism, which in Russia is absolutely a no no.)

Walking away from the catastrophe as if it never happened and he wasn't culpable, Jeffrey Sachs remakes himself into an international humanitarian. He's a champion of the poor, promoting mosquito nets in Africa, etc. He's now saint Sachs. In a land of no judgment or memory there's no responsibility either, and certainly no penalty.

Anyway I won the investing in imploding Russia argument. But I was no more a good winner then I had been a good loser. I went on about the idiocy of throwing money into chaos. Paul and I never spoke privately after that. It began to dawn on everyone that contrary to expectations Japan wasn't going to pull out of its slump anytime soon, and I won't say he was encouraged to move on, but the signal was sent that he would be allowed to go, which he did, and we lost touch.

Dear Paul:

I'm so sorry I didn't shake your hand, and I regret so much that crack I made. Our differences on Russian opportunities should have had nothing to do with our friendship. The only thing I proved was that I was as poor a winner as I was a loser. If you knew how often I had regretted the cost: not knowing how you and Terri, and the girls, are doing, you might be mollified. I had a psychological condition that stopped me from admitting I was wrong. It was absolute. Overriding everything. It doesn't excuse my behavior, or what I said, but it's the reason I didn't seek you out afterwards and apologize. I was in the middle of the worst of it – in the wake of Karen's leaving. I was so screwed up at the time that it slid over into having trouble even thanking people. I guess because there'd be some implication that I had been in need, and now I was in their debt? I don't really know.

With all the world full of potential healthy friends I couldn't blame you for avoiding me. Still it's important that you know there was a cause, and it would mean a lot to me if you would correct your picture of your old pal. I did and do care. The way I acted has haunted me ever since.

> *Your penitent friend,*
> *Richard*

Since my divorce I've basically had two socializing centers. The neighborhood Episcopal church, and the local Democratic Club, which is affiliated with the California Democratic Council. In both places I am viewed as someone they're happy to have, but someone who doesn't naturally belong there. I should add for those unaware of this that today's Episcopal church is a far cry from yesterday's institution of the establishment. This isn't a complaint, they're far closer to the mission of Jesus than they were as the inheritors keeping royalist discipline. Both the church and the club, though they're fond of me personally, pigeonhole me by my profession as enmeshed in the opposition to progress and humane programs: as one associated with 'greed' is the engine, the ethos of the businessman, and bigots, jingoists – the Establishment. I'm one of the creatures on top, the corporate officer, paid and involved in manipulating the innocent, pulling the strings. They know I work at Lenz Holliston so that means I'm with the wheeler-dealers, and I have to rationalize my part in the exploitation of the suckers; the influence buying, slanted ads, 'dog whistles', gerrymandered districts, purchased politicians. They think it's a happy fluke that I want to hang out with them, a possible compensating. But they never forget where I come from, what I do – my role in 'the real world'. They're always alert for little giveaways, telltale slips. There's nothing I can do to dispel this image. Believe me I've tried.

To have your views discounted, in particular on economic matters, when let's be honest, I'm the only person in the room who understands what he's talking about - the nitty-gritty of the mechanisms in play, is aggravating. For instance on the financial crisis I committed the sin of telling them the truth: you can't tell a Clinton – and for that matter Obama - investment banker from a Republican investment banker. Average Americans are always going to lose. Sorry, not only is there no difference in the advice (to deregulate), to make the insiders richer, but when the bubble pops the recommended remedies are the same. Look at when the leveraged mortgage derivatives scam collapsed, what guidance did Wall Street's guardians first give Bush, and then Obama? 'It's a shame about those little people now in foreclosure. But (shrug) what can you do? Let's be honest, they couldn't afford those homes, they are going to lose them - and all their equity. There's nothing to be done for them but for the general economy the quicker it's all settled and we can move on the better. Who knew real estate values wouldn't always go up? The important thing now is to make the banks whole, in order to safeguard the entire system, and get credit flowing again.' The figurehead president complies, a Democrat acting exactly like the Republican, as if only the top was crucial. Is it coincidence that that's the class can give large donations? The classes are further apart than ever, and 'too big to fail' hasn't been corrected. Of course the fact that the population is ignorant and apathetic doesn't help. All this is obvious but you'd think I'd said something blasphemous. My friends, both at church and in the Democratic club, never directly challenge what I say. There's a resigned sigh, a pause, a looking about, then a changing of the subject. As if corporate Richard can't appreciate the intractable opposition Clinton and Obama faced, the vile treachery of Republican obstruction.

I started out with sympathy for both Clinton and Obama. I contributed and worked hard for their elections (their first elections I should point out). Their personal stories were compelling. Clinton never met his biological father and the only thing he inherited from him was his animalistic libido. Obama's relationship was also tragic. The African father who existed like a myth but turned out to be a spoiled self-centered drunk. Brilliant, but despicable. Both their mothers struggled. They had to study hard to qualify for scholarships because they lacked money and connections. So I started in their corner. But because they started with nothing and ended up on top they quite naturally think the system's pretty good. Which is a bad joke. They went to Yale and Harvard, which, like all Ivy League schools (and Stanford) are good for 'networking', brainwashing, and little else. Present and future elites are groomed to run the country via success in closed hierarchies easily rigged. Where infighting, inside knowledge and connections are rewarded, but nothing beyond figures in. Getting filthy rich from game-playing and skimming is the norm, not from being productive. The reason we have the sort of Wall Street we have is because it's run by Ivy Leaguers. Game players. Hence all the comparisons to casinos, which is very apt. Though I would stipulate even by casino standards their games are extremely crooked. Insiders start with the most chips, then the rules are bent in their favor so they can't really lose.

The key to understanding the complacent attitude of both Clinton and Obama, is to reduce it to this: 'How bad can a system be if it allows someone like me, with no money or connections, by dint of hard work, to rise to the top?' You know why Teddy and Franklin Roosevelt instituted real reforms? Because they came from the plutocracy. They had no illusions about fairness or the benevolence of the rich. They knew firsthand the attitude of 'They're lucky to have a job at any pay. A roof over their head and food to eat. They're only scum.' Teddy and Franklin Roosevelt, because of their background, inside knowledge of America's ruling class, couldn't be bought, hoodwinked or intimidated. Anyway it's important that you know what a source of frustration it is when my criticism is dismissed as elitist - we can't expect Richard to understand - when its really progressive.

I take pride in the fact that at this time in my life I believe I have as many women friends as men. I think a balance is preferable. For anyone. For myself I take it as a mark of maturity. A recognition of what I need. Not that I want to spend all day shopping. But I've come to the realization, at least I think it's a realization, that women's outward occupations are misleading – at least to men. They may not form or express it in a way men can accept, but I think women tend to base their lives on deeper qualities. In my clearer moments I can see the application to Karen. I won on points on all the small particular arguments, but big picture she was right in what she felt. She was married to a creep who was verbally, and probably psychologically, abusive. Would it have been smart to have children with such a man? No. Was it smart to leave him? Yes.

Beth was special. I should say is special, since technically she's still my friend. She hasn't told me to drop dead yet. Though I fear that could be coming around the next bend. We hit it off immediately. She was with one of her disposable boyfriends. I laughed at her wry comments, she laughed at mine. She doesn't care how her judgments or tastes strike others, there is never any hesitation, as if everyone has a right to their perspective. (Though later I would find out there are moments when she herself is hyper-sensitive. What triggers this change is a mystery.)

The only bad thing about Beth was she encouraged my sarcasm. Guffawing at my harsher strokes. It's a tendency I would do well to curb, or eliminate altogether. It's a wholly negative. However all in all Beth stands out. So many people believe they think for themselves – but how many really do? Not many. Usually their vaunted independence in thought boils down to nothing more than their character and experiences, adorned with borrowed ideas that justify their inclinations. Its wrong to call it thought. They turn the dial ever so slightly from the course their parents charted, and consider it daring. Most lives are spent reacting. Beth really thinks. Constantly. You can see it. And this appraisal of things, from the ground up, her frankness about reservations, is not only sometimes embarrassing, being so unusual, it's startling. An indication of how rare it truly is and how often our standard wiring prevails.

I can tell you it's wonderful and stimulating, if a little exhausting, to have an acquaintance who really thinks. As long as they aren't bombastic with their conclusions. Because it prods you to re-examine your own received opinions. Tenets you think you subscribe to, personalities you assume are admirable. I think of myself as rather blunt, but compared to Beth I'm the soul of tact. Yet, unlike Susan, I can't remember her ever making a disparaging remark about Karen. Though she was definitely my friend, and so dissimilar, for some reason Karen elicited her sympathy. Early on in the marriage Beth was the one who made that observation (whose aptness and heft I didn't get until it was too late), that people entering a relationship or marriage make a tragic mistake when they plan, and are confident they will be able to change the other. They find out the hard way that they can't, and then there's dissatisfaction. I know I fell into that mistake, and so did Karen, but at the time I assumed if Beth was referring to us she was getting us wrong.

Well I blew it with Beth. Some time after Karen left for good, finding myself in a libidinous state, I fixed on her. Probably for no better reason than that she happened to be around. And to this day I don't have a clue what her attitude towards me was. That night she seemed passively reserved, in a sort of 'I'll wait and see what this turns out to be' attitude. This is someone who shuffles boyfriends to the point where you give up on trying to remember their names. Who would think she'd get hurt? But the next morning it was clear she had shifted into some kind of romantic fantasy. And of course lust satisfied, I had flipped into preparing for the future. Telling myself don't send a false signal that can complicate and entangle. This is Beth your friend.

Though this may come off as a self-serving rationalization, this time my non-communication, mixed up with my block, was deliberate. A conscious choosing of what I conceived to be the lesser evil. Even now I don't know what else I could have done. Yes I was doubtful of my feelings, beyond the physical. I think I said appreciative things and acted I hope appropriately. At no point did I utter "I love you" or suggest this should go on. I woke knowing it had been a mistake, giving in to weakness. Motivated I swear primarily by the desire to minimize Beth's letdown I intentionally adopted a somewhat brusque nothing has happened pose. I got up and dressed in a businesslike just-another-day manner. She looked at me languorously from the bed, expecting a kiss or vow, and I pretended not to notice, and asked what she'd like for breakfast.

I know that morning, her apparent disappointment, has left the impression that I'm some kind of cad. Having satisfied myself I dropped the wooing. Yet anything romantic would have been more misleading and long run crueler. What was I to do? I should have been more considerate of her feelings, but with all her boyfriends who could have anticipated this reaction? To me it was obvious that once you took sex out of the equation we were simply friends. Women that you see as love interests have to have a certain combination of qualities that match yours in some mysterious way, and usually you pick up pretty quickly on if there's that promising chemistry or not. I think there is something animal deep in us that alerts us to who might be right, and you know when it's lacking. So how had Beth seen me all along?

I have found I don't stay friends with ex-girlfriends. I know others do. But I see it, not as finding out something bad, but just like evaluating a person for a certain position and finally deciding 'no'. As judger and judged you have to deal with the consequences of that, and it's pretty hard to ignore. There's also the reminder of the high hopes you once had. Not to mention the embarrassing exaggerated attempts you made in order to impress. I'm not putting Beth in this category, because I never saw her that way. I see her as a friend. A friend I value above all others, or at least in a unique way. I have a suspicion that part of her animus has to do with the guy she was seeing at the time of our tryst. An okay fellow, with a fair sense of humor, good job, children half-grown. After our encounter she closed him off without any explanation. Her pattern, then and now, is to get bored by her boyfriends. But she is free to imagine this guy was the right guy, and it was only selfish Richard whose bad timing intrusion sabotaged the perfect match. I'm not buying it.

I believe most of us, when buffeted by desire, are capable of conning ourselves into believing a lower appeal is really a higher. Obviously I was not immune to this weakness. However I don't think Beth is either. Since 'feeling it out' encounters are often inside-out, an aloofness at first can create an attraction, and an easy conquest contempt. I'm not saying it should be that way, but because it is, we naturally find ourselves playing roles, whether we want to or not. To attract the right person we try a balance: independent and social, nonchalant and interested, different but not strange.

I know I gave in to weakness. I'm sorry but I can't, as a man, see it as something extraordinary. Beth is a mature, experienced woman. Has it not been true for ages, when brute force was no longer permissible, that men have tried sweet talking women into mating? Not something you'd think an intelligent woman would need a explanation about. And dare I bring up - what was so heinous after all? Relative to Beth, her lifestyle and values? Here is an admirer of Anais Nin and that whole dreadful Bloomsbury gang. By her sullen pouting attitude you'd imagine I'd seduced an innocent virgin. 'Violated' her somehow. Or that it changed my regard for her, when no one respects her mind as much as I do.

Dearest Beth:

What do you do when for several years you suffer a psychological knot that stops you from admitting any mistake, and then along comes a really serious mistake towards someone you care deeply for? It's important that you know that I talked myself into it before I talked you into it. It was false, but more self-deception than manipulation. It was selfish. But I risked a friendship I daresay that is more important to me than it is to you. I know I betrayed weakness. The realization of what had happened came afterwards, and late, to me, but then it hit hard. You must know if I gave the wrong impression it was completely unintentional. I don't want to believe my short-sightedness has forfeited our friendship. I know my behavior has put an asterisk on it, but I pray over time you'll give me the chance to prove my trustworthiness. I will measure up. In the long run. Everyone makes mistakes – don't they?

While I regret misleading you, if I did, and I certainly regret the hurt that ensued, since the experience itself was great. Doesn't that have some mitigation? You have such a succulent body Beth. What can I say? I gave in to the moment. Is it wrong now to confess at being surprised at how passionate and natural you were. So on the positive side I think it increased my understanding of your sensuous depth. Now I know why all your beaus are so smitten. Of all my friends truly you are the one I value most. Please don't let one lapse of my self-deception destroy our friendship. I sincerely beg your pardon.

A True Admirer,
Richard

This is one virtual letter I could send. Though I don't think I will. Not simply cowardice. I feel I'm barely hanging on by my fingertips. I'm hoping time will soften her attitude. Really why should a moment of weakness annul a whole history? Why can't Beth remember the person she liked, whose company she enjoyed, and fold an admitted mistake into that larger picture?

The next incident I hesitate to include because it concerns a dog, and you might think my list is drifting to the petty. Yet if we judge our trespasses by how much they haunt our conscience, this episode must rate very highly, because I think about it all the time. And to be honest I always cringe at the memory.

The Watters were my next-door neighbors. A very nice couple and I need to add very old. Their dog, Darwin, was a mix, but obviously there was a lot of wire terrier in him, and they're smart dogs. On our block, while the backyards are fenced and private, the fronts, dominated by lawns, are more or less open, with shrubs, perennials and roses, little hedges, some trees, that indicate property boundaries, but there's a nice free and flowing aspect to it all. Unfortunately Darwin, who in good weather was out of the house and free to wander wherever he pleased, had decided that my front yard should be his lavatory. I understood the Watters, once they opened the front screen-door and he darted out, were unable to restrain him. But it didn't matter how many times I shooed or chased him, when he didn't see me standing on the grounds he'd return and do his business. I didn't feel it was right to complain to the Watters, though if they'd been younger you can bet I would have. I found it very irksome. No one else had a problem with the dog. He never barked at anyone. Though it was odd that a dog should be loose, he was accepted in the neighborhood. Everyone liked him, the kids all called out his name.

So one day I'm back deadheading roses when I spy him entering the other side of the front of the yard. It always irritated me, but for some reason that day his undaunted persistence triggered real anger at his boldness in continuing to pick my yard, and that nothing I did could deter him. He hadn't seen me so I had the advantage. I picked up a fairly large rock and threw it as hard as I could. I don't know if I was trying to hit him – I probably was. Anyway it landed close and the ricochet gave him a fright. He jumped back and tore for his yard. As fate would have it someone was turning around in the Watters driveway at that precise moment. Brakes screech – too late – there's a thud, and then a squeal from Darwin. As the driver and passenger opened their doors I skulked away, on tiptoe, around the other side of my house, entering the backdoor without making a sound, praying no one had witnessed my part in what had just happened. The people in the car were decent. You never know how someone will react to their pet getting injured, yet (peering through my curtain I watched them try to comfort him, read his tag, knocked on the door, and then left a note relaying the unhappy accident. The Watters had gone for the day with their son, but I didn't know if they'd meant to leave dog out or it was just an oversight.

If Darwin had died right then it would have been bad enough. But he didn't. It was awful. He lingered, whimpering this plaintive cry, in pain, for hours. It seemed to go on forever, until finally, as his strength ebbed, it grew weaker and weaker, and then there was silence. I think it's that cry that has engraved itself so deeply in me. If he had just died quickly, crushed beneath the tire, it would have been regrettable but not haunting. I can't purge the sound of that helpless whimpering from my memory. I never intended to kill him of course. If the rock had hit him, and really hurt him, I would have felt bad enough about that. After the consequence of the anger impulse of the moment. That he was dead was simply horrible.

I think a lot of our behavior which in hindsight we find mortifying, occurs when we're not really thinking. When we let emotions we are sure are justified rule our actions. Unprepared we lose our bearings and then sometimes there's shock at what we've done after we've done it. You have to take my word, I like animals, I like dogs in particular. If I didn't travel so much I'd probably have one. Nor am I a person who peers out of the corner of his window, hiding in the dark. That's not me. But in one second I'd gone from being a homeowner righteously provoked beyond his limit, to an out-of-control maniac precipitating a cruel chain reaction. You can understand it was a staggering switch. We were in our yards, in our petty little quarrel, and then suddenly there was pain and death for one of the antagonists. (The driver of the car must bear a little responsibility for not hitting his brakes quicker when the peripheral blur appeared.)

Of course the Watters were crushed. They loved that dog like a member of the family. Their son buried him that evening. I was never honest about it, but I tried to make it up to them with little good deeds. I think I'd always been a good neighbor, but I became more solicitous, volunteering to drive them anywhere they needed to go, or shop for them. It was the purest accident. I've never hurt a dog in my life. (And I will only accept judgment on this from people who don't own a dog and yet have had the repeated insult of stepping in dog shit on their own property.) I think a fair arbiter would have told the Watters: look either you must train - break your dog of this habit, or you must confine him to your backyard.

Mr. and Mrs. Watter:

You were always such good neighbors to me, I hope you found me to be a good neighbor to you. I have something to confess. At the time it happened I had a problem admitting mistakes, so I didn't come forward. I was ashamed and horrified by what occurred.

Darwin was a neat dog. But for some reason he picked my yard to be his bathroom if you know what I mean. I did not appreciate at the time having to clean up after him. I would yell at him when he was doing it but it made no difference. One day I saw him before he saw me. So I threw a rock – merely to scare him. That was when he ran in front of that car turning around in your driveway. It was all bad luck. I felt terrible. About his suffering and your grief on discovering him dead. If I told you the truth I think it would have made your suffering the loss harder. You would have dwelt on it being avoidable. And of course your opinion of me would have fallen. But I need you to know that I was ambushed by fate just like Darwin and yourselves. Please forgive me. It was an accident.

Your Deeply Sorry Neighbor,
Richard Upton

I met Cynthia in a somewhat odd way, though on reflection how else could we have met? The assistant minister asked for volunteers to walk the neighborhood and calm fears about a homeless shelter the church had proposed. It was at the height of the homeless crisis. The plan was to take in about 20 people, Monday through Friday nights. Some fearmonger had circulated an alarmist flier on how the church was going to become a magnet drawing undesirables in, who, when dispersed in the morning into the community, could eye property or children. Our uphill fight was not successful, local officials caved in to the pressure, and disallowed the experiment. But Cynthia and I, who had been paired for canvassing, became friends.

I would describe her as a cute person. More by dint of personality, than physical appearance. Gentle, smart, but burdened with a railcar of self-doubt. More than a normal person should have. It didn't function as a friendship between equals, because of her habit of deferring to me. Though I fear my mentioning it will leave the wrong impression. About both of us. I will admit I think my greater affluence played a part in this deference. I tended to listen to her stories as an analyst would, with pretty much the same sort of expectation and responsibility: to render an objective reading. She had a good education, but had become a social worker; so a lot of conscience, pressure and unpleasantness, in exchange for a civil servant's salary. In the course of her work she found herself in the middle of a lot of human dramas. Because of her wonderful empathy I have no doubt that she was an exemplary civil servant. She was the sort of person who stays a friend, not out of shared interests, tastes, or mind; but because they appreciate knowing you. On your side you become used to their attendance, there's a fondness familiarity like a family member's. And I value loyalty.

As I said my job and appearance are misleading. I'm not stuffy or conservative. From mother's side of the family (in significant ways skipping poor mother) came culture. It was assumed that in due course you would read the 'great books'. Appreciation of drama, art and classical music was also expected. I was a business major because that was what Dad had wanted. However every semester, even back in high school, I always took an extra literature or history class. On both sides was an emphasis on staying within ethical boundaries whatever you were doing. Your morality could acknowledge human limitations, the rules of the world, but these could not be used as excuses. And my father was a good model, a man who was a success while staying scrupulously honest.

The rift in what was regarded as acceptable that opened my eyes came from two of Dad's friends. I think I was probably between ten and twelve. Kevin was the kind of person everyone enjoys. A sense of humor that pushes the envelope, but knows where the limits are and always stops short. A bit of the rascal, that adds a little spice to life. But Kevin used the 'n' word too often, long after it was no longer acceptable for self-respecting people to use it. Especially educated people. There weren't any Black people in our circle, yet it was still quite discordant. And honestly I don't know why he did it. He wasn't a hater. He seemed to think it was funny, maybe in a provocative way? Getting a little rise reaction out of people. These were adults and they were taken aback, but the reaction was tittering to an etiquette violation. I can't recall anyone ever getting serious and telling him "Look Kevin that's wrong. You've got to stop using that term." As a kid I knew it was wrong and I was perplexed.

Art was the more significant person of the two. A substantial, respectable pillar of the community. I thought of him as right up there with Dad. A great guy, super father. He was a realtor. One day, I've forgotten what the errand was that brought me to his office, but I was there, and as he wasn't busy, he decided to give me a little tour. Towards the end he opens a drawer and pulls out a check. What was this for? If Negroes came by to see a house you had listed, you pulled this check out and said, 'Oh, I'm sorry, I just got a down-payment on that'. He didn't tell me this with any glee, more like part of showing me the ropes. Nevertheless I was shocked. It was a moment when I grasped that with all of America's ideals the game still wasn't being played on the up and up. Our circle weren't descended from Southern segregationists; our ancestors had fought for the Union. We were all good Christians. Decent people. Yet evidently we were compelled to lie to Black people, resorting to phony checks to deceive them. (As a kid I didn't realize that Blacks were well aware how rigged everything was). I kept thinking of the dirty trick, the disappointment of Blacks looking for a nice house. The dishonesty and unfairness of it all. I think combined with how it contradicted all the ideals I had been taught at home, at church, and in the history and civic classes at school, it was the beginning of the stirring of a broader social conscience in me.

After Cynthia got to know me she came to trust that on fundamental issues she could rely on my judgment, that we shared the same values and goals. My problem stemmed from a personal trait she had. I began to type her as a hypochondriac. I do realize some people have inherited a weaker constitution, they're not imagining their afflictions, they really are more susceptible to illness. And I know it can be unfair to base your view from the center of your own good health. However when you're around someone long enough, and they seem to constantly magnify every little ailment, you do begin to wonder if a lot of it isn't simply in their head. I think I can say that - from the outside - her symptoms were not convincing. Yet she always made them out to be serious and threatening. Her exaggeration of everything extended to the healing side. Every new miracle drug, or expert, or alternative treatment was an exciting breakthrough. The new specialist had caught something all the other doctors had missed! Or this brand new drug was entirely different from anything ever discovered! It never stopped, and somehow she always cranked up the same enthusiasm.

How someone, while maybe not very deep, but above average intelligence, could venture forth on this wheel without ever stopping and reflecting, 'Hey, is there a pattern here?', is a mystery to me. I guess it was all consuming – the drama so compelling she was always in the present; all the ailments and doctors, and panaceas of the past, blocked from view by the urgency of the present affliction. I tried my best to be the supportive friend. I asked about the latest problem, and then put on a concerned face. Listened to the latest treatment, nodding my head, acting impressed.

Then of course one day it was for real. Lung cancer. I don't understand with all the tests she was constantly undergoing how it was possible for anything to sneak up on her. But somehow they missed the initial stage. As far as I can determine there was no connection between all her earlier maladies and this real one. But that's just my opinion. Cynthia had never been a smoker in case you're wondering.

In the beginning I did come through. Suddenly my sympathy was real, my listening genuine. I would do anything she asked. I was glad to. I have that as my consolation. But then we started to go through cycles reminiscent of all her previous enthusiasms. A new approach. A need to believe in it (an obliged earnest profession from you that you too believed in it). The unmentioned turning of our backs to the possibility of death, even though both of us were believers. This will sound petty but I could have hung in there if it had been a matter of weeks. But it wasn't, it was a matter of months. If at the beginning of an ordeal parties were allowed to be honest about realistic perimeters, wouldn't that be a better system? Then we could avoid disappointing people. If I could have asked, "Cynthia, how much time do you think it's reasonable of you, to expect me to devote to you, because of your illness?" I knew her, she would have selected a modest figure, which I would have been happy to exceed. But we would have had an idea, a ballpark figure. Not an open-ended unlimited commitment. Naturally patients lose perspective with the threatening traumatic prospect of extinction, and they assume family and friends are equally compelled. This may be harsh, but we're not. And I'm not pretending that if it was me I wouldn't act just as myopically. I probably would. However when we all pretend that compassion is unlimited (and it isn't) we are inevitably setting ourselves up for serious disappointment.

As it dragged on I found myself making the most inexcusable rationalizations. We weren't that good of friends. We hadn't been that close, for that long. What did we really have in common? It would be better for Cynthia to spend this precious time with her family and real friends. People more on her wavelength, with a longer history, who could muster more genuine sympathy than I could. It would be better for her, and truer, if I played a lesser role. Awful.

All the earlier phantom illnesses had taken their toll I believe. It's too bad, but I think I was somewhat drained in the sympathy tank. By what I had been obliged to show for all the illusory illnesses. The prospect of going over to her apartment became so dreary that I would fumble for any distraction as an excuse why I couldn't go right then. Procrastination took over. At the time the obligation seemed endless, and dodging it brought temporary relief. Denial developed further. And Cynthia didn't prod me. She was probably concerned that I had burned out. I'm not certain I hadn't. Anyway it was a horrible transition: from almost daily visits to no visits. And I didn't call either. I became ashamed of my conduct. Then it transpired that I couldn't even think about going back over there. How could I explain it? I couldn't.

One day out of the blue a little card came. All it said was, "Miss you. Love, Cynthia". My reaction to this was perverse - I became incensed, as if she had violated some protocol, an understood - though never spoken, agreement we had. I should have been forced, no matter how resentfully, to face the music at that point. And I intended to. I would try to come up with an explanation. Yet I simply couldn't bring myself to actually go. The same procrastination kicked in, I wasn't quite ready. I really did have to do this or that. After enough time passed in the wake of the card, the mountain of guilt accumulated to an unassailable height. The space, the disgrace of it all. I abandoned any hope. It had become insurmountable.

I never quite figured out her longtime boyfriend. I was on Cynthia's side, not that she ever complained, but I assumed their relationship was loose because he wanted it loose. I didn't think it fit her personality, but this isn't based on any real knowledge. By what right I have to judge him I don't know, because in his way he did come through for her. Certainly measured by the abridged standards he'd established. Interestingly though he didn't accompany her to Mexico. But I don't know the particulars, and that could have been her call I guess. She never came back. Alive that is. Even today it hurts to run into him. He works at the grocery store closest to my house. We exchange furtive glances and subdued waves. Often I will drive out of my way just to avoid bumping into him.

After she died her sister called me up as if our relationship had never changed. She wanted to know if I felt like saying anything at the service. I lied, said regretfully I had to be out of town on that day. I was surprised but shouldn't have been. Cynthia always went with the best interpretation of people, making excuses for them. I'm sure she made excuses for me. She refused to judge any of her clients or friends, and always forgave.

Dear Cynthia:

I'm sorry I chickened out on you like that. You were such a wonderful giving person. That day we were teamed up at church was a lucky day for me. If only I could have taken the opportunity, when I received your typically gracious note, to eat humble pie and make amends. Everything in that period was exacerbated by a psychological complex that beset me, which didn't allow me to acknowledge mistakes. You can see the problem, what greater fault could there be than the cowardice of bailing on a dying friend? I'd resolve 'I'm going to visit Cynthia today', and then I just couldn't bring myself - my body - to follow through.

Your earlier alarms, under whatever rubric we want to give them, took their toll on me. I say this not as an excuse, I have none. But as you remember each symptom was treated as if it was the onset of something life-threatening. I tried to go along, no matter how half-heartedly it might have appeared to an objective party. Then you'd tell me about a new proposed treatment, and I would do my best to act like I too was convinced and was completely behind it. I'm just saying that some of us, most of us I do believe, are not bottomless reservoirs of empathy. You were always an exception, with your true Christian charity.

Someone once said it doesn't matter who's in the room, we all die alone. I assume you found this to be true. I will always regret my cowardice and letting you down. Somehow being sure you wouldn't judge me, and wouldn't want me to feel guilty doesn't make it better, but only makes my failure worse.

Cynthia I ask for your forgiveness, knowing you will grant it.

Your Chastened Friend,
Richard

Long before I worked at Lenz Holliston I had my first real job in the investment field back east. It was the perfect introduction in a lot of ways. I shared my internship with another young man, Gerald Whitehurst. We got along well, there was none of the jealousy, or cutting the other down behind his back. Our mentor was Sam Rosenthal. A wonderful man. Vast experience, brilliant with analysis and portfolios, and very patient with us. His problem was he was probably the most disorganized person I've ever met. You could never find anything. If people called he would have to call them back because a search needed to be mounted for documentation. Everyone adjusted to this quirk and it did make life exciting. I set out to organize files into some sort of system. It was while doing this that I ran across a drawer with a file labeled "CASH". I kid you not. Even it was not organized, envelopes with money, money paper-clipped, just a mess, like everything else. Plus there was no reason that Sam should have been handling cash anyway. I didn't know what to do with it, so I left it to the side. For awhile.

As I've said I was brought up with certain ethics. Of course theft was a no no. Thou shall not steal. And I did recognize the temptation: unknown amounts of cash that would never be missed. It's the temptations that hang around, that wear us down, that attract in our weak moments. It's no problem when you're strong, but they're still there when you're weak. Need some money? Take it - pay it back when you can. What's the problem? No one will notice. You succumb. Once you breach that prohibition it's easy to repeat. There was a lot of money in that drawer. I think Sam kept dumping it but never took any out. I don't know why. Maybe he didn't like walking around with cash. So over time I probably took several hundred dollars.

When I started addressing my transgressions I thought the best way to deal with this one was to confess to Gerald, since Sam had passed away a long time ago, and the firm had been swallowed up. Truth to say I didn't want to get in trouble. I figured out an estimated sum, with the years times the interest, and included that in my letter of admission to Gerald. In the letter I attempted a little humor by referring to it as 'one of the late-est settling of accounts on record'. I got a nice note back but he returned the check. I got his number and called him up.

"Hello. I'd like to speak to Gerald Whitehurst if he's around."

"You've got him."

"Gerry, it's me Richard."

"Hi."

"Hi. I need you to keep this check."

"It wasn't my money. It was Sam's money. You know he wouldn't have begrudged you - any of it. Don't let it bother you."

"Gerry I'm trying to do a restitution thing. It wasn't my money and I took it. I secretly took it. I didn't ask. Until I confessed to you in that letter I've never admitted it to anyone. How wrong does something have to be? It's the only time in my entire life that I've ever stolen anything. It's important to me."

"Alright but who did you hurt? Not Sam – he would have given you the money if you'd asked. He would have said take it – take it all. You certainly didn't hurt me. It wasn't my money, I didn't even know about it, that's why I can't accept the check."

"But I need you to accept it. You're the only one I've got."

"Don't worry about it. No one was hurt."

"But it was wrong."

"It wasn't my money, so how can I take a payment like it was?"

"Please take it for your girls. Think of it as coming from Sam. Now that's something he would have liked. Maybe knowing Richard's trying to make amends, getting something off his conscience. If your girls receive a little bonus from this nut case in their father's past is that so terrible? Can't you do that?"

After a long pause he agreed to take the check for his girls. I sent a new one back to him and achieved some peace of mind on this score.

Obviously my biggest admission is the one due Karen. In the best of all possible worlds I would deliver this in person. If she just looked at me as I spoke, heard my voice, she'd know it was sincere. Believe me I've tried. I call, just to see if the timing is right, if I can get permission to come over. The second she makes out that it's my voice on the line she hangs up. I suspect she knows what I'm about, and she wants to short-circuit it. If she lets me confess that I acted like a heel and bully, that most of our problems were my fault, she'll be stuck with two unpleasant choices. She can refuse to forgive me, even after I've taken all the blame, and come off as the one who couldn't move past it. Or forgive - and lose her all-purpose heavy. How would that impact her victim status? It would be greatly diminished. If her ex-husband acknowledges the fault was all his then he can't be as dark as she's portrayed him. She doesn't want the consequences that follow either of these outcomes, so she forecloses any opportunity for me to make my admission.

On my part how many times can you solicit someone before it becomes harassment? I've worked out this little fantasy I play in my mind. In it I just drive over there – to heck with permission or notification. Push the door open, walk through. See their little girl off to the side playing, and mention in passing, "You could have been my daughter. You would have been smarter. But your mother said she wasn't ready for children." Burst in upon Karen, hold her - not violently - and say everything I have to say, while she throws her head from side to side, trying not to hear - but she does. I of course triumph as tears flow down her cheeks, knowing the game is up. Don't be disturbed. I would never enact such a thing. I'm not like that. It's simply a daydream release. That's all.

Ask yourself if I'm such a bad guy why, when we were dividing things, did she rely on me? Solely. Why didn't she hire a lawyer? That's what people do when they don't trust the other party. No, she knew she could trust my honesty and fairness. I'd go over to consult, with Gary (they were together but not married) hovering in the background, as I checked to make sure she understood whatever I was proposing and it had her consent. Yes I was so attached to the house that I would have gone further, but it was my house in the first place, and I ended up giving her well more than half the appraised value. A lawyer would have cost her. I know exactly when the break occurred. After everything was signed and agreed to she asked me to buy her a new car. She knew that every year I traded in Mom's car for that year's model. (It's a waste because she never puts any miles on them.) But I was taken aback. It was as if she was asking for a parting gift. If you're divorcing someone, a divorce you initiated, your action says I want this over, it made me unhappy, I want to start a new life. Not 'Oh by the way, can you buy me a new car on top of everything?' It was such a weird and inappropriate request. I said either Gary pays for it or you get a job, it's no longer my business. I could have been more tactful, but it was only after that exchange that I became the abusive monster.

Who is she now? Gary's a nice enough guy. Albeit with the brains of a fish. A hard-working carpenter who has to work for others because he isn't together enough to work independently. They struggle every month to make ends meet. You know the type, pickup truck, cowboy hat, pretending to be country in the city. Because Karen has no clue who she really is she's probably convinced her latest persona, improvised to fit with him, is her true self. How can a person go from an appreciation of classical music to Country schlock? She wasn't putting me on, I know she really got it. Now it's Mary Lou wailing for fickle Billy Bob, while guilt-ridden Billy Bob sobs in his beer at losing poor Mary Lou. Read a book? Are you kidding! Go to a play? For drama she'll have soap operas and football games. Country music, TV, rifle range, bowling, stock car racing and junk food: barbecue, beers & sodas. That's her new 'culture'. That's the milieu in which she's going to raise her daughter so that at 15 she gets pregnant because she's bored out of her mind.

Dear Karen:

I was unfaithful only once during our marriage. I'm not proud of it, though it occurred during the worst of our relationship. Susan. It didn't mean anything to her, and it didn't mean anything to me. Still I'm ashamed and I regretted it immediately.

I know you think I took advantage of your naiveté, and I can't deny it. I can deny that it was premeditated. I fell into my part gradually and came to believe it was natural. Given the difference in our ages what role would I play besides authority figure? I was horribly wrong but you must believe I didn't set out to establish myself in sadistic control. I admit over time the bully came out. Yet a lot of the energy came from exasperation and high expectations. At the same time I was struggling with a psychological condition that didn't allow me to admit I'd made a mistake. You see how that would make everything worse.

I wish at some point I could have said No I'm not behaving like this any longer. Considering how many years it takes dysfunctional dynamics to set up though it seems unrealistic to think you can change while still engaged in the old relationship. So in hindsight I see your wisdom in just running away. If you had stayed and argued for a separation I would have argued point by point, mocking your reasoning. But at the time it was a stab to the heart. I ramped up the rationalizations, self-deceptions, and feverishly told myself you'd come home with your tail between your legs. You saw my darker sides, how can I pretend you didn't. I saw some of your shallower sides, and latched onto them. In the end why didn't I help you in a loving way? Why did we slide into becoming antagonists? I don't know. I have no excuse. We weren't equally at fault. It was probably 80% me – at least. I behaved like a louse.

All you ever had to say was 'I don't love you anymore'.

Richard

The paradox is that if my complex hadn't been so bad I think I would have wiggled out of ever facing it. Because it was so extreme I was forced to confront it. In AA you are made to stand and identify yourself like, "Hi, I'm John and I'm an alcoholic." Public admission is important, because it's real world and it's witnessed.

76

It's harder to backslide and deny, you admitted it. I hope you take this account as a public admission.

I'm not claiming metamorphosis. Not pretending that I've altered my nature. When I slip up I'm still hesitant, disinclined to cop to responsibility. But the difference now is I prod myself to speak. I recognize what's going down and I give myself a kick. Due to this self-prodding my timing can be a little off because it's delayed. People look at me as if I've been asleep, or maybe English isn't my first language. But that's all right. Compared to the risk of falling back into the track of the rigid denier I will gladly endure looking a little odd or out of it. I know how important it is now.

Justice

I'd like to thank the Albuquerque Journal for allowing me to write this week's Reader's Perspective. I'm Claire Kingdon. I'm 77 years old. I've lived in New Mexico most of my adult life. My husband and I met in college and two years after we were married we decided to move here. We were always happy about that decision. We raised three children, and there are now 7 grandchildren. I've been a widow for the last 13 years. I think of myself as a New Mexican.

I would like to offer a different perspective on the Delfino Moses Ortega story from last Saturday's front page. [Ed. "Local Barber Charged In Colorado Slayings" by John J. Lumpkin and Jeremy Pawloski.] Because I don't believe its one of those incidents where it has to be one of two choices. Either those who are sure he's innocent are right, so he's that person. Or those who accept that he's guilty are right and he's a completely opposite person. Most likely to me is that he's both of these people. For those of you who missed last Saturday's paper it told of the arrest of Ortega by Colorado authorities for killing two women a quarter century ago. He made one look like a botched carjacking, and the other a botched burglary. The only thing they had in common was the appearance being botched robberies, so the murders would seem like unintended consequences. The charge in both cases is that the husbands paid Ortega $10,000 to kill their wives. The reaction by the townspeople in Rio Rancho to this horrible charge against their most popular barber, was one of disbelief. "He loves everybody." "He loves children." "He'd do anything for you." "He'd help you out any way he could." "He's a pillar of the community and a wonderful person." "A good friend and a good gabber. He keeps you amused while you're in his chair and before you know it he's all finished and you had a good laugh."

What I deduced from people's reactions was our instinctual presumption that it has to be an either/or choice. Either he was the person they knew and liked, and these accusations therefore were unfounded and pernicious; or the charges were true, and the friendly barber was just an act, a false front. Relying on what I've witnessed in the world, and in people, I'd like to propose that it's most likely both are true. That he is guilty – there must be pretty damning 'new' evidence for a Colorado Springs district attorney to bring up charges 25 years after the crime. Yet that doesn't mean he wasn't genuinely the friendly barber people in Rio Rancho have known and liked. It wasn't an act. (I don't even want to think about the cruelty of it all if Mr. Ortega were innocent. It's too horrible to contemplate. Thankfully there's little chance that's the case. No doubt - after 25 years - he was caught off guard, but he would have quickly surmised the source of this trouble.)

There is an advantage to the perspective age can give one. Most of us start off in life with clear categories and definite lines of separation. We decide not only on classifications that make sense to us but we gradually establish how seriously we weigh different things. Not only what is wrong but beyond that what is unforgivable. Yet as the years mount up, unless you become one of the rigid, you find, against your own resistance, the sureness of categorical judgment has eroded. As they say instead of black and white you find out everything's gray. This has to effect how you come down morally on offenders. You see standards bending depending on the person, and you end up making offsetting adjustments.

Even with close friends you notice quirks. I have a very dear friend who is as tight as the bark on a tree. I know how she is, and I just go around it. You factor in and anticipate how she will react to anything that costs money. She's a great person in all other respects. I have another close friend who can't stop talking. You know that when you get together with her that it's going to be pretty much non-stop blabbing, and she's going to be the one dominating the conversation. That's just how she is. It will be entertaining and tiresome at the same time. Another friend is undependable. You learn this the hard way, but after a few disappointments you make an adjustment in your expectations. You learn to treasure a person's good sides, and not dwell of their deficiencies. Maybe laugh about them. Most of us have friends whose politics aren't ours, or whose religion is not ours. These are important differences, yet we don't allow it to nullify the friendship. And how many of us have really good friends who are fond of us but for whatever reason can't tolerate each other? In these relationships you are required to do a balancing act, and you do.

How often do we hastily apply a label to something and never bother to go back and reexamine it? Along this line how often do we decide that something is simple when, if we took the time to study it more closely, we'd find that in fact it was pretty complicated? I think it's in this sort of blithe simplification wherein 'a lie is a lie' falls, and the following presumption that anyone you discover lying is nothing but a liar. That their core nature has now been revealed, no need to go further. Is that really the case? I don't think so.

Following black and white logic we decide, when we think we catch a person covering up something with a fictional explanation, since this qualifies as deception, then they must be deceivers. They're bad. After all they're boldly presenting a false appearance; and maybe impersonating in an emotional manner what we'd expect from an innocent person if falsely accused. But we are convinced, and let us say for the sake of argument that we are right about this, that they're not as they pretend to be. Does that mean we are justified in our condemnation of them? For a moment pull back and consider their dilemma from their point of view. Let us say that for most of their life they have behaved in a correct manner. Yes they've gone off course in this instance. Who hasn't made a mistake? And technically they are lying. But they are well aware of the consequences for their image and reputation if the accusation were to stick. That would be the end. The lapse would define them. It would be everything they were known for. That is the source of the passion in their denial. Not because they're practiced liars or actors, but from the terror of the consequences of being stigmatized. Of being branded forever. If you can see this as unfair and disproportionate, you can glimpse how the emotion, even their indignation, could be real, even if they were hiding the truth. Panic because the result of exposure would misrepresent who they are.

I wouldn't want anyone, especially any surviving relatives of either wife, to think I'm attempting to downplay the heinous nature of these crimes. For husbands to commission the murder of their wives is terrible. And likewise Mr. Ortega, agreeing to do it for money, was odious. This is solely a plea to consider realistically who Mr. Ortega is now, 25 years on. The grounds for mitigation that I contemplate relate to:

    1) The passage of Time.
    2) The tendencies of Human Psychology.
    3) The very nature of true Justice.

A person who because of the nature of their job come into contact with many people, say someone working in a government office that issues licenses or permits; a bus driver; waiter at a restaurant; or a barber; might tend to have a flooded, possibly jaundiced view of humanity. Which isn't to say they wouldn't like people, they'd simply know so many - so many types they were forced to work with. I don't think it's mere imagination, or going too far, in presuming that Mr. Ortega would only have heard the worst about the two wives from their husbands. The husbands had every incentive to prejudice him and justify themselves. Maybe this started even before they hatched any plan. (One can't help wondering if in the second case, after hearing out the husband's complaints Mr. Ortega wasn't the one who – cautiously – brought up that for $10,000 he'd solved a similar problem.) So Ortega heard one-sided biased accounts of what the women were like, which not hearing the other side, he accepted uncritically. The husbands were free to give only exaggerated disparaging versions of their wives. To describe them as ghastly harpies. I know how the reverse works at my beauty parlor where it's just women. Often the gossip dwells on the defects of men: boyfriends and husbands. How they are lazy, cheap, dull, or a zero as far as romance.

Most likely Ortega had no contact with the women. Maybe he didn't even know what they looked like. The first husband would have set things up by saying this is the time we close the nightclub. This is the make of our car. This is the road I will drive on. Use a flashing red light so she'll think it's the police pulling us over. Strike me hard so the authorities will believe it was a robbery attempt, and I was knocked out. Make sure you shoot her dead.

Having gotten away with the first one (March) must have led to the commission to do the second (November). This one would have been easier, because the husband and wife had separated, and she had moved into a separate house. The motivation I think was obvious - to avoid the financial loss a divorce would have entailed. All the husband had to do was give Ortega her new address.

No matter how cool Mr. Ortega might have acted back then, unless he is a psychopathic monster, these executions must have entailed heart-pounding adrenaline spikes. I'm fully aware that $10,000 was worth more then than it is now, but still there was always the risk that something could go wrong. That an unanticipated third party might intervene, just by bad luck. Or incriminating evidence would get accidentally left behind. Even after he pulled the murders off, he had to worry that one of the husbands might slip up and then implicate him in a plea bargain. He couldn't control that. We don't need to speculate about his conscience to state that a cloud of anxiety would have descended upon him after he committed these crimes. That is some measure of punishment, spread over so many years, even if it's in a ghostly proportion.

Part of the old definition of tragedy was having the central figure inherit, or achieve by merit, a high station, distinction or honor; before they fell. Falling from a height defined it, qualified it as a tragedy. I don't think it a stretch to say, that in a New Mexican way, Mr. Ortega's story qualifies in this way as a tragedy. The Albuquerque Journal [in the West Side edition] less than two months ago featured Mr. Ortega for the service he renders fellow veterans. On his days off he would go to the homes of disabled veterans and cut their hair. In the article he related that he came from a long line of barbers. Both sets of grandparents, along with seven uncles and aunts. If that's not an inheritance I don't know what is. He was quoted as saying he liked being a barber because he enjoyed "meeting and talking to people". Four years ago the Governor appointed him to the State Board of Barbers and Cosmetologists. For the last year and a half he's been the Chairman. So relative to his vocation he'd reached the top, with the past seemingly safely hidden from view.

If we're honest we should admit that our reaction to the news of misfortune befalling others (strangers) often evokes an ugly side. Usually whatever sympathy we manage is pro forma, outweighed by unbecoming curiosity, relief that it isn't us, and even satisfaction, as if 'they got what was coming to them'. This is our smaller self rising up and taking over. Something bad happened, but it didn't happen to us. There's an instinctive relief to this with an animal aspect, especially a herd animal, as when a predator catches one but it isn't you - you are still alive with all the others in the herd who survive. The satisfaction part is worse. Our jealousy of the elevated explains our gratification at seeing them brought down.

This is most obvious in the delight with which people devour celebrity exposes. Nasty scandals, divorces and custody battles; the never ending alcohol and drug problems. Or the financial bust, after lavish 'conspicuous consumption'. Voyeurism done in the mean spirit of 'Well look, they turn out not to be so superior after all - they're getting cut down to size'. Most of us struggle on with some broken dreams, and as the saying goes, misery loves company. Feasting on the tidbits of celebrities fumbling allows us to see life as mere luck. It was just luck that raised them up, and they thought they were so high and mighty; and now luck – with an assist from their inner character flaws - has brought them down. From our own disappointments comes the motive to discount success as due to dumb luck and a willingness to do the unscrupulous. Nothing to do with merit.

(I agree that society's evolution away from old notions of 'sin' has overall been good and healthy. I draw the line though at dispensing with all standards of behavior. While there's always been gossip, and it always contained a strong negative element, people used to be ashamed to show their gloating glee at the plight of others. It was a sign of poor upbringing. Now they couldn't be more open about it. Every ugly attack is fair. As if because we made the famous famous, we retain the right to bring them down and joy in it. In a love/hate way as much as we're drawn to it we resent their success; we presume it's gone to their heads; so we relish seeing them taught a lesson: that they're no better than us, their comeuppance viewed as overdue. Somehow this goes towards balancing things - for our not having their fortune. It's all perfectly awful and tawdry if you ask me.)

In our system of justice final determination of guilt or innocence is left to judge or jury. I like our system, particularly the 'jury of one's peers'. Over the years I've had the honor to serve on a few juries because, as it happened, I had the time, and neither the prosecution or defense saw any reason to excuse me. One thing that's always made a deep impression on me occurs early in the process. The judge will ask prospective jurors: despite what you may have heard or read about this case, can you be fair, can you lay it aside and follow my instruction to weigh only legally submitted evidence and testimony? (There are always some who will exploit this opportunity to worm out of their duty, pretending that they aren't able to disregard what they heard or read.)

For those of you who didn't read the story last Saturday, I should probably mention that Mr. Ortega was tried for murder once before. For shooting an ex-employee over the left eye with a .357. The jury accepted his version - that it was self-defense. I'm afraid some of you might jump on this and say, "Well that's it! Coupled with what we now know about the wives, that makes three cold-blooded killings this guy's perpetrated. It reveals the true darkness of his soul, and what sort of a villain he really is." But I would beg you to please hold on for a minute. The date is important. This killing took place exactly 17 days after the second wife's murder. Now this may not have been classic 'self-defense'. Granted. But it occurred in this same dark period and couldn't we speculate that the disgruntled ex-employee knew about, overheard some things, or figured what had happened? That then he confronted Ortega, I would assume to blackmail him. Threats. Demanding either his old job back or cash. Ortega would have been prompted by fear - where will this end? He was compelled to act. Unlike the case of the two wives there would have been little or no premeditation. And let's not forget that while technically this victim was a victim, he had opted not to go to the police, which is what an honest person would have done.

Justice seems simple in the abstract but when encountering real human beings it gets very complicated. For example the matter of sentencing. In my opinion where there is mandatory sentencing, leaving the judge no discretion, there is injustice all across the board - in every direction. Let's say two people have been found guilty of the exact same crime. From a distance you might think that they should receive the same sentence. But the more you know the particulars the more you realize that wouldn't be right. While the crime might have been the same the individuals are very different, the circumstances are very different, and the sentence should be what is appropriate to each, not a generalized punishment.

I ran into a man some time after we'd both served together on a jury. He surprised me by telling me that if he had known at the time of our deliberations the cost of incarceration – approximately $25,000 a year, it would have affected where he came down. At first I was shocked and appalled, because I presumed that cost was extraneous to our assignment to assess the evidence and decide the case within the perimeters the law dictated. But the more I thought about it the more I could see if this man thought it was important in the big picture, and apparently he did, he had every right to include it in his determination. A judge can instruct in the law, telling a jury what they should accept, and what they should rule out of their consideration. But the jury is the final arbiter; so they can ignore the judge's instruction if they so wish, and decide on any grounds they chose. Think of the jury as a little cell representing our democracy. This man was a taxpayer, and he saw himself paying a price, and he considered the price too high; so he had every right to see it as a factor to be included. I also think though he should have considered, as a good citizen and a member of society, whether he wanted the accused unpunished scot-free to return to mix in society.

Why do we say that "justice should be swift"? Does it show that we value expediency over everything else? Of course not. So is it because we always bow to the authorities; if they've decided something we assume there must be a good reason? No. While there is some deference and respect we have no illusions that they're infallible. Is it a sop to a primal vengeance, to get our bloodlust satisfied before the beast gets really agitated? Again no. Though its true if you rolled all these elements together you would get a profile of cases where the system doesn't function properly, and the innocent can be railroaded. Most wrongful convictions arise from police and prosecutors stubbornly sticking to their first hunch - they want this suspect to be guilty to quiet the public. Coercing confessions, leading eyewitnesses, coordinating expert witnesses, and burying troublesome – even exculpatory – evidence. But vengeance isn't the underlying reason in the profound interpretation of the aphorism 'justice should be swift'. That originates in an understanding of the changeableness of the world. And the changeableness of human beings. And this doesn't exclude ourselves – the people who make up the jury. Nor the judge – nor the judged.

In our everyday lives we encounter this principle of justice even if we don't notice it. Take for example a child being naughty. Let's say your son has broken an expensive object you told him never to touch. Or your daughter has watched television after you expressly told her she wasn't allowed until she'd done all her homework. However, at that moment, for whatever reason, you don't want to get engaged in disciplining. But you don't forget either. You remember, and a month later, when you are in the mood, you dole out some punishment. Most of us would sense something faulty in this action. An exhibition of poor parenting; demonstrating a lack of self-discipline and/or the ability to achieve the proper perspective on what you were doing, and the disconnected message you were sending. And – this is crucial – it would strike us as unfair. Why? There had been a deliberate violation and some penalty had been warranted. It's because we naturally recognize that the punishment must occur in the same time frame as the transgression to be just. Otherwise it's not fitting.

With Ortega and the passage of a quarter century, the crimes and the perpetrator have become separated over a vast expanse. I'm not saying that the crime has changed. It's as heinous as it ever was. But the individual is certain to have changed. Remember it all happened during one relatively brief block of time – less than a year – 25 years ago. Yes one can argue Mr. Ortega is the one who evaded detection, so the responsibility for this great delay falls on him. But what creature doesn't run from pain and possible captivity? Anyway it's beside the point whose fault it is. Part of the lessons learned, by the survivor Ortega, came from the bad acts of his younger self preying on his conscience. The over-riding fact is that we are dealing with a different person than the one who committed the murders. No we can't prove this 'beyond a shadow of a doubt', but that's an impossible standard.

Negative stays negative. Just because we now have Mr. Ortega in our power and at our mercy, and can exact a terrible recompense if we want to, make him a prisoner for the rest of his life, doesn't mean we should. True justice rises above an eye for an eye. Positive is still positive. I would recommend the Colorado authorities forebear. Let Ortega take a plea. Of course he must confess his crimes. He must repent. But in exchange he should receive a relatively light sentence. There should be a general acknowledgment that punishment didn't come in time, and a public expression of regret, a separate apology from the jurisdiction to the families of the victims for this lapse. But the recognition that Ortega has changed, that he is not the same person as the perpetrator; that he has in fact become a model citizen, should also be publicly acknowledged. As a good that arose from something foul. As the article mentioned a man who, on his days off, would go to the homes of disabled vets to cut their hair. (I don't know for a fact that he did this for free, though the way I read the article it seemed to be implied. But I don't know.)

Always remember, 'Judge not, that ye be not judged'. If we want people to believe that we can change, and we most certainly do, then we must allow that possibility in others. In life one should struggle against growing hard and closed-minded. Since Ortega is no longer a threat to anyone, why not let him live the balance of his days in the exemplary style in which he has been living in recent years. Let him exist, as a felon, not as someone who got away with crime and escaped punishment, but as an example of human redemption, mercy and improvement. As a reminder of the great variety in humanity, and how inside every individual there can be several different people. How this is true of ourselves.

Structuring

"Look sweetie, I want to talk to you about some serious things, for a little while, okay?"

"Okay."

"See you're just the right age. When you were younger you were too young to understand, and later you'll be tired of listening to adults.

"The birds!"

"Yeah."

"They saw us."

"Those are ducks. Did you know that? They have swans, but I don't see any today. Swans are huge. Geese are pretty big, a lot bigger than ducks, but swans are even bigger. And beautiful. You want some of the bread to throw them?"

"Yes."

"Here. That's enough. A little at a time."

"That one has funny colors. Why does it?"

"I don't know."

"Is it different?"

"No, I don't think so. Just a different color for some reason. Shapes the same. Emmy were you listening to me?"

"Yes."

"I want you to pay attention. Let's sit on the bench. We'll still be close."

"Can I have some more?"

"Alright. But scatter it out so they all get some. What about that one out there?"

"Yeah. There."

"Good. Alright come, sit. Now what I was saying is I've waited until you were old enough to understand what I'm going to say. Deep inside of us we hold onto our memories of things. Everything exactly as it happened. A lot of times we can't reach those memories, we forget or make up poor versions that aren't right, but somewhere they're still down there. So I know, even if you forget this, it'll still be inside you."

"Uh-huh."

"What I'm going to say is there are important rules in life. Like you know: doing good and not doing bad - that guide a person in their life. Right?"

"Yeah."

"First off develop good habits. You know when I tell Nana not to spoil you, it's not because I don't want you to enjoy things. Of course I do. But too much candy, too much playing video games or whatever are bad; and get you into the habit of wanting – expecting – to have too much. A little candy is a treat. It's enjoyable. But too much candy or too much TV is bad, and you know what – eventually they'll make you feel bad. Rotten and grumpy. Developing the habit of wanting too much can really get a person in trouble. Spoiled. The spoiled aren't happy. If you stay up all night you won't be bright for school. If we let you drink sodas, like some parents let their kids, it'll be bad for your body – and bad for your teeth. The important thing to know so you're alert is that's it's a lot easier to never start a bad habit, than it is to stop one once it's grabbed hold of you. A habit can be bad or it can be a good habit. Either way it's hard to break it once its established. Understand?"

"Yes."

"As you grow up you'll see people can't just do what they like. Like going to school. Why do you have to go to school?"

"I like school."

"I know, but let's say all you wanted to do was play. Even if it was fun to do nothing but play, that would be for what we call the short term, right at the moment. Going to school, learning things, developing good habits, improving your mind, these are long-term things, for the rest of your life. They will help you when you're grown up. So in the long run you can arrive at a good life. You try to get good grades – you try to do well – so in the future, after school, you can get a good job and that supports your family, with a nice house in a nice neighborhood. A mommy or daddy are always thinking how will what I'm doing appear to my kids? Because even parents who have bad habits themselves want to set a good example. Someone who swears when they get angry is setting a bad example. There's a good chance that their kids will swear also. You can say over and over 'swearing is bad, don't do it', but if you do it whenever you're mad, that's a stronger influence than giving good advice. The same with smoking. People will tell their children, 'Don't take up this nasty habit', but if they go on smoking they're setting a bad example and there's a good chance that when their children grow up they'll be smokers too. They imitate their parents."

"You and Mommy don't smoke."

"No. But I hope if we did we would stop, so we wouldn't set a bad example for you. I think showing your kids that you work hard, and you believe in working hard, is another good example. Why should people work hard?'

"To make money."

"Well I guess that's part of it, in the sense that you need to provide – support your family – by doing a job that other people will pay you for. But it's not the money. That's just what is exchanged for doing your job you know. There are plenty of people who work, who keep their job, just barely, but don't work hard. Do enough to keep their job and not get fired. And they get paid too."

"Can we get a boat sometime?"

"Are you listening to me Emmy? Sure, sometime, but let's do it when Mom and Timmy are with us. That'd be more fun wouldn't it?"

"Yeah."

"What I'm saying is the real reason to work hard, to do a good job - no matter what it is you do - is self-satisfaction. Knowing you are doing your best. And not just for yourself – or even your family. But we're all in this together – dependent on each other. What would happen if everyone did a half-hearted job? Things would fall apart. We'd all suffer. And people who work hard feel better about themselves – knowing they are giving it their all. You follow that?"

"Yes."

"Let's say there's a father. Who's not a bad man. He wants to do what's right, but for whatever reason he does something wrong."

"What?"

"I don't know, just something not good. We'll say a mistake." Okay he doesn't tell his family, because he wants them to go on respecting him, and he's worried that if they knew the truth about what he did, they wouldn't respect him anymore. So he doesn't tell the truth. Which we know isn't good. We won't call it a lie, we'll just say he avoids mentioning it. Because he's the only one who knows what he did, no one else knows about it to bring it up. But it messes him up. It troubles him. He can't stop thinking about it – and imaging how his wife and children would react if they really knew. And know what? He starts getting cross with them. Yelling when he shouldn't. Snapping at them over very little things. This really happens. So what is he doing?"

"Yelling at them."

"Well – yeah. But by releasing this pressure – from having done something wrong, then concealing that he's done something wrong, now he's doing another wrong: yelling at his family. And he's setting a bad example Em. All because he has a bad conscience. Which means he feels bad - guilty - about what he's hiding from them. And he reacts to this bad feeling by acting bad. So everything gets worse and he becomes a bad role model, a bad example. We feel sorry for these people, but I wouldn't want you going over to a house where your friends parents acted like that. Right?"

"Yeah. Who?"

"What?"

"Who's parents?"

"No I'm not talking about someone we know. I'm talking about people we don't know. I'm just saying – as an example – if we did know parents like that, I wouldn't want you to be around them. Honesty is so important. And not being honest can get you into trouble. When you say something you want people to take your word. 'We know Emmy is honest.' Sometimes, in little ways, being honest can cost you. If the teacher asks, Emmy did you do this assignment all by yourself, and you reply honestly, no my mother and father helped me a little, all right, you might not receive as good a grade. But you're doing the right thing. You're establishing a good habit – of telling the truth. There are people who get away with things – some are very good at getting away with things. But you don't want to be one of them do you?"

"No."

"In the long run they're headed for trouble."

"Can we feed the ducks some more?"

"Honey we've thrown all the bread we brought. See the bag's empty. Let me finish what I'm saying okay?"

"Okay."

"Loyalty. You know what loyalty is? Staying loyal? It's a person knowing that I mean so much to you that if I was in trouble – and called for you to come – no matter what you were doing you'd come. Even if I was interrupting something that you wanted to do – wanted to finish. Even if it made you look bad, in the eyes of some other people. You'd still do it, you wouldn't care – well you might care - but you'd still do it. Because your higher loyalty would be to me. People are loyal to their country. Often we think of dogs as exemplifying this trait. You know their loyalty to their owner, to the family they live with; barking at strangers, warning: someone's coming. Guarding the home. The way they follow you around wagging their tail, wanting to please you. You remember Grandma's Fritzi – how protective he would get? That kind of attachment. Faithfulness – there are a lot of words for this, but it's being loyal. And being loyal is staying loyal."

"Daddy can we go to a movie?"

"When?"

"Now."

"No, I'm trying to tell you something. It won't be long. Let me finish. Okay, maybe later, if we see something suitable. For kids, alright? Do you need to go to the bathroom?"

"No."

"Are you listening to what I'm saying?"

"Yes."

"Okay what did I just say?"

"You can depend on someone who is loyal like Fritzi."

"Alright. Okay. It won't be long Em, but I want to try to finish what I'm trying to tell you about conduct. I'm trying to give you a picture of what's important to a person in life. Okay?"

"Okay."

"Fairness is also very important. If someone does something good, be fair, give them credit. Don't try to horn in and get part of the credit for yourself, when you didn't deserve it. And don't try to shrink what they did, so it appears smaller than it was. That's not nice, and people do this all the time. Especially at work, but also at home. Do you give credit to your friends when they do something good?"

"I think so."

"I think so too. My father, your grandfather, had a neat way of capturing the problem. He'd say there are traps for the weak, and there are traps for the strong. The traps for the weak are what we've been talking about: not developing good habits, laziness; failing to be honest, or loyal, when you're tested. And I mean tested by a real things in the world – circumstances in life – not a test at school. But your grandfather would also tell us when we were your age that there are traps for the strong as well. It's easy to become proud when you're strong. Vain. Do you know what vanity is?"

"No."

"Thinking 'O I'm really great. I'm better than other people.'"

"Which movie?"

"I don't know. I said we'd have to see. One for children Em, and one you haven't already seen. We're not going to a movie you've already seen. Be patient just a minute, let me finish what I'm saying. Let's say you're looking at some poor person who has fallen into trouble of some sort. Instead of thinking they must have done something wrong - to have brought this misfortune on themselves, you should think if I'd been born in their place, had the same life they had, that could be me. And this is true. Only, as they say, 'by the grace of God' did I avoid it. It wasn't anything I did, I was just fortunate to have my life, my circumstances. So you steer clear of the 'I'm better', and you think instead 'how fortunate I am'. Understand?"

"Yes."

"You have a mother and father who are smart, so the odds were in your favor. And you are smart. Did you do anything to bring that about?"

"No."

"No, you were just born. You're fortunate, but that doesn't make you superior to children who may not be as smart. Vanity – vain, proud people, have a hard time caring about other people. Because they only care about themselves. In consequence they have few friends – people just don't like vain people. Mostly they end up unhappy. It's sad, but you know there's some justice to that. And they blame everyone else – but it's their fault."

"Can we get more bread?"

"Not today. Emmy are you paying attention?"

"Yes."

"The next time we come we'll try to bring more bread. It depends, you don't give them fresh bread. We brought a lot. If there were geese here – they're big and pushy. Let's sit for just a little longer, and I'll finish what I'm trying to say. Come on. Look Em there's something inside of us that tells us when we're doing right or doing wrong."

"Even bad people?"

"Yeah. They ignore it, or make excuses; but they know what they're doing is wrong. There are very few people who don't know what is wrong or right. Crazy people. There are really very few people that are crazy."

"Why don't they?"

"Well they're confused. Let's not worry about them. That's very few people. And they're easy to spot, talking to themselves, imagining things. Let's talk about the vast majority of people. Most people if they do something wrong, let's say they're greedy and they take something that doesn't belong to them. Inside they know that they've done something wrong. They tell themselves excuses: I need it more, they owe me, they have plenty, they won't miss it; stuff like that. But deep inside they know what they did was wrong. They try to convince themselves that it wasn't. You know what that's called, that thing deep inside of us that tells us we've done wrong?"

"No."

"Well I told you that's the conscience. Your conscience will remind you that you had no right to take something that wasn't properly yours. Or you should have been nicer to that person. I want you to always pay attention to your conscience Em. Don't ignore or lie to yourself. Dealing with your conscience is being guided by the Golden Rule. You know the Golden Rule?"

"No."

"I'm sure you do. I'm sure we've told you. The Golden Rule is look at what you're doing and if its something you wouldn't want someone to do to you, then stop. Do you want people to be nice to you or mean?"

"Nice."

"Then the Golden Rule tells you that you, in turn, should be nice to others. You know why it's the Golden rule?"

"Why?"

"Because you can't go wrong with it. You can depend on it to guide you. So it's thought of as golden – because gold is valuable. That's the way people used to talk about something - because gold was so valuable in the old days, because it wouldn't rust. A way of saying this is the best. The best rule. If you forget everything else, and remember the Golden Rule, you can't go wrong. Say you have a toy. A doll. And a good friend is visiting. Let's say Amelia. And this is a very special doll you don't want to share. But Amelia is your guest and she asks to play with the doll. You ask yourself, if I were a visitor at Amelia's house, and she had a special doll I wanted to play with, what would I want her to say?"

"To let me."

"Right. So what does that tell you you should say, when she asks at your house to play with your doll?"

"Sometimes she doesn't ask."

"Alright that's wrong. But when she does ask politely?"

"To let her."

"Good."

"What if she brought her own doll from home?"

"Then there's no problem. Ready to go?"

"Yeah. For a movie?"

"If we see a good one."

Going Last

[editors NEW NETHERLAND QUARTERLY REVIEW]

One objective the founders of our quarterly hoped to perpetuate was that in important matters the editors would abstain from abridging discussion due to space considerations. Thanks to the generosity of our early benefactors the New Netherland Quarterly Review is still able to observe this goal. We believe at present we are among a select few retaining this ability. Yes we are aware that other serious journals indulge in lengthy exchanges on their on-line appendages. To our, undoubtedly antiquated sensibilities however while 'virtual' existence has much to recommend it - miraculous in its speed-of-light efficiency, it doesn't suggest substance or permanence of sustained thought. Not compared to the old 'actual' form on the paper. Even if pulp is fated to join papyrus and sheepskin, let us indulge this harmless luxury a little while longer.

In our Fall issue we featured the article, "Lincoln Crossed Out" by Professor James Helton. A review of Professor Luigi Baccala's "Cross of the Christlike President", published by the University of California Press. Doctor Baccala has registered exception to the review, believing points were slanted and misleading, and he has asked for space to respond. We informed him that our policy inclines to place no limits on an exchange, but he has chosen, for his own reasons, to measure his remarks. Doctor Helton on the other hand has taken full advantage of our liberality. He has informed us that while he sees no reason to retract his critique of the book in question, he does regret the narrowness of his focus, since he believes that Baccala's writing and thought, beyond this particular book, deserves serious consideration.

Luigi Baccala
(Santa Cruz, California)

I must confess that when I first heard the New Netherland Quarterly Review, an esteemed journal by anyone's standards, had deemed my little book worthy of notice, I couldn't help but feel flattered. It's rather unfortunate that in whatever shuffle took place after the initial decision to review it, that my book got assigned to someone too busy to actually read it. This happens in life, I don't feel persecuted. Busy people with too much already on their plate are told to deal with something that for whatever reason doesn't happen to interest them. There's also the not inconsequential fact that I am not a member of the historian's guild. Where the allegiance is to dues paying members supporting other members, waiting their turn to receive their moment in the spotlight. Everyone protecting the turf from non-credentialed outsiders. I'm not even a member of the political or journalist guilds, which though viewed as inferior fraternities, still have some claim on the territory.

As I said in the book President Wilson loved the lunatic glorification of the Klan and their terror campaign by the pedophile GW Griffith. In a weird way that vile film with its celebration of racist terrorists did mark, exactly as the two principals thought, the rebirth of their nation, and the eclipse of ours. If Professor Helton wants to stand with Wilson I'm happy to stand with Debs. Wilson's unrelenting grudge against Debs' stemmed from the latter's daring to dismiss the president's rationales for the sacrifice of thousands of lives in the dumb carnage of World War I as nothing more than the usual lies that exploit nationalistic fervor. I for one can't pretend the link between Lincoln and Wilson doesn't exist. In the face of what we'd all agree was a national emergency, Lincoln established extra-constitutional executive powers that had not existed before. Wilson exploited those powers for the war he wanted, after an election he won by deception: promising to keep us out of the European conflict. All the propaganda, coercion, security statism, American empire, we have now are the contours we inherited from Wilson, which he did not invent, but borrowed in turn from Lincoln.

I commence my little refutation here in full knowledge of how the odds are stacked against me. Simply contesting the review of a book creates a first impression of someone so vain they can't admit that their work contains mistakes. It's the image of a special pleading whiner. Even more prejudicial to the reviewed is the format of the exchange. The reviewed is allowed to protest, but must go first. The reviewer is to have the last word. After all he or she must defend not only their own opinion, but the judgment of the journal as well, which nominated them for this assignment.

The little drama has a set pattern. A book, the product of protracted research and long labor, gets short shrift and is misrepresented in grotesque caricature. The indignant author feels obligated, for the record and their own reputation, to un-bias as many readers as he or she can reach - to pen a rejoinder. They will have to struggle to keep signs of emotion out of the response or it will be taken as evidence of a poor soul who couldn't rise above the investment in their own work, partiality, unable to admit the errors and weaknesses helpfully pointed out, in other words unwilling to 'take their medicine'.

Yet the foolhardy author is sure that some of the facts to hand are incontrovertible, and they will effectively refute the review. Also direct quotes from the review can be demonstrated to be false or used misleadingly. The inference that this misrepresentation was probably deliberate is hard to avoid. So at least the fair-minded will be allowed to see that the book has been abused. The author will attempt to maintain an unperturbed air so as to suggest mastery of the material and a continuing confidence in what was written. None of this will profit in the least. Because the reviewer goes last. Whether the reviewer capably answers the points thrown back at him is less important than the 'optics' the position confers. There's back and forth, but to end is to finish. To have the last word is the honor given authority. All the worried business the reviewed brought up will come to be seen, as it shrinks, as trivial quibbles. The reviewer might diminish it further by pretending to offer us the bigger picture. If the review had a few misses they were minor, and who would make a fuss about such trivia? They were immaterial to the main thrust of the criticism, which remains an indictment that cannot be shook off. Readers will accept this as a fair and final summation of the matter.

A reviewer has another advantage in being able to study the major points of the complaint, and then tailor his refutation to its shape. He can dismissively skip quickly through the parts where his critique might be weakest - make a gesture of generalized defense; and then emphasize at great length the parts where he feels his strength lies. He or she can act above the fray. Pretending real surprise, and a little sadness, that X should find the simple enumeration of blatant deficiencies offensive, instead of regarding these corrections as beneficial to seeing the subject correctly. Isn't fealty to the subject the important thing? And while the reviewed must be very careful to constrain and hide emotion, a reviewer is free to provoke and mock if so inclined. Unless the discussion lies in a reader's particular field of study, and they have an independent opinion, most will accept the reviewer's emphasis as defining what is important and germane. And there is that added factor that vicious reviews are a guilty pleasure. There's something in us entertained at watching a presumptuous pompous expert getting their bubble popped. No matter how much a reader might have been swayed when they first read the author's complaint, count on them getting moved back across the same terrain as they read the reviewer's counter. And it will be accepted as fair, after all both parties had their say. I bring all this up preemptively, before mustering my foredoomed protest, so you will know as you watch me struggle to mount my defense that I do so without any delusion or expectation of vindication.

Let me commence by stating that I did not set out to *get* Lincoln. Helton refers to the "Christlike" in my title as sarcastic. It was not sarcastic. As the author I think here at least I might be allowed to claim inside knowledge of my own attitude. I believe the mature Lincoln was extremely empathetic, patient, understanding and forgiving. He could even forgive enemies and traitors (something wonderful and at the same time deeply disturbing in a country's leader). There's a long record of his interactions with people and the manifestations of attributes we have always designated as 'saintly'. Inferior people could insult him and he would forebear. It's true that as a young man he had a mean-streak, and that along with the storytelling, and jokes at his own expense, he could be pretty savage towards targets. But this means he deserves more credit for deliberately rejecting the impulse towards viciousness, turning away from it and towards becoming the compassionate person we know him as. Lincoln would turn the other cheek. One famous example: the monstrous abuse he endured from the insufferable Gen. McClellan. When Lincoln and the Secretary of War came to call at the general's house, they were made to wait, and when the egomaniac finally came home he went straight upstairs to bed, sending word down that he had retired for the night. It's unthinkable that any other president would have tolerated such insubordination, let alone during wartime. Except for the treasonous MacArthur in Korea I can think of no other American commander who has behaved like that. And Truman fired MacArthur.

Nor, contrary to what Helton says I imply, do I hold that ambition automatically disqualifies one from spiritual being. I honestly don't know where he got that. Who was more ambitious than Jesus? To incarnate the Jewish messiah, but to do so in an inside-out way: a revolution in the individual soul, not leading an army of independence. I think we'd all agree Jesus was both ambitious and spiritual. Often it would seem to accomplish a great task it helps to have commensurate ambition. It's not just the Alexander the Greats and Napoleons; it's also the reformers: Jane Addams, Dorothy Day, Ralph Nader.

By the way, though I know there are more books published on the subject than anyone can possibly read, it would surprise me if Prof. Helton had never come across Harry S. Stout's 2006 "Upon the Altar of the Nation: A Moral History of the American Civil War". Like me Stout is not only critical of Lincoln's actions, he's also critical of his legacy. Yet he too refers to him as "Christlike". As the Jonathan Edwards Professor of American Religious History at Yale, I think we might allow this to serve as some sort of precedent. (Though I must add that as much as I admire moral absolutism, it's mind-boggling to me how anyone can end up with a parity between North and South. Because some individuals on the Union side did despicable acts we'd all condemn, and war means spilling blood, Stout allows himself to drift into an unreality where its sinners all.)

Of Lincoln's depression, I did not "exaggerate his condition". I'm not sure that's possible. If Helton wants to join those who romanticize depression, I'll have you note this rarely includes people who have actually suffered from the affliction. I chose to regard it as a dangerous disability (as in disabling). I won't be derailed or intimidated by Helton's injunction that we try to understand values and behaviors in the context of a period that had "different standards and beliefs". Of course in principle that's sound, but it's being used here to obfuscate something that is clear by any sober standard. There is **no** period in man's history, there is no country, where Lincoln's behavior would not have marked him as deeply disturbed. As a youth living in the country, where every young man carried a pocketknife, he abstained out of fear that the temptation - at any moment - to cut his own throat, would prove too overwhelming to resist. Does Helton seriously suggest that there were a lot of young men back then who walked around with a similar fear? (The poem young Lincoln writes, published anonymously, is all about an individual committing suicide.) Later, when he had grown up, and he'd have his spells, his friends took turns keeping suicide watches on him. Are we to imagine that this too was something common in nineteenth century

America? Among the various ridiculous insinuations ad hominem that Helton forks in my direction, the one I take the most exception to is his slyly suggesting that I plagiarized Joshua Shenk's "Lincoln's Melancholy". I don't know what I can do beyond what I did; citing Shenk, naming his book, bringing it up in the appropriate place in my text. I honestly can't go beyond that since obviously I don't agree with his thesis: that Lincoln's depression was his source of greatness.

Helton disputes that the one piece of hard evidence that's survived - a pharmacy account listing drugs ordered for the Lincoln family - as dispositive of anything. He says they could have all been for Mrs. Lincoln. Since Helton refuses to concede that Lincoln's perennial funks were 'crippling', that they would significantly impact anyone's ability to concentrate and think, it follows that he won't consider the effects of the drugs Lincoln took to cope with his depressions. Remember we're talking about someone, and there are contemporary witnesses to this, who at times could barely function, sometimes for protracted periods. Then factor in that this same person was tricked into doing the 'honorable' thing and marrying a woman he had developed reservations about. It's clear to anyone with an open mind that he medicated himself with opiates, mercury and chloroform. Compounded no doubt by the medieval medical treatments of the day: administered bleedings; blistering of the skin; forced stomach and bowel purging.

If you want an insight into a person's political philosophy find out who their heroes are. With Lincoln it's very clear, it was the most famous Whig Henry Clay, 'The Great Compromiser'. He held the union together by compromising (I'd say all principles); from the beginning of Clay's career: the 'Missouri Compromise' of 1820; until the end: the 'Compromise of 1850' - think fugitive slave act. Lincoln made no bones that he was "an avowed Clay man". It should be said in fairness to Clay, that though he came from Kentucky, a slave state, and he owned slaves, he thought it an evil. As did Lincoln of course. But where did their real sympathies lie? With the Whites. Even in the slave states. What would happen to them, if and when the Africans were freed? They'd be swamped. That was their ultimate concern. Clay's solution was Lincoln's solution, purchase the slaves from their owners and transport Blacks overseas somewhere.

Clay, a direct descendent of Hamilton's philosophy, believed the nation needed concentrated power and powerful banks. Clay and Lincoln's vision of the future was a combining of the economic prowess of the Northeast, with the workforce of the West. We like to think of Lincoln as a rail-splitter and homespun philosopher, not a railroad lawyer. But he was also a railroad lawyer. One of the things I like about Richard White's new book, "The Republic for Which It Stands" is that he draws no artificial boundary between Reconstruction and the Gilded Age.

Readers who assume Helton's review was written in good faith are going to believe "Baccala refuses to grant that Lincoln found slavery an odious institution, when obviously the South knew this, that's why they seceded at his election." The whole intent of this is to make my position seem beyond the pale. I defy Helton, or anyone else, to find one line in Cross of the Christlike President that suggests Lincoln was not revolted by slavery. Is any nuance too subtle for Helton? The emphasis I made in the book, and stand by, follows the distinct tenor of Lincoln's revulsion. From the age of 8 until he was 23, Lincoln's father used him as free labor. Even going so far as to hire him out to others and pocket the money. While I can't say if Lincoln ever hated anyone, more specifically his father, at the very least he disliked the man intensely. Refusing to even go to his bedside as he was dying. (This is the one instance when the mature Lincoln may have failed to act Christlike. Though he loved his stepmother, nothing could get him to forgive his father.) This is how he saw slavery: as theft of labor. Slave owners were thieves. "It may seem strange that any men should dare to ask a just God's assistance in wringing their bread from the sweat of other men's faces". Now maybe to Helton Lincoln's perceiving slavery as a theft of labor is a sufficient response to the absolute evil that owning another human being is. For me it falls short.

Helton implies that I will resort to anything to impugn Lincoln. For example the way I bring up an incident in his youth. "When he was nineteen, still residing in Indiana, he made his first trip upon a flatboat to New Orleans. He was a hired hand merely, and he and a son of the owner, without other assistance, made the trip. The nature of part of the 'cargo-load,' as it was called, made it necessary for them to linger and trade along the sugar coast; and one night they were attacked by seven Negroes with intent to kill and rob them. They were hurt some in the melee, but succeeded in driving the Negroes from the boat, and then 'cut cable,' 'weighed anchor,' and left." I did not bring this up to infer a possible source of prejudice. As Helton well knows I am not the author of this, Abraham Lincoln is. And again this is the mature Lincoln, circa 1860. He'd been asked to sketch his life in order to aid others in putting together a campaign biography. He seems to have considered this incident worth including. If I presumed that it might have had some impact on him, please forgive me, for a moment I forgot about his divine birth. Obviously Helton is perturbed that I brought this up, but why? I dare say it's not my motive in retelling this story that bothers him, its the disturbing thought of what were Lincoln's motives in bringing it up? To show he wasn't naïve about the danger posed by Negros?

You can search my book and you will never find anywhere that I dispute that Lincoln came to the presidency "at a time of great crisis". Who would? Nor do I dispute that he believed letting the South go would jeopardize our experiment in democracy. The fact that he believed this, and "he was alive at the time", for Helton is sufficient, and settles the question. Well Horace Greeley was alive at the time and his view is my view. What Helton doesn't bother to relate to readers - let alone refute - is my contention that the Confederate states would have fallen apart in no time. That afterward it would have been easy to sweep up the pieces – as one by one they begged to get back in, willing to give up slavery to do it. The only thing that kept them together, as poorly as they were together, was the war. Say goodbye and with no opposition to bind them they would have begun disintegrating immediately. And if every state has a right to secession, why not different sections? Why not different counties? Why not any township that wants to govern itself? Every cotton baron would have set up his own little army of thugs, not simply to crack – the literal – whip on the slaves, but to insure that there was no interference in the operation. There would have been fights from the fields to ships. How fast would their currency have lost all value? It would be feudal gangsterism, with no police because all would refuse to pay taxes.

He says I'm inconsistent, that I don't attack the framers, the Virginian slaveholders: Washington, Jefferson and Madison. This is because I happen to make two distinctions. One should make an allowance for different times. Is it that difficult to perceive that the 18th century was a different age than the 19th century? Secondly it's important to note that the founders made no bones about the fact that slavery was evil. They all confessed this. Later after the contagion had festered too long for recovery you get wretches like John C Calhoun, Jefferson Davis, Robert E. Lee and the rest of that ilk, demonically touting slavery as good, an institution found in the Bible, therefore sanctioned by God. And in Lee's case Blacks weren't ready - another 500 years might be needed. As Lincoln sharply observed at Cooper Union, when he asked rhetorically what would satisfy the South - the answer: "This, and only this: cease to call slavery wrong, and join them in calling it right."

Finally I would like to reassure NNQR readers that while I'm always on the lookout for group-think, I am not hostile to historians or researchers. I depend on their accounts. And I respect their discipline, both in rigorous scrutiny of all evidence, and adherence to the methodology they were schooled in. It's no slap to say I don't feel that I'm in a competition with that approach. The historian's scope covers the people and times they've selected. What was their history, their beliefs, goals; who they were, and what happened that resulted in the actions they took. Influences can be traced back, with great care, but never too far forward. Any historian tempted to show strong parallels with the circumstances of his own age to any particular past will quickly be brought to heel by his peers for violating self control. And I'm sure there are good reasons for this caution.

But I am not interested in slowly building a sound edifice for later scholars to add to as additional information comes in. Nor have I taken an oath only to make the smallest assertions and avoid at all costs any final judgments. I want to know how the people of the past relate to us. I'm not intimidated by the historian's guidelines because I believe we *can* put ourselves in the place of people of the past. I know for instance that in the 19th century death stalked families, Lincoln's family, almost every family. Many children dying young, women dying in childbirth, TB, smallpox. But I say we can imagine these conditions. And because I believe basic humanity hasn't changed that much in 35,000 years, we can also imagine what they went through. Yes their conditions were different, what they knew was different. Don't we employ our imagination to bring novels to life? Plays and movies would have no power except we are able to will ourselves to accept their artificial frameworks. And further I say the posture of being 'scientific' and 'objective' that treats people of the past as beyond our imagination & identification is not only an insult to them and to us, its false. They weren't that different, nor were their circumstances. We can put ourselves in their place.

James Helton replies
(New York, New York)

I have to begin by correcting Professor Baccala's assumption that his book got haphazardly assigned to someone without the time or interest to read it. I not only read this book, I believe I've read everything that Baccala has ever written. I subscribe to a Santa Cruz alternative weekly for no other reason than to catch his occasional columns. I'm probably one of his few (dare I say?) fans living outside of Santa Cruz. Certainly no one else here at NNQR knew who he was. It happened that when I saw that his latest book fell under American history I thought here is my chance to nominate one of his works. Unfortunately the prerogative I exercised, because it was in my field, rebounded as a review assignment.

Like most of his recent books this one too turned out to be polemical, with little pretense at dispassion. He had one overarching motive in writing this book. To prove that had it not been for the "children of darkness" the United States could have fulfilled the ideals of the people he admires, like Emerson and Whitman. Instead of falling to earth as just another devouring empire. I feel not just a duty to my field, but to my NNQR readers, if I see an agenda that pushes history aside, interpretations that lack sufficient substantiation, only the author's certainty that he is right. I'm obliged to note all that. If you are conscientious about your field, and your role as a reviewer, you have no choice. Your regard for the author cannot affect rendering an honest assay. My review ended up going in the opposite direction of my original intention, which was to introduce Baccala to a wider audience.

He says his title, "Cross of the Christlike President", wasn't sarcastic. I must take his word for it, and I do. I will leave it to readers to judge by the tenor of his response why I might have jumped to the conclusion I did. However I don't think its conjecture that the average person browsing books, seeing one centered around Abraham Lincoln, titled

"Cross of the Christlike President" is going to assume that it deals with the burdens Lincoln bore for the country, not the burdens that he (inadvertently) left as his legacy to the nation.

Historians are wary of scapegoating, and for very good reasons. I will postpone for now a fuller exploration of Baccala's views on Nature versus Nurture. Suffice to say he believes inheritance by far the more dominant influence, "Studies have shown that conservatives are born with a conservative predisposition." To Baccala people aren't that different from dogs except that we control our own breeding. We self-select for traits we find desirable. Over time a character gets engraved deeper and deeper. "Dogs will each have dog nature and their own unique personality; yet they'll also have the characteristic of their breed. Guard dogs will have a guarding bent, hunting dogs a hunting bent, lap dogs a domestic inclination, shepherding dogs a shepherding impulse." It's important to understand that to Baccala dog breeds are an exact parallel to human ethnicities.

Baccala says humanity hasn't changed in 35,000 years. How he knows this I don't know, but he goes on to say this allows us to put ourselves - through acts of imagination - in the place of others, even if historians tut-tut the endeavor. Yet he has posited a subset of humanity that is born evil and will always practice evil no matter what. His villain in America is the South. Though he leaves the illusion uncorrected that he shares the position others have taken, that the Confederates should only have been allowed back into the union after punishment, penalty, and admission of guilt. In other words after they were rehabilitated. But his real position is that they should never have been allowed back in. Until they (in essence) no longer existed as they were. Is this not a roundabout way of saying never?

Who is more responsible than anyone else for this grave mistake? Lincoln of course. "His goal of reconciliation was insane. His belief that disunion would be a severe blow to the experiment of democracy was exactly backwards. As time showed, letting the contagion back in untreated is what proved fatal to the hope of America championing equality, liberty, and universal justice throughout the world." Not that we, as just another part of humanity, succumbed, as all great nations have, to the arrogance that flows from unchecked wealth and power. No, we alone, the anointed, started with an advantage, as we were purer, from our Founders we saw how power corrupted even good men; we were more modest, we could have succeeded. But alas there were demons within. "Defeated at the greatest cost, but were treated like prodigal brothers by a delusional saint".

Baccala is prickly that I should have pointed at Thomas Jefferson. This was deliberate, knowing he is one of Baccala's favorites. The man he credits, past Thomas Paine, as the creator of the American conception of liberty. Which I actually agree with. But I stand behind what I said in the review. We know he's the greatest hypocrite in American history, the question remains is he the greatest hypocrite in all of world history? One can't pick and chose and have it both ways. You can't say, "There wasn't a Southern traitor from Calhoun to Robert E. Lee with a mind or soul worth spit." then turn around and prevaricate about how Jefferson conducted his life. Yes early on Jefferson declared slavery to be evil. And he suspected his racism towards Africans was self-serving. But on Bacalla's scale this proves he was a conscious person, one whose actions could be held to a higher standard than the unconscious. Yes, Sally Hemings may well have resembled his late wife. They had the same father. So making her his concubine is all right? (And one is tempted to ask if D.W. Griffith was a pedophile why wasn't Thomas Jefferson?) Yes he was born into early Virginia plantation life. Weren't Baccala's villains also born into that same world? Jefferson was not only gifted, he was one of the best-educated men in the New World. He spent 5 years in France. Yet to the end he went on remodeling, rebuilding Monticello (all the work done by his slaves); buying books, the most expensive French wine; piling up debt; not ever freeing anyone except those who were related to him.

For the record, if this nettled Baccala, the title of the review, "Crossing Off Lincoln", was not my idea but that of the editors. Though I did find it pithy and apt. And I take a back seat to no one in my admiration for Debs. I wasn't, nor would I ever, defend Wilson's authoritarianism - as exhibited during World War I, nor his racism. If Professor Baccala was attempting to make a point about conscription, Lincoln's and Wilson's, he should have been more explicit. I was simply trying to bring some balance, alerting readers that Baccala's emphasis of events was problematic to say the least. Baccala states as fact, that D.W. Griffith coming to Wilson's White House and screening for him "The Birth of a Nation/The Klansman", marks the ultimate victory of the Confederacy, and that both of these men somehow knew and celebrated this as fact "just as Hitler danced with glee in Paris".

It's always walking on thin ice to criticize the Roosevelts in NNQR, but I have to say, when it comes to "imperialism" and "the glorification of war", Wilson can't hold a candle to McKinley and

Teddy. And FDR wasn't naïve about his alliance with Southern segregationists. He was a political realist. I narrowly corrected Baccala's tirade about Wilson's Southern origin, his being a wolf in sheep's clothing, "pretending to be the former governor of New Jersey and president of Princeton". He *had* been governor of New Jersey, and president of Princeton. These were his credentials; did he not have a right to put them forward?

Its possible, a 150 years after events, to draw whatever lines you want. You can cite Clay, 'railroad lawyer', and the Gilded Age. Implying the ground was being set for the modern USA: "run by and for the super-rich"; a state that can go out anywhere in the world "entitled to police and manipulate, answering to no one." What if the line I want to draw goes back to Lincoln's resistance to the very popular Mexican war? He only served one term in the House and his stance against the war may well have contributed as the most important reason why. I would say how he reacted to this challenge shows his real character and integrity. Not that I think we need evidence on that score. But then I would draw my lines to the modern anti-war dissenters. No, Lincoln was not a pacifist opposed to all wars. But he did oppose the immoral wars – seizing territory while dressing it up as righteous and patriotic.

Let me be crystal clear on another point. I never insinuated that Baccala plagiarized Joshua Shenk[1]. Baccala's faults, on which (involuntarily) I have become expert over the years, certainly do not include the need to borrow the writing or ideas of anyone else. He has too many ideas of his own to leave any room for others – who he usually

---

[1] "Lincoln's Melancholy" by Joshua Wolf Shenk 2005 Houghton Mifflin Company.

disparages. What I presumed, and I labeled it in the review a "speculation", was that as he was trying to formulate how a good and brilliant man like Lincoln, could, in his view, calculate everything wrong; he boiled it down to three essential elements: ambition, prejudice and pride. Maybe depression was floating around as a fourth possibility - obviously I don't know. But it seemed to me that late in the process of forming his thoughts on his own book he ran across Shenk's, and this spurred him to add depression to the other factors. And if it was as severe as Baccala construes it to be - a death wish to be blunt - riding around on his own without a guard - this makes the appointment to Vice President of the villain who would scuttle Reconstruction, even more egregious.

I directed most of my fire at refuting the assertion itself, i.e. that Lincoln's mental state was debilitating. As I said in the review, for some people depression is a dark pit from which they can't escape, but for a lot of others it isn't. It's something they deal with. In a way overcome. Sometimes Nietzsche's "That which doesn't kill us makes us stronger" applies. Whether we want to go as far as Shenk did or not it's obvious to me that Lincoln belongs with those who overcame. It doesn't matter if you apply the 19th century term 'melancholy' to it, or our more modern medical 'depression'. Since Baccala begins with the conclusion that Lincoln's decisions were unsound, indeed led to the unraveling of the republic, he works backward to have depression (along with ambition, prejudice, and pride) explain Lincoln's impaired thinking. As one who certainly doesn't see Lincoln as perfect, yet is unwilling to grant that his decisions were faulty, the tendencies Baccala points to, which he regards as significant symptoms of debilitation, I see as obstacles that were dealt with. From where I sit they did not prevent him from "performing as a rational actor". Baccala is infuriated that I give more weight to Lincoln's take of conditions, when he was an 'identifying subject', buffeted about by the blindness and passions of the age, over Baccala's presumably more coolly neutral assessment. But I'm choosing to trust an intelligent observant participant who lived in that age and felt the pulse of the people as it happened, over an opinionated tourist from a far different age who I know for a fact has several axes he intends to grind.

I am not unaware of the clever trap Baccala has prepared by telling our readers the very conventions of our exchange are unfair. The reviewed must go first explaining how he thinks his work was wronged. The reviewer gets to answer and that placement itself tips the balance. He wants you to check your swaying convictions so even if you find my rebuttal persuasive the echo of his prediction will make you wonder if its on the merits, or merely my advantage in positioning. Well I have a point I'd like to raise. If we only hear one side of an argument aren't we likely to agree with it? Would that be fair or wise? Yes the reviewer is granted the place of responding. How could it be otherwise? Should I, could I, refute points before they're made? Talk about confusing the readers.

I will stop here, not that I couldn't go on, but I don't want to go down the same road I regret going down the first time around. I will only say that forcing a template you bring with you onto events of the past is not proper history, its historical fiction. We grant latitude to the authors of historical fiction so they can bring to life their figures and scenes. And I think these imaginative journeys can help us understand people and situations. They can also mislead in the direction of fantasy. There's a huge divide between historical fiction and scholarly history.

What I can tell you as someone whose read everything he's ever written, at least that's publicly available, is that the cynic we encounter today was not the young Baccala. Then it was more optimistic. A mixture of Walt Whitman's vision for America, a beckoning example to the world of democracy/equality/freedom; coupled with an unstoppable spiritual groundswell in the hearts of Americans building to an Emerson - William James transcendence. The young Baccala declared that the signs and trends were unmistakable. A true spiritual realization would occur ("not a dumb revival"), America was destined to be inhabited by that light and to take that light – 'lamp of enlightenment' - around the globe. Obviously we were the only ones qualified as an advanced country & racial melting pot. The tired Europeans were spiritually deflated. The rest of the world's people were stuck in primitive traditions imprinted in their minds.

What happened was a result of inflated expectations meeting indifferent reality. In America the intelligent and informed increasingly relied on science, and as Baccala said, "because they had concrete answers it was assumed that science had all the answers, and they were all concrete." While those with any spiritual intuition, instead of evolving as he had predicted in a progressive way, in the face of the cold unfeeling modern world, retreated into the old and rigid, even into archaic and literal religiosity. The tiny set that fulfilled his idea of spiritual transcendence were too small numerically to be significant. As he bitterly put it the contest was left to "the spiritual zeros versus the brainless". This disappointment, combined with his career setbacks,

124

and his tendency to look for something or someone to blame, explains all his later work, including "Cross of the Christlike President". Baccala requires not only the agents of darkness, the Southerners, he needs someone high to let the low in. Hence the never properly punished South was let back in to dispense its poison. If only Lincoln hadn't been such a sappy saint.

I will tell you how I first became acquainted with Baccala's work. For whatever reason it's always been a struggle for me to stay awake in a darkened theater watching a play all the way through to its completion. This is awkward because my wife, who teaches English, happens to enjoy 'serious' theatre. And it's a little funny because when I try to nap, say on buses, trains or jets, I can't. And I don't think it's the darkness in the space of a theatre which can explain it. Concert halls are just as dark and spacious, and music would seem to be more conducive to sleep than speeches, but I seldom nod off during a concert. And above all others, the playwright sure to set me to dozing is William Shakespeare. I never dreamt I could justify my drowsiness to my spouse. I was resigned to the fact that the tendency made me appear culturally shallow.

After one such night though, refreshed if embarrassed by my long nap, and after delivering another apology, my wife started hunting for a book she said I should read. I assumed it would be some jeremiad against Philistinism. Instead it was Baccala's book "Separation", and his chapter on Shakespeare: "Bardolatry". It was exactly the opposite of what I had expected. In essence it said my response was actually a natural one. "That all of Shakespeare should be as gaudily artificial as a beaded gewgaw is no impediment to the literati.

After all they are well trained to be well strained. And don't think for a minute that they aren't as romantically sentimental as the average person they look down on. They are more. Only they need a properly sanctified hallow object for their worship, with permission from fellow sophisticates to let go. Give them something with a pedigree and reputation no matter how exaggerated, and they will swoon. They will get intoxicated. They will declare it plumbs the very depths. Yet while the average person is apt to fall for whatever piffle is popular in their day, arranged as it is to ride current taste, they are not equally susceptible to yesterday's piffle. Quite the opposite of the literati. As bad as the diet of the average American is, loaded with junk, washed down with soda, if you told them dinner was to be nothing but cake, they'd balk, 'No, that would be sickening!' Shakespeare is not only all cake, it's a cake that's almost completely frosting (and what little cake hides submerged was actually mixed and baked by someone else)."

I was shocked. It never occurred to me that you could question Shakespeare's greatness. Baccala said with the human need to worship the search is less for a truly worthy person, more for someone not obviously disqualified. In that light Shakespeare's elevation makes sense. He knew how to twirl language. He knew the ups and downs, the rhythms of entertainment. There was his breadth: comedies, histories, tragedies, "he stole from every kind of source". But Baccala said the depth was always an illusion with Shakespeare. The galaxy of characters are really the same old tried and true stock figures taken from the earlier morality plays, with a flimsy Elizabethan costume draped over them. Whereas if you examine the 'larger than life figures' - always male – Henry IV, Macbeth, Othello, Hamlet or Lear, they don't hold together. Despite what the worshippers say they are "neither coherent nor convincing" as real people. This is because they're contrivances - plot contrivances. Any given response is more likely to hinge on a plot need then on their character. "Shakespeare, unique among writers of reputation in any language, lacked the creativity to make up his own stories. Its not that he wasn't smart in picking what he stole, or clever in weaving together 2 or 3 different stories stolen from entirely disparate sources. Today his work would be categorized as script adaptation. Story by so and so (the real author), adaptation by William Shakespeare."

"The key figure in Shakespeare's formative years was his father John. When he was young, his father, a successful glover, was a well respected man in the town, a top alderman. It's important to note that the gloves John Shakespeare fashioned were not work gloves. They were dress gloves: ostentatious, ornate, fabricated solely to impress the eye. The lesson of what people desired, what sort of 'show' impressed and satisfied them, was not lost on the boy. He was to become an embellisher too, but in a different realm. For whatever cause (black market wool deals gone bad, or drink?) when Shakespeare was about thirteen his father lost his place in Stratford society. In a reverse of what would be the son's fate, the townspeople seem to have always stayed fond of John; but it is clear from the town records that he fell out of money, and out of being 'respectable'. John's fall may be the reason that William was so keen on success and grasped money so tightly; and later took such pains to impress everyone that he wasn't common, no he was a gentleman. The lesson of outward form sufficing to impress every class stayed with him. Into it blended the beginning of his career that started as an actor, which reinforced his belief that you could dazzle with mere outward form. The reason actors love performing Shakespeare is because its an excuse to 'chew the scenery and ham it up', whether in thrilling fights or emotional melodrama, and yet do it all under the guise of the most respected legitimate theater."

"In all of history in the arts, it's somewhat rare that an artist will have an intimate who is also a recognized master. We can say Mozart had something of a peer and friend in the older Haydn. Hawthorne and Melville were friends. It doesn't happen often. Yet it did occur with Shakespeare. For him it was a younger friend, Ben Jonson, considered the second best playwright of the Elizabethan age. Yet Jonson's insights are disparaged by the Shakespeare priesthood. Why? Because he actually knew the man. He knew his weaknesses as well as his strengths. They became friends after Shakespeare helped the younger Jonson break into the theater world. But Jonson is not allowed to be seen as he was as someone who benefited from Shakespeare's mentoring, and was grateful to him for it. No, he has to be regarded as a competitor, so his observations can be dismissed as prompted by petty jealousy and envy. This of a man who professed he loved the late Shakespeare 'just this side of idolatry'. Not to mention that it's Jonson's elegy that is the famous one: 'Soule of the Age! The applause! delight! the wonder of our Stage!'. He even went further: 'He was not of an age, but for all time!' It's true that Jonson favored a different kind of theater - one as he put it, with a little dig at Shakespeare - with "deeds and language such as men do use". And yes he had a fiery temperament, he had been a soldier, and killed a man in a duel. But what he felt towards Shakespeare, besides friendship and appreciation, was loyalty and gratitude. When they talk of the company of 'wits' at the Mermaid Tavern – it was Jonson and Shakespeare chiefly. At the end in Stratford, who was there of the old London crew, celebrating with Shakespeare at the marriage of his daughter - as he drank himself into his final fever and death? Only the poet Michael Drayton and Jonson."

"Jonson's unforgivable sin was his familiarity with Shakespeare's real tendencies. He knew that Shakespeare's ease in writing led him to doodle out springy lines of nonsense: 'Many times he fell into those things that could not escape laughter.' It's not just Jonson who knows this of course, there are long speeches in Shakespeare's plays that are so muddled that to this day no scholar has ever been able to make any sense of them. Jonson knew, Shakespeare's gift for penmanship aside, his sloppy approach marred even his best work. An excellent example of this is the crucial moment of Hamlet at the graveyard. When it turns out to be Ophelia's internment, Shakespeare has Hamlet surprised that Laertes' should try to throttle him. After nicely telling Laertes 40,000 brothers couldn't have loved her as much as I did, he protests, 'What is the reason that you use me thus? I loved you ever'. The idiocy of this, if taken seriously, would go: 'Hey man be cool. Yeah I murdered your father, but that was an honest mistake. He was hiding behind the curtain, and I thought it was the king. And let's be honest he was a meddling fool. Yeah I drove your sister mad, by spurning her and killing your father, but these things happen. I didn't know she had drowned until right now.' The Bardic apologists will tell you Hamlet has cracked when that suits their argument. Or he is pretending to have cracked, but is really wily, when that is preferable. They can and do have it both ways. But the truth is that Hamlet, like all of Shakespeare's characters, beyond being a recognizable type, is simply a vehicle to deliver lines and advance the plot."

"A defense for Shakespeare's approach could be made. Obviously he got away with doing what he did. Jonson belongs to those people that expect, and therefore demand, that language have meaning. Language originated to convey, we assume, important information, from one party to another. There is an assumption by this group that language not only should resemble what is actually spoken by people but that it should have substance and make sense. Its true that a lot has developed in the use of language since it became part of human life. Scholars tell us that Elizabethan performances were amazingly rapid-fire. Apparently their tongues, ears and minds were quicker than ours. What Shakespeare grasped was that he could use dialogue decoratively, as part of the scenery. Especially since it was a show of stock characters with known roles, most of them right out of morality plays. Employed in a story that he'd stolen, that had an obvious thrust or moral. And who was the audience? There were a few well educated aristocrats and gentlemen. They'd be entertained by the wordplay. The majority of the audience will accept that this is the sort of dialogue these characters speak, whether they grasp it or not. While the groundlings have even fewer requirements, satisfied to watch the action unfolding on stage; or the drama and emotions swelling; while the humor – something like 'Midsummer's Night Dream' - is low burlesque anyone can get."

"Jonson also knew Shakespeare's faults as a man. Chief among them being his pretentiousness. Shakespeare paid for a coat of arms for his family with the motto, 'Non sanz droict', which means: 'not without right'. Jonson, in his play 'Every Man Out of His Humour', lampoons this folly by having a preposterous country bumpkin buy a coat of arms with the motto: 'Not Without Mustard'. Well the priesthood that can't have their deity teased for concocting ridiculous dialogue or writing sloppily, certainly can't have him mocked for being a fop. So Jonson is summarily demoted to envious competitor. Though you'll notice they still cite his praise of Shakespeare, because of course it's the best anyone's ever written. This is the quality of our literary jurors. We can see a similar stiltedness in their appraisals of contemporary poetry. Our literati select the intellectually clever but extremely empty for their highest praise. Stuff so artificial that no sane person would waste their time on it."

Baccala mapped out the process in Shakespeare's deification. He drew an interesting parallel with a similar process in ancient Greece that ended in Homer's elevation to semi-divine status. We tend to think of ancient Greece as one period but it wasn't. The language of Homer to later Greeks was impressively archaic. This was a great help on the way to divine status. The world and the lives Homer evoked were different, starker, primeval - with truths and upright manners more direct. Everything seemed to hone in to essence. With a grand language appropriate to the heroic. In the same way the Tyndale/King James Bible's archaic phrasing, distinct and evocative, worked so well to convince people in the West over the years that it was relating a world more significant, with heavier personages also more significant. That sense of otherness enhanced because it was a translation from a completely different language, two or three in fact. That heritage, producing an oddly different structure, added to the effect.

Baccala said a similar process works on us with the Elizabethan phrasing and vocabulary. It's distant enough so we don't question it, the way we do current dialogue when we can hear it doesn't ring true. We tag it as false. We find the Elizabethan reversals, especially with all the unusual words Shakespeare liked to decorate his speeches with, impressive, evocative and poetic. We can suspend disbelief and pretend that in its Elizabethan context people spoke this way. Of course the air of the artificial is inescapable, but we can tell ourselves maybe artificial was the fashion. Possibly set by the court. We are curious about this Elizabethan world, and the task of the bardolaters is made easier by the fact that for most people the only Elizabethan lingo they will ever encounter is Shakespeare.

"Originating from an important country is also essential. Alexander the Great created a Greek speaking Mediterranean world that led directly to the Roman world. What if Homer had been Phoenician or Assyrian, believing whatever they believed; and their tales were his raw material? Do you think there would be endless translations of those works over the generations? No. What if Shakespeare had been born in Belgium? His entry in a book of Artists Lives would be very short indeed. '1564 – 1616. Popular inventive Belgian impresario; adopted stories from various sources for the theater. Plays in all genres: comedy, history and tragedy. Unfortunately the obviously contrived plots, archly effete dialogue, with an unmistakable whiff of obsequious court flattery, have discouraged revivals.'"

"Shakespeare's survival has two primary supports in the theater; the reputation the sentimental pedants engender; and actors who see a chance at prestigious weighty parts, that at the same time allow them to ham it up. We can precisely date the origin of Shakespeare's ascendancy to 1737, a hundred and twenty years after his death, when two personifications of these types made their way to London. Samuel Johnson, the pedant, and his student, David Garrick, an actor, who would become the star of 18th century British theater. Together they established the divine Shakespeare we all know now. Johnson, a conservative, thought of himself as a writer. His admiration for Shakespeare was as towards another writer-as-athlete, he was dazzled by the difficult acrobatic moves. He had no problem with verbal inflation, word art in the specialized craft. Manipulation and self-promotion? Isn't that part of life, especially interpersonal relations? He probably knew John Donne's poetry was superior, but as a teacher he was interested in reaching the maximum audience. How many people could ever comprehend Donne, give them as much time as you like? Dr. Johnson as the author of the first professional dictionary of English. By filling it with quotes from Shakespeare to demonstrate how a word should be used, the statue of Shakespeare got bronzed. Johnson's endorsement remained unchallenged because in due course he was elevated to Olympus himself, through being the lead character in Boswell's 'Life of Johnson'. Lucky for his legacy his exaggerated poetry and fiction are not read. If they were, reliance on his taste might come to an abrupt halt."

"There is nothing wrong with entertainment. Maybe there's nothing wrong per se with having our emotions manipulated in order to be entertained. But wouldn't we prefer something higher in real art?

Let's make a comparison to the musical realm. Its fine for novices to be attracted to classical music by more sensational pieces, a la 1812 Overture, Flight of the Bumble Bee, Bolero, Scheherazade, et cetera. These are fine for drawing someone in. But we expect a gradual movement towards deeper, more introspective compositions. What used to be called absolute music. Like Bach's organ and Beethoven's string quartets. If the arbiters of classical music said no, stay with the surface baubles, they are the apexes, you would have something approximating the cult of Shakespeare. If a student in a writing class submitted 'Shall I compare thee to a summer's day? Thou art more lovely and more temperate', the teacher would return it with the comment 'Nice, but please try a little harder.' Yet as the work of the immortal Bard its regarded as divine inspiration, and its tag line, 'So long as men can breathe, or eyes can see, So long lives this, and this gives life to thee' makes them all sigh because they are part of that process. To elevate the flowery and artificial is to instruct normal people about a god they will feel they have no choice but to acknowledge, but its one they won't worship and will avoid attending."

I was astonished. The thought had never crossed my mind, even after all the times I had nodded off, that Shakespeare could be challenged. Wasn't he unanimously proclaimed 'the greatest writer of all time'? Yet Baccala asserted that one play by Chekhov, Ibsen, or O'Neill, told you more about humanity than all of Shakespeare rolled together. His real point was that there was a human need to elevate something above, to have something to worship. He believed if you toppled Shakespeare from his pedestal someone else would be drafted to fill the spot, and they would be just as inadequate in their own – different - way. The pedestal was the problem. He wasn't one of these people who targets a member of a pantheon because they have their own favorite in mind to substitute-switch to fill that space.

The larger theme of "Separation", all of which I turned to read after this middle chapter, dealt with the misconception that great art issued from the heart of culture. Baccala said on the contrary, where art has been concentrated for a long time it becomes entangled in mirroring itself, instead of its proper subjects: the world and human nature. That's what the title refers to. Great literature coming from the periphery - great writers separated from the culture centers, primarily Russian and American. Tolstoy, Dostoevsky, and Chekhov in Russia; with Melville, Emerson, Twain, Whitman, and Dickinson in America. The separation is usually not voluntary. The Russians desired to join and win respect from European culture exemplified by the French; the Americans from English speaking European culture centered in Britain. Both regarded the Europeans as more culturally developed and refined. The real became a reluctant fallback choice, as if their sad fate, when it seemed they couldn't keep up with the out of reach artificial fashion. At a time when distance still mattered. Even their own critics tended to deprecate the far superior native work as crude, because it didn't match the stylishness of the European centers. Baccala noted the "vast desolated spaces" in both Russia and the United States were "sources of strength and sobriety", which he contrasts with "parlors" of Europe, "indoors/inbred". He also mentioned other writers on the periphery, like Ibsen in Norway, and the Spanish poets.

I have to admit though that along with his commentary on Shakespeare, which of course I latched onto for personal reasons, what served as a clincher for me was his quoting of a 1761 letter from Benjamin Franklin, then in London, to his brother Peter. It's all about the artificial nature of the fashionable popular song. Franklin didn't chose some dilettante to illustrate his points, but the great Handel. I remembered coming across this letter when I was studying Franklin. How exquisitely perceptive – and funny - it was. And shrewd: "Do not imagine that I mean to depreciate the skill of our composers of music here: they are admirable at pleasing practiced ears, and know how to delight one another; but, in composing for songs, the reigning taste seems to be quite out of nature..." He enumerates the defects in just one popular song of Handel's 1. Wrong placing the accent or emphasis, by laying it on words of no importance, or on wrong syllables 2. Drawling; or extending the sound of words or syllables beyond their natural length. 3. Stuttering; or making many syllables one. 4. Unintelligibleness; the result of the three foregoing united... 5. Tautology." It's all quite wonderful. For some reason in the intervening years I'd completely forgotten about it. (Maybe because it had no historical political relevancy.) Reacquainted I remembered why I had laughed so hard - while agreeing with him. And Baccala tied it seamlessly into his larger theme. However the fact that he would know this letter, and deploy it here so perfectly, had me hooked.

With him serious music was only classical, saying as a separate idiom it had some immunity from the forces he was speaking of. Though he did point out that Germany and Italy were late to unify as states; and for symphonic music after Mahler in the 20th century it came down to Sibelius and Shostakovich. The 'anticipatory intellectualizing' that came into music with Schoenberg and the other 12 toners he disdained. "Schoenberg, Webern and Berg were very good at alienation, and if we grant existential alienation is a 20th century theme, we must give it some credit I guess. However as that's pretty much the only thing it can express: an atmosphere of anxiety and alienation, its limited range is tiresome." He was likewise dismissive of the 'anticipatory intellectualized justifications' for 20th century visual art, especially abstraction and abstract expressionism.

He ended the book by taking photography as the ultimate example to prove where art really came from. The interaction of the soul in a work of art. He said fair people will concede that some photography is art. But an intellectually rigorous person would dispute that a piece of equipment, a machine that captures light images, could yield art. How to reconcile these two perspectives? It wasn't merely the functioning of a machine, nor was it the skill of the photographer in manipulating it, choosing the right angle or light, the speed or focus, or the skill in developing or framing. To Baccala the instrument – the camera - allowed the act of photography, but the act of photography allowed the individual influence of the presence of the photographer's being - their soul. Only later, after I read his other books, did I fully comprehend how literally he meant this. When I first read it I wasn't sure. Even more than using photography to say something about art, he was using photography and art to say something about the soul. Art as an example of how the soul interacted with reality.

When I had finished Separation, a book which as I said I found in every way remarkable, I was naturally curious to see what else this Luigi Baccala had written. His first book, "2 Universes", I was surprised to learn was listed as a science book. In fact it turned out to be a cosmology. There had been no hint in Separation that his first career had been as a theoretical physicist. But that was the case. And since I was intrigued by the way his mind worked I decided to investigate this earlier book.

2 Universes turned out to be a difficult book to locate. Though written for a general audience, it was a comprehensive rendering of his cosmology. (It's remarkable that over the years whatever books he writes, with one exception - a novel, the University of California Press faithfully publishes. Although as far as I could determine not one has ever gone into a second printing.) The only copy I could locate of 2 Universes was at a rare bookstore in New York, one whose specialty was antiquarian science books. Though at the time I resented paying what I considered an exorbitant price for a book that was not that old, as the years have passed I've consoled myself with making what I consider to be the greatest deal of my life. As iconoclastic – and to me unexpected - as I found the viewpoint in Separation, I have to say 2 Universes is even more staggering. Now the term 'alternate reality' is bandied about a lot, but Baccala actually delivered not only an alternate reality for the one we thought we knew; but alternative explanations for pretty much everything. I can only describe the experience as starting to read something you assume is science, then at a certain point you go 'No, its science fiction', then as you read on you realize it isn't - this is a breakdown of our world; he's describing how it all works. There's a consistency and he's included everything.

I learned later that one of the principal factors that got him in trouble was including consciousness in his theory. Apparently to all 'hard science' scientists, including physicists, this was a suspicious inclusion of a nebulous alien element that had no place in quantifiable evidence-based theories about the cosmos. Maybe it was okay for a biologist in the early 70's involved in brain research. Not theoretical physics, or any 'real' science. But I didn't know enough at the time about these separate categories to let this bother me. And later I came to agree with Baccala. How comprehensive was any cosmological theory if it didn't include consciousness and life?

As you will see there were many other facets of his theory that got him into trouble with the 'quantifying' physicist community. His first cause was nothing, which he frequently referred to as the Void. It came first. Which made sense to me. Baccala said we needed to contemplate aspects of nothing that come from the contradictory nature of its character. The Void has none of the qualities we think of as qualities, because its essence is negation, yet its impulse to self-cancel has very important consequences. (According to Baccala 'compromise' is built into Creation, but it was unavoidable.)

The establishment of space came about from two cancellations. One evacuating outward, one evacuating inward. This is strange but it creates the 3 dimensions we associate with space, even though Baccala regards space here in the first universe as largely an illusion. Anyway the inward and outward expansions meet and create what we call the Big Bang. He says that explosion expansion is only half. The contraction that ends the universe originally occurred at the same instant. We need to note that in Baccala's conception there's also no real time in this first universe in the Void.

However a strange synergistic process has been set in motion. The Void, by being nothing, *is*. But the

Void, as nothing, can't be. So it separates from Being, and that is the embryo of the 2nd universe, left to the side of the Void. Baccala says because the Void has no resistance – to Being – Being pries open the space between the explosion and the contraction that originally happened together. Importantly Being from the 2nd universe can serve here as time - as the 4th dimension. What he terms a 'mutual creation' occurs. He further stipulates that this 'excess' Being from the 2nd universe serving as time, comes not from the direction we think (of course he's constantly reminding the reader that there's no real time, "it all happens at once"), from the chronological beginning towards what we think of as later. No, he says Being enters and flows from what we consider the end and goes toward the beginning. We, and all of Creation, roll back on it in what we think of as the normal direction of time, harvesting experience into our Being (consciousness/life).

If what I say about Being and Time (here) and Life seem confused, or worse I've made it appear that Baccala's proposition was sloppy, I have to say in my defense I don't think he placed much importance on making a distinction. As it was an excess of Being from the next (open eternal) universe that served in this (closed limited finite) one as the fourth dimension: time. And as life & consciousness were the concentration of this being/time. So really it was a case of $A = A = A$. Being and time and life were all one.

Humanity has always conceived of Creation as what happens here. Baccala says the truth is it's a duel process. A telescoping down of billions of years of the 2nd universe into concentrated images sculpted by the demands of the Void. That is what we have here. And at the same time a telescoping out from the images created here to the 2nd universe. Each depends on the other, hence the 'mutual creation'. Though it's hard for us to imagine, in this simultaneous 'chicken or egg' neither is first or second. In a way they're both first and second. Yet there is a great contrast. This universe is finite. Closed. Limited. The next (allow me to call it that even though according to Baccala it only *seems* that way) is open – eternal; with Being empowered.

There's continuation in Baccala's scheme, the creatures of Creation (as beings) continue from this universe to the next as they are. But the realities are reversed, the order is opposite. In the Void's world being is on the receiving end. Circumstances are what they are – deal with it. In the next world, with real space and real time, being is free to create any environment it wants. Out of 'real space' and 'real time'. The order is reversed and the powers quite changed.

Another of his heretical notions was the concept of a Whole in this universe. It corresponded to the Being of the next universe considered whole, as one. It came from that initial move of the Void's being. But it was also tied to consciousness and it used consciousness. Since human self-consciousness was the highest we had more to do with the programming the set up then any other player. With the exception of a handful of 'masters', humans, like all the other living creatures, were unaware of their participation. If we think of the 1st universe as a field (in a physicist's understanding) of Being then any individual was a particle.

The Void lacks, along with everything else, any volition. It can spawn a negativity, which Baccala says humanity has often called 'evil'; which can sneak into a space left open, and if unchecked by a nearby positive, develop a momentum. Yet all of this is mindless, there's no volition. However the Whole, even though it lacks identity, since it's a conglomerate programmed by all the living, does have a bias toward being, and has established aims. Which we would call constructive and good. It has to work around the conditions the Void, with a 50% vote, dictates. After all it is working in the Void. Yet the Whole has always created, monitored and coordinated – within those conditions – what happens. Baccala proposes that instinct in animals is a prime example of the practice. Its like radio signals guiding a subject as to what to do next. Baccala scoffs at Darwin's vision of nature. He says if the wild world really was such a pristine random experiment "very few species would have arisen, fewer would survive, and development would be a fraction of what we behold". Even though Baccala says all of the 1st universe, strictly speaking, happens at once, he says reaching the maximum magnitude of being, a culmination which occurs at what we deem the end, is not optional. It's a mandatory condition.

Though his heresies were numerous it seems that the proverbial last straw was Baccala's assertion that this universe had a boundary and a center. Since the center was concentrated Being, and this meant Earth, to those who presumed he was a religious nut, this was proof that his real aim was to go back to before Copernicus. To justify restoring a human-centered cosmos. He had always been considered eccentric and eclectic, but brilliant. Reading his far out cosmology, opinion swung decidedly against him. He might be a religious reactionary, possibly unhinged, certainly an enemy of science.

The suspicion that he had some hidden religious agenda was false. But if we rephrased or framed it as his interpretations possessed a spiritual element, I think that would have been accurate. Most modern scientists regard the material world as what is real. Baccala followed the ancient Indians in labeling the whole material universe as maya – illusion. The Being was real. The images came from the next world. But the chamber was in the Void. The fact that all the objects made of maya respected each other as equal – they were equal – didn't make them substantial. To him the only things that he would call really substantial were what a scientist would label subjective intangibles: consciousness, life, souls, and the experiences those souls had.

In the normal course of offering a theory, you are supposed to suggest experiments or findings that might confirm your hypothesis. Baccala held that the nature of quantum confirmed his theory. But he was willing to offer two specific predictions. The first concerned checking the history of the universe. Baccala said at the same time as the formation of the solar system, Earth, the onset of bacterial life, there should be found an observable alteration in the laws of the universe. At the time this occasioned much mirth among his critics. One wit mocked the idea by asking, 'Should we look for a bumper crop of white dwarfs?' (Of course Baccala meant the sort of adjusting reaction elsewhere in an entity when its energy is put into developing a center.)

His second prediction concerned confirming that the universe as a whole had a boundary. You have to understand to modern physics, since the vision of Einstein, this too is all wrong. Galaxies so far away from us that, relative to us, they reach the speed of light, no longer exist as far as we are concerned. But since its all relative that doesn't mean they hit a wall and burn up. There isn't a real boundary, there's only curvature of space. They don't exist any longer in our reality, but since everything is relative, in their reality they continue on their merry way with no incident. Because there is no real boundary. But Baccala maintains that there is, and eventually we'll examine something containing evidence that galaxies reaching the boundary get disintegrated. His prime candidates for carrying this information were cosmic rays. It was only after he'd been ridiculed and misrepresented that he decided to write his book and appeal to a wider audience. Unfortunately at that point he had already been branded in the field and no one outside the field dared to associate themselves with the ideas of someone who might one day be exposed as a charlatan. No one wanted to be on record as having said they even found his ideas interesting. So U.C. published his book, but no one reviewed it, and no authority recommended it.

When it comes to science I need to admit that I am a layperson. Though I do my best to keep up – with medical breakthroughs, scientific advances and new technology. What really appealed to me about Baccala's system was that it was the only one I've ever encountered that took on explaining quantum, not what it was, a description, but why it was - the weird way it was. Relativity applies to how the greater universe operates; quantum operates on the opposite scale: the smallest basic building blocks of the universe. Everything else you read about quantum will speak of how baffling it is, all the paradoxes and strangeness. But none will risk hazarding a reason why it's the way it is. Baccala does. And to me, someone I must remind you without a degree in any science, his explanation makes sense. It fits the phenomenon.

Of all its odd aspects the very oddest thing about quantum is that in its essence it's a statistical probability. Not mind you that this is a formula for using it in equations or running experiments. No, when you get down to what it is, it is a statistical probability. Think of Baccala's 2 universes and his mutual creation, like two mirrors facing each other, the images going back and forth. The one here, though it is the source of the 'next' - of all its players and qualities – in turn needs for its own creation to have the images from the 2nd universe (going through the conditions and restrictions the Void imposes) etched in here.

Baccala had only a few of what you could call time or duration equivalents in his theory. But he does have, in a way, an equivalence between the two universes. (Remember not to be confused by my using 1st and 2nd. That's the way we see it, and will see it in the next world, but they're actually occurring simultaneously.) This universe is a flat enclosed once-only plane; and the next a fully dimensioned reality, with real space and real time, that goes on forever. There's the rub, obviously the plate that is our present universe can't wait forever to finalize Creation. So the measure of the next universe that is 'good enough' to establish a stable image, equals the duration of this universe. (Now estimated to be roughly 13.8 billion years.) It boils down to a tautology: the reason quantum, the foundation of the material universe, is a statistical probability, is because it's a statistical probability exposure refracted coming and going through the Void. Imagine a deflected compression of [13.8] billions of years of eternity. That mutuality yields a 1st universe that is long enough, detailed enough, for the 2nd to accept its beings as the enactors and shapes of eternity. So you see the balance with the 13.8 billion years of captured images from the 2nd as a sufficiently long enough sample of behavior for the 1st to be confident that – again cognizant of how everything's bent to what the Void allows - that with that proviso, it has captured things correctly.

When I had finished this most remarkable book I was determined to find out who this fellow Luigi Baccala was. I actually ran across more material about his father, Odo Baccala, a famous humanities lecturer and author at Yale. There was scarcely anything about the son. My wife had told me that of the things that had turned the Lit Crit crowd against him it wasn't his attack on Shakespeare, or even his penchant for metaphysics; that was all permissible. What wasn't acceptable was the obvious fact that Separation had been written for a general audience, not the cognoscente. Their snobbery contained the suspicion that a person only wrote for a popular audience if 1) they were so ambitious they couldn't be trusted, or 2) they resorted to this because they lacked the goods to fool those with detailed knowledge of the material.

This turned out not to be the route he had taken earlier. As a physicist at Berkeley he had submitted papers with his thesis for peer review. It was only after it was attacked that he finally opted to try for a general readership. His career has been plagued by bad luck, regrettable decisions, all made the worse by an antagonistic attitude. The Physics Department mounted pressure to move him elsewhere. Their reputation was, and is, second to none, and they were worried about the association with someone they viewed as either reactionary or insane.

I haven't yet encountered anyone who says they studied with him at Yale. The only academics I could find who knew who Baccala was, were all originally from the West Coast. They spoke of his '3 strikes'. First was getting the boot from the Berkeley physics department. Good luck putting that in your resume.

Second strike came when UC, for whatever reason, moved Baccala from the Physics department into Education, under the psychologist Arthur Jensen. Jensen had already become a pariah, suspected of being a racist. The 3rd strike came when he went to work for Marvin Mudrick in Santa Barbara. Mudrick was a brilliant 'man of letters', but the academic establishment had decided that the reputation of iconoclast had gone to his head. That his tone had too much swagger - deliberately provocative. The prime example was kicking dirt on Shakespeare. (This is how Mudrick and Baccala first met. Baccala wrote to compliment a dissenting article written by the elder Mudrick.)

College of Creative Studies

Mudrick's experimental college was an appendage of UC Santa Barbara. Limited to a few students, a complete contrast to the huge and indifferent classes which are the norm for undergraduates. Students were told to rise above concerning themselves with academic merits, focus only on what they were interested in. The subjects were limited: Physics, Literature, Biology, Mathematics, Chemistry, Art, and Music. The science students could do research. The art students were encouraged to paint. Music students to compose. Mudrick himself led a writing class where everyone had to write and present their work.

I searched through the CCS archives until I found pay dirt. Art Tenace had written a memoir of the school. He had been a student there and later a teacher. Most of the memoir centered around the alternative schooling and Mudrick - which makes sense since CCS was Mudrick's creation - and he was by all accounts a charismatic personality. But Tenace has one whole chapter, and not a short one, dedicated to Baccala. I asked, and he graciously consented, to excerpt it here in its entirety.

The Voice in the Wilderness

B was a human singularity. Not really a good teacher. Which was odd as his father was world famous. Two things seem necessary for a good teacher. Enthusiasm for teaching (and your subject), and a belief in your students. A basic belief in their ability to learn. He had neither, and he didn't bother to hide it. And while most educators will show some tact in pushing personal slants, especially if they're controversial minority views; B not only showed no hesitation in presenting his views, he presented them as the law, the revealed truth. And he was the only teacher at CCS who flaunted the protocol of engaging with students. You could ask a question - good luck to you. He'd usually cut the questioner to ribbons. With B there were always exceptions. If you were Black (the 'Real People'), or Hispanic (the 'New People'), he would pause and respond cordially. Usually these students would discontinue when they realized they were getting special treatment. Grading was on the casual side at CCS, but B carried it to an extreme. If you simply showed up for most of a class he'd give you the credits. He believed our whole generation was brain damaged (from environmental toxins). So his bar was as low as it could go. I did have to drop out of his Mathematics class though. It was way over my head and I knew he wasn't about to circle back to help me - or anyone else.

His parents fled Italy before World War II. Both their families were well off. But they were Socialists who refused to bow to Mussolini. They encouraged the young couple to go to America. In Italy both had been teachers. His father made the transition and was a huge success in the humanities. Famous as a teacher and author. Ending up at Yale. His mother apparently had difficulty with English. She refused the teaching jobs she was offered as beneath her. But she tutored B in physics and mathematics. Also insisting he take piano lessons. Which he did until he left for college. (Yale of course.) He said his mother dreamt of him playing Frescobaldi on a pipe organ one day. But it was not to be.

They had several children but B was always considered the prodigy. His father introduced him to the philosophers he always loved. The 'Enlightened' Europeans like Leibniz and Kant. And the American 'Transcendentalists' like Emerson and William James. With Priestly and Berkeley in both camps and both continents. The parents taught him at home at first, with the cream of visiting tutors. Then they worried, I think for good reason, about his socializing aptitude. So they enrolled him in a strict Catholic school. A choice which seems to have been a serious mistake. It didn't help that he was much younger than his classmates. Or that he knew everything going in.

Some of the staunchest atheists I've ever met were ex-Catholics. Not that B was an atheist. But he did end up very anti-Catholic despite his family. He said the nuns at the school were sadistically cruel. And many of them were from Ireland. Once in one of his Literature classes a group of us made up a chart. Dividing Irish writers into Catholic and Protestant backgrounds. The ones he disdained were all Catholic. The ones he liked were all Protestant. There wasn't one exception. You learned quickly that B played favorites. After all who could be more Catholic than Italians? But that didn't matter, they got a pass. Everyone knows the Axis powers were Germany, Italy and Japan. With B you would have thought it was only Germany and Japan. Even though Mussolini became a dictator long before Hitler, and Hitler copied many of Mussolini's techniques.

He graduated from Yale with honors. Then Berkeley won the bidding war for his services. (Something which they came to regret in due course.) Yet even those who didn't like him had to admit he was brilliant. And as a general rule physicists and mathematicians peak young. I don't think anyone knows why. But it wasn't long before he started alienating people. At first it was his off putting personality, which was always abrasive. Though there are plenty of oddballs and eccentrics in modern science you must work with others. There's no going it alone anymore. Every field is simply too complicated. But B had no patience for working with others. An even bigger problem was the direction of his ideas. Against the norms for theoretical physicists he seemed to be straying. He started bringing consciousness into his theories. Then he promulgated a coordinating Whole, an inexpilicably existent collective Being. And it got worse. He started proposing that Earth/Life was the center of the universe. And human consciousness was some sort of godhead. Berkeley's physics department started to worry about their reputation. This B fellow turns out to be a religious nut. They had to get rid of him.

The university administration responded to the pressure. They lured him away by saying don't you want to get away from the hostility? You can write your theories anywhere. They had to worry that B could appeal. Or go to the press. Possibly even file a lawsuit. After all it could have been argued he wasn't being moved for cause, as bad as a teacher as he was. It was his scientific speculations they found unendurable. The Physics department heads thought his ideas proved him unstable but it could be seen as a violation of academic free thought. But why in the world he agreed to be assigned to Arthur Jensen is a mystery. Some self-destructive impulse? Or arrogance maybe. Even back then Jensen was controversial. To make matters worse shortly after arriving, quite in character, B decided to write a memorandum on Jensen's work: 'The Albino Imbecile Choir'. It was typical B savagery. "Imagine that a party of the blind decide that they are the perfect group to winnow out who can really see. The tests have to be in Braille of course, to make sure the judging is fair. The judges assume no problem, and are triumphant when all their predictions are borne out. The favored group, the blind, tested far above anyone else. The non-blind subjects, as predicted, did poorly. Remedial help is recommended. This is similar to what the delusional Albinos, in a proud day for psychology, are doing with their imbecilic IQ tests. The machine minds have predetermined that machine mind is the very pinnacle of intelligence, though it actually doesn't deserve the name. Their idiotic tests, stamped scientific and objective, demonstrate machine minds at work. Gears whirring, Caucasians and Asians receive blue ribbons. Who would have thunk? Then in an unfelt gesture of the generosity and compassion swelling in their robotic hearts they recommend special programs, possibly even special schools, for the poor laggard populations that aren't cyborgs."

Sometimes in class when a topic might bring Jensen to mind B would muse, "How long do you think Jensen and his ilk would survive in the ghetto? One day? Two days tops. How about him measuring up in a jazz ensemble? They'd give him the floor and he'd improvise some drivel and they'd ask 'Man you feeling okay?' Those are tests of real intelligence." What the UC administrators thought of all this is anyone's guess. But when news of the memo got back to Jensen and his team the relationship had to be terminated. They naturally saw it as proving what they had suspected. That B was a hostile spy planted to discredit them. Though I doubt that whoever received the memorandum would have known what he meant by 'machine mind'. I doubt they would have known that B believed it was a calculating talent the primitive forerunners of Homo sapiens had developed. Anyway the UC administrators were now in an even worse bind. They'd already moved him once, who would want this eccentric malcontent? Then someone came up with Mudrick at CCS. This was perfect for both B and Mudrick. Mudrick liked iconoclasts, he was one himself. And he was always fascinated by cross discipline pollination. B was sui generis. A master of physics, mathematics and all the humanities. And no one in the world was smarter, and no one in the world was better read.

Mudrick was very loose with all the teachers. But the latitude he gave B was different, not in degree but kind. B could do whatever he liked. He didn't even pretend to follow the school procedure. Often you weren't sure what the class was. Everything except mathematics was called either Physics or Literature. You had to find out on your own beforehand because it could be philosophy, metaphysics, or history (World, European, or American). I don't know this for a fact but I believe Mudrick never informed the UC Santa Barbara brass of what was really going on. Allowing B to rove wherever he wanted. (Much later some of us even wondered what the terms of his employment were.) Because of his personality B quickly turned most of the teachers against him. But never Mudrick. He thought brilliant people were often arrogant. I don't think Mudrick was into spirituality. I never heard anything that suggested it. Certainly not like B. But he loved the B story for what it elicited. The small-minded reactions he provoked and the ideals he proclaimed. To get excommunicated from the physics fraternity for bringing life into his conception of the universe. Not giving ground because he thought it essential for a theory attempting to be comprehensive. For someone firmly in the humanities Mudrick found that story appealing. Probably never bothered to learn the particulars of B's cosmology. Nevertheless he was always in B's corner and B knew it.

B had an unholy trinity of modern error. They were Karl Marx, Charles Darwin, and Sigmund Freud. Unfortunately two of the three were Jewish. (Not that B was an Anti-Semite. But one of his ideas was that the good Jews came to America and the bad Jews went to Israel - still believing they were 'chosen'. So the association with Jensen, plus his view of ethnicities as breeds, brought up uncomfortable thoughts.) The unholy trinity exemplified the modern mind disconnecting from the soul. Though the only one he really disliked was Freud. He thought all psychologists were frauds. He would say its fitting that 'ego' should be Freud's downfall. Inflicting his hang-ups onto millions of gullible troubled people. Darwin he always referred to as 'Iceberg Chuck' for some reason. He said you could draw a direct line from Darwin through Nietzsche to Hitler and the Nazis. And you could draw a direct line from Marx to Stalin and Mao. Personally I never understood, if you accepted B's postulates, how Freud was the worst. So he projected his personal neuroses onto innocent patients. How does that measure against millions of people dead? Yet B would say Darwin and Marx were well intentioned.

To B Marxists, Freudians, and Darwinists were all cultists. Indistinguishable from any other wacky belief system; any religious cult, the Shakespeare cult, or the Ayn Rand cult. Anyway he thought they were three fools with a negative sway on modern thought. Marx was a well meaning myopic groping for an atheists' utopia on earth. Unlike the Founding Fathers he had no clue how power could corrupt any individual. Which history showed when elites under his name devolved into totalitarian tyrannies. Being a good critic of capitalism didn't qualify you to redesign society from the ground up. B had read in depth all three of the unholy trinity of course. He said Darwin had no clue that there was a Whole monitoring all life. He had no clue there was a Whole. It was noticeable though that the beginning of "The Origin of Species" had left its mark on B. The part about breeding. How quickly characteristics can be developed. I think that's where he got his concept of different human ethnicities being comparable to dog breeds. B didn't believe Nature's evolution was uncontrolled. "Its all coordinated." He said if it had been random it would have taken eons. "The people who know numbers have no interest in gritty nature. Those invested in nature have no interest in abstract numbers." B said Darwin got the idea of evolution from his grandfather Erasmus. "A far superior thinker to Iceberg Chuck." As to Darwin's absurd reliance on mutation and sexual selection "you'd need billions of extra years for that rickety theory to work."

The first class of B's I took was Philosophy. Which was really the history of Western philosophy. What struck me was how quickly Wittgenstein was dismissed as rubbish. He was at the high watermark of his prestige. B said the older Wittgenstein was less crazy than the young Wittgenstein but he was still

152

crazy. In fact his whole family was nuts. And it was a mark against Bertrand Russell that he would defer to such a madman. What I understood by the later Wittgenstein was the one that made language central. In an epistemological way. And what he meant by the young Wittgenstein was the one who thought we must translate everything into mathematics/logic. Which was the course modern philosophy took. At least in Great Britain and the U.S.

The next thing that surprised me was his contempt for scientists. Here was a man who had started in science. Yet he called them all cripples. He said asking them any deep question was no better than asking your car mechanic. In fact you might get lucky with the car mechanic. B said there was a truth buried in the primitive Genesis story of the Tree of Knowledge. He said only a 'traditional' person now would be intuitively open to the concept that the acquisition of knowledge had a cost. To modern minds that was a bad joke. The modern presumption is that finding out something we didn't know has no cost at all. It's all positive. B said not necessarily.

I taped some of the classes at CCS and I always asked permission. But I didn't with B. I just had the sense that he'd turn the request down. Arbitrarily, for no good reason. So I hid my little recorder. I wasn't too worried that he'd discover it. He had little curiosity about his students. He thought if one out of 50 comprehended what he meant it would be stroke of luck. Yet he would occasionally tell us that everything he said would stick with us. Because our souls knew it was true. For me this turned out to be close to the case. I don't know why. Strength of assertion? I never committed myself to accepting his views. And not that I have now, but I've noticed over the years I started framing subjects the way he did. With the exception of Mudrick I've forgotten the lectures by the teachers I esteemed at the time. As time passed I discarded their tapes because they no longer seemed like something I'd listen to again. The funny thing is I remember B's condescending harangues, and I've recopied all the tapes I have of him, in order to preserve them. I would never have predicted that, and I'm not sure I even understand why.

B cut through one of the primary philosopher's puzzles: why is reality knowable? He said it was no mystery. Our reality was molded around human sensibilities. The Whole had to do a balancing act. Submitting to some of the conditions of the Void because that is where this universe is set. It used the negatives to cut shapes as it desired. He asserted no two people were the same. That all experiences and qualities had been or were being mapped. He had another weird notion about modern humans disconnecting from their souls. As a development that had to occur. And among the advanced elite. He was a determinist who believed there was a reason for divisions. As in religion: Buddhist, Hindu, Catholic, Protestant, Sunni Muslim, Shia Muslim, Taoist, Animist. The uber rationalist *scientific* materialists were a discrete group. With a destined number of adherents that had to live out that view. "The modern intellectual deals with incredible complexities. Yet because the intellectuals are myopic they don't think the complexity signifies anything in itself. It's just the way things are: 'Naturally the deeper we dig the more we discover.' They can't pull back. Yet these fools think they know all they need to know to make pronouncements on the perimeters of the search. As to the meaning of life anyone you run into in the street will have a better clue because they lack the delusion that they know things they don't."

Nor was the existence of evil a problem for him. He did believe evil existed. Not evil entities; no Satan or devils. Though in different times you could project such manifestations – as people did in the time of Jesus. B said that the Void had not been able to resist beings entering its space. The prying open of the Big Bang. But its nature is self-cancellation. It's not conscious, but nevertheless its nature wants the circle to be closed. This force appears to us as negative, as evil, because to us it is destructive. B said it shouldn't be underestimated.

The history of philosophy was laid out. From its beginning in the ancient Greek world to an end. Really to a specific person to be exact. Martin Heidegger. He brought philosophy to its last turn. Then by going along with the Nazis discredited it and killed it. Heidegger, according to B, rationalized his conduct by saying he believed in being 'involved'. He got his appointment as rector of Freiburg in 1933 by joining the Nazi party. When he realized they were thugs he withdrew his membership. After the war he refused to acknowledge and admit his entanglement with the huge surge of evil. His fatal flaw was that his view of Germany and the Nazi's were parallel. His tone deafness continued afterward. He really thought that the Germans kicked out of adjoining countries after the war, and splitting Germany into East and West, was as great a tragedy – if not greater – than all the millions murdered by his countrymen. Heidegger had dedicated his masterwork "Being And Time" in 1926 to his mentor Edmund Husserl. Yet while the Nazis ruled he had that dedication removed. Because Husserl was Jewish. B subscribed to the Eastern idea that the life proved or disproved the value of a person's philosophy. He also said Heidegger was to philosophy what Einstein was to physics. Working backwards, by the process of elimination, both ended up with ultimate elements. Neither knew what the elements really were, or how they fit and worked together.

B thought it entirely appropriate that the last philosopher should be German. His theory on the Germans was one of his most extreme. All ethnic groups except Africans below the Sahara had crossbred with more primitive species. In Germany there were Neanderthals and others. B speculated that when a Cro-Magnon baby resembled a Neanderthal it was immediately slain. However babies with a Cro-Magnon exterior but the beast within survived. That trick became dominant. Remember he believed machine mind was not a late development but an earlier one. Which explained the German obsession with files and ordering. Good for science and engineering. He said they would never produce great art or novels. (He was no fan of Durer or Goethe.) However the internal struggle between man and beast was fruitful for philosophy, poetry and music. His most provocative point addressed the appeal of the Nazi racism to the average German. He said deep within they felt the shadow of the beast. What could be more liberating than to be told the great lie that you were the pure race? Nietzsche and some supposed lunatic law of nature proclaims you, through superior power, protect that inherited superiority. Command and kill inferior races. Ironically by their cold-blooded mass murder they revealed the beast hidden within. You have to understand that this was long before DNA testing proved B was correct, only Black Africans hadn't mixed with pre Homo sapiens. At the time we all thought this was just more of his far out craziness.

B said Heidegger couldn't be de-Nazified because he was never honest to himself about his capitulation. He lacked empathy. "He could seriously compare the industrialization of food production, in its soullessness, as an exact equivalent to the death camps. And he refused to back down." Though as Heidegger aged he began to have doubts about his approach. Major doubts about Nietzsche. That Being could be expressed in language. That the tools and methods of philosophy were up to the job. Poetry might be better. B said his dilemma was

155

ending up approaching the spiritual while denying the spiritual. A philosophy that didn't believe in answers. That neither helped you to understand the world or become a better person. But was a pretty perfect embodiment of an end.

Jacques Derrida, and his 'always already' deconstruction, was 'post-philosophy'. B liked Derrida, he said he had a touch of the poet in him. (The truth is he sort of liked Heidegger too, with all his faults.) He didn't necessarily agree with Derrida that deconstruction had brought about the end of philosophy. But he did agree that philosophy had ended, and deconstruction was not philosophy. "You are not a philosopher if your business is dissecting texts. You are not constructive, you are not a participant. You come after. You can have a clear eye, a good mind and intuition, but you are a critic. A commentator."

The beginning of philosophy was also different. The three great Greeks were there, Socrates, teacher of Plato. Plato, teacher of Aristotle. From Socrates and Plato the questioning inquiry position. To Aristotle, 'the modern machine mind', teacher of Alexander the Great. Insuring Western history as we know it. But B followed Hegel saying the first philosopher came the generation before – in the figure of Parmenides. And to B Parmenides was the greatest philosopher. Before philosophy and religion split, when reason and revelation co-existed, and Being could be understood. Not as famous as the Athenian three. The overview of it all didn't dawn on me at first. But the second time I took his class I began to see how he had laid out philosophy's history. There was a high mesa at the beginning of the epoch. (The advantage of this position was an idea of Heidegger's.) Parmenides, with the advantage of that clear perspective, had the 'vision' of what would come. With that perfect balance of the spiritual and reason (logos) he understood Being as indivisible and unbreakable. Much of his argument was against the teaching of Heracleitus, a favorite of Nietzsche. Heracleitus majored in paradoxes and flux. One can't step into the same stream twice, the waters are different. Parmenides on the other hand stressed the dismissal of non-being and the elevation of Being, with its unity and immortality.

Starting with the 3 Greeks there was a descent from Parmenides and his pupil Zeno. The charge against Socrates that he was irreligious was absurd. Most of his life he was attended by a guardian spirit. But the charge that he was an enemy of the state was true. Even though he had fought for Athens in the past he was against democracy. His parables recommended elite control. His ideal was closer to fascist

Sparta where his philosophizing wouldn't have been tolerated one day. Plato who came from an aristocratic family also believed in elite rule.

Down in the valley of the 2500 years were many of B's favorites. Leibniz, Hegel, Berkeley, Priestly, Emerson, et al. To be fair he didn't require total agreement. He admired Spinoza and David Hume, and Hume was an atheist. But as great as these thinkers were, there was a milling fog in that valley. It was only at the end of the epoch that the other mesa rose. And I don't think I have to tell you who was standing on the top of it. Though B never made it explicit, he didn't have to. Parmenides benefitted in coming before. Vision aided by pure light with no interference by the subjects, who would come to fill and play the parts. (Parenthetically I should add, though B esteemed the Greeks, it didn't hurt that Parmenides and Zeno were Italians.) B standing on the opposite mesa was aided by everything coming to an end. Everything significant filled in, he was able to put it all together and understand it as a tangible whole. Parmenides faced forward with nothing obstructing his view. That was an advantage. B faced backwards with pretty close to all the contents present. That was his advantage.

To B it was clear that what Parmenides meant by 'unity' was what B thought of as a quality of Being. Parmenides, in his own vocabulary, taught the primacy and indivisibility of Being. All as One. The universe as motionless. Every entity – the many – having to be whole ones in themselves. So when B talked of the 'step down from knowing to questioning' the implication was clear. Not only Parmenides to Socrates, and everyone forward. But himself to Heidegger and everyone back. Socrates' advocacy of fascism was explicit, Heidegger's shameful collaboration a historical fact. There was only one aspect that B thought Parmenides and Zeno had missed. "They got so much right in regards to Being. They were the originators of 'to be or not-to-be', not Hamlet or Shakespeare. But in their zealotry for Being I think we have to admit they missed the role the Void played as first cause. Beginning the chain reaction of all that followed. And providing the non-existent space where Creation occurs. And even if we cede that spacetime is a 50:50 proposition, there's no overlooking the Void's part in the non-existent matter that makes up all the material here. Not to mention all the forces – energies – in this universe. Or where are we?"

I need to mention one item of dispute. A book by Plato titled "Parmenides". Now most classicists regard it as fiction. As they do many of Plato's later books. But B took it as a faithful account of an encounter between Socrates and Parmenides. As close to verbatim as something could be written years after an event. Like the N.T.'s synoptic gospels. A discussion that definitely would have been memorable. Not because of Socrates' participation. He was at the time a fairly undistinguished young man. Witnesses would initially value and remember the exchange because Parmenides and Zeno were famous.

Now it's possible that I was influenced by B's forceful conviction. He could be persuasive. Making his interpretation seem the only logical conclusion. Yet I found that the text did resonate with his explanation. His conjecture was Athens was not a great metropolis. By modern standards it was tiny. And the educated, mostly aristocratic elite interested in philosophy, were an even smaller subset. Plato had achieved fame with his dialogues. As he intended he'd made Socrates into a beloved figure. And made most Athenians ashamed that their city had condemned him to chose exile or death. But the story of the exchange between the Italians and the young Socrates existed among the elites. If only in oral form, which would have been the norm. Anyway Plato would have been rebuked for leaving out the first, and maybe the most formative encounter in Socrates development. After all in the aftermath of this exchange Socrates forswore metaphysical speculation. But it's easy to see why Plato would be reluctant to record this conversation. It goes against his project of elevating his late teacher to immortal, if quirky, sage status. Parmenides and Zeno use him as a plaything. And they're not hostile. They like him, they hope he pursues philosophy. The unavoidable fact is this book is like no other in Plato's canon. Sometimes he would portray Socrates showing some deference to an older sophist. But usually he couldn't long resist the punctuating-needling-tearing apart of poorly thought out suppositions. Granted that Socrates is young, in this book he comes off as helpless and far out of his depth. So to me B's version of it accorded with the peculiarities of the text. The classic scholars' dismissal of it as fiction doesn't make sense. Why would Plato make up such a story? What could be the possible motive?

While Parmenides combined the spiritual and rational, that wasn't the norm in the West. B taught that the first great spiritual awakening occurred in ancient India. Their gurus were real masters. And their scriptures – like the Upanishads – were real scriptures. B said a pantheon of gods can be created out of the Whole, simply divide characteristics. The Greeks and Romans did. As did the Egyptians, Babylonians, Syrians and everyone else. Until the Abrahamic religions, with the possible exception of the Persians, this is what everyone East or West did. B said the Indians hold the copyright to the epoch's deep spirituality. Buddha came from the Indian tradition. Being *first* with B meant you would also come in *last*. Self-satisfaction and complacency leading to stagnation. "Its tricky because everything *is* divine. When an Indian put his or her hands together they are recognizing the god in you. But we see in the rigor mortis of the archaic where 'the die is caste'. There is a truth in karma. But if god is in everyone how do you explain a quarter of your population at the bottom being born into a condemned 'untouchable' state? This is why, no matter what they might say out loud, all educated and decent people around the world despise Indian society. The height of spirituality did not come alone, it brought the curse of dungeon darkness with it."

B believed as history evolved and our populations grew in numbers and rationality, the physical world got more set. That is more concrete – solidified. Therefore we looked back with contempt at different groups' origin stories and holy myths. But he believed the past - with people separated and sparser in number - was more plastic. And many of the stories we scoffed at had in some form occurred. He in general respected traditional people. "Feelings have gotten so attenuated, and assigned roles so rigid, that many believe the idea of the soul came from organized religion. But it's not true. Traditional people all knew there was a soul. Hence ancestor worship. To this day traditional people haven't been cut off from their soul. Its only modern advanced humanity, so far into the mind, that we don't know who we are. What we are."

One of his principles was that you didn't get things for free. While there was good in all of mankind's great religions, "You never get the Truth free. Humanity needs structure - doctrines - that are also heavy chains." Then he'd talk about the Great Lie. And he maintained all religions featured the Great Lie. What it purports is that nothing essentially has changed over time. What was true in the past stays exactly as true and right. Not only does the deity remain unchanged, but whatever rules were issued are as appropriate now as when they were formulated. Anyone with any intelligence can see how things have changed. Yet the fundamentalist of every religion demands that the Great Lie be accepted. Many of your average believers however make an accommodation. While they might not take a public stand about precepts that are outdated, they pay them little mind.

"All religions have an expiration date on them. Without exception, in the present age, that date is past. You can say I respect people who grew up in a certain tradition, treasure what is 'higher', have a sense of loyalty and identity. Or you may say I understand people searching for spiritual answers and settling for a belief system that in most respects approximates what they believe - as close enough that they can live with it. There's no disputing the value of community. And having a spiritual ethical program to share with your children. That's why I'm a Unitarian. Nevertheless if we don't admit that the day is past for going along with incredible nonsense and primitive fear mongering, simply because every religion has a history, then we're not being honest. And we shouldn't 'respect' others if they're capitulating to special assertions no longer plausible or ethical. The privileging of earlier people, the leaders and followers of Buddha, Moses, Jesus or Mohammed; may look like reverence and modesty. But it's actually cowardly avoidance – not making your own decisions. Look at your world. Not theirs. Then examine your own soul and decide what you think."

The skeptics were wrong. The great religions, even the tribal religions, hadn't been made up. They came from the Whole. But they were designed to be partial, to fit the partiality of those receiving them. And all apologists for ancient religions that featured a commanding God or gods had two questions they had to answer. That B said they couldn't honestly answer. 1) Why weren't there any follow-ups in our day? Why can't the God or gods manifest and communicate today? (Because this assertion & relationship is no longer appropriate.) 2) What are we to make of the majority of humanity that doesn't follow our religion? What's wrong? Are these surplus people unimportant, merely foils to show the chosen's superiority? (Everyone is equal, but different truths & stories were given to match different needs.) People are children and they can swallow nonsense if they need to. B taught that the Whole had designed the particulars of religions to make it hard for someone in one box to be attracted to another box. His prime example was a Muslim and a Christian. The Muslim would find the whole idea of a Trinity as heresy. To imagine someone being the Son of Allah. Whereas a Christian would hear about all the wives of Mohammed and be instantly turned off. B said these divisions were not accidental.

There was the paradox that Western religions had erred in personifying God. Whereas the East had erred in making the divine too inhuman. And the idea that evil, that negating force from the Void, 'doesn't pay', could be misleading. It was true that it diminished the malefactor's soul, so in that sense it didn't pay. But here on the material plane, judged by material gains, it often did pay. American history was a prime example. Grabbing the land – often stealing it – from the natives paid off. Forcing African slaves to work, through cotton, created the nation's initial wealth. "The evildoers looked on their work and declared it good. 'We were able to push the Indians off the land. Killing any who rebelled. Claiming it as ours, because that is what God wanted. It was the Divine plan. We used African slaves to do the hard work because that was also God's will. Part of the Divine plan. Our prosperity is proof of God's blessing.'" To B the fear, prejudice, hatred against people who are different, was always one of the prime giveaway signs of evil. As was selfishness and greed.

In truth he devoted more time to Christianity than any other religion. Sometimes I thought this was due to his upbringing as a Catholic. Other times I thought it was the residue of his old belief in the United States destiny, as the 'melting pot' leading all nations towards enlightenment. Despite separation of church and state America was predominately Christian. But on the other hand he had already started to become disillusioned. So it might simply have been that he presumed if his students had a foundation in any religion it would be Christianity. And for most of us that was true. He would admit that in light of the Trinitarian doctrine both Judaism and Islam were purer forms of monotheism. However on the positive side the idea of the Trinity was a way of suggesting participation in Creation, which he held to be an important truth. "We're not just animals in an experiment. We participate in setting it up, even if unconsciously. It's interesting to me that this problem seems to have never occurred in the East. Because their religious practices involve consciousness as the way in. As opposed to the West where it would be prayers to a God outside of you. I think those who argue that the East is far ahead of the West in spiritual sophistication because they've been studying consciousness for centuries & millennia are correct. I think of their initiates as going through their own soul to access the Greater Soul."

One of our group, that took B's classes, had a brainstorm. A way to override his resistance to questions. Inspired by the British House of Commons where he said if you backed the next speaker's point you rose briefly. He said we could do a version of this if we acted together. First we'd agree on what we wanted to know. Then we'd all raise our hands at the same time when B happened to come close to the subject. Whoever he called on would ask their version of the question we'd all agreed on. It actually worked. He assumed since there were so many hands all at once something significant had been tripped. Believing we were ignorant and dense, not to mention poisoned, he expected we needed remedial explanations. One time, and I've forgotten why, we wanted to know the person in history he found the most *astonishing*. One of our group thought it would be a political figure; a George Washington, Giuseppe Garibaldi, or Simon Bolivar. But most of us thought it had to be Parmenides.

Yet we were wrong. Without hesitation he said it was Jesus. "An unexpected mystical eruption in Roman Palestine, as if directly from India. To revolutionize the concept of the Jewish Messiah. Devout Jews expected a kinglike personage, victoriously battling for an independent Israel. To say no to that. To come as a poor preaching teacher and healer. To say that the soul's what's important. Its immortal. 'The Kingdom of God is within.' The material world and the body are not important. Just that would be remarkable. But for a Jew to tell other Jews I'll do what I want on the Sabbath. 'The law was made for man, not man for the law.' 'What you have done to the least of our brethren you have done onto me.' Personally B thought Jesus *was* the Jewish Messiah. Though he said such things are not only not settled here, they aren't settled in eternity. He also believed most of the miracles and healings recorded in the bible did take place. And that included the resurrection.

"The four gospels each possessed their own hazards. Mark, though very stark, was the most reliable. With verbatim quotes like 'Why do you call me good? No one is good except God alone.' You knew you were getting the real Jesus before the churchmen began tampering. They were unhappy with Mark's brusque ending so they made up their own and tacked it on. Mathew gives a Jewish centered perspective on the ministry. John could not be trusted at all. Not just that it was written by a Greek disciple of John's, who really didn't like Jews. And his beginning, while impressive, has little to do with Jesus but a lot to do with Plato. But that's what the Whole wanted. No, the real problems come from John's character, not the Greek who wrote down his gospel for him. While John no doubt had a lot of positive attributes his ambition casts a shadow on them. Jesus announces to his apostles that the Son of Man is going to Jerusalem where the chief priests and the doctors of law will condemn him to death, hand him over to a foreign power to be mocked, flogged and killed, but three days later he shall rise. So John and his brother James seize this as an opportune time to come up to Jesus and ask for a little favor. Along the lines of getting your request in early. They suggest that when he comes into his kingdom they'd like thrones alongside his - to his left and right. You can tell Jesus finds this request a little startling. We talk about Peter being dense. So Jesus tries to explain to the whole group, who are not real happy with John and James, that spirituality isn't about lording it over others. The highest serves everyone else. But these brothers, John and James, are like that. Luke has the brothers encountering someone casting out demons in Jesus's name, but because he wasn't really one of their group they tried to stop him. Jesus tells them that he who is not against you is on your side. John's Gospel has that very famous 'No one comes to the Father except through me', but that's not Jesus – that's John. In the gospels its solely in John where you get 'only Jesus is God' claims. Jesus and the Apostles come to a Samaritan town and they want lodging for the night. But when the Samaritans learn they're headed to Jerusalem, a place where Samaritans are banned, they refuse them. John and James want to call down fire on them, burn them all up, until Jesus rebukes them. This is who they are."

"Throughout this book John is constantly dropping not very subtle hints that he was Jesus's favorite, 'the disciple whom he loved'. I'm sure this is how John talked to his group. This is years later so brother James has been dropped from the act. It's given with that whole charade: modesty prevents me from uttering my own name. But he doesn't stop there. On the cross Jesus addresses his mother, tells her now John is her son; then turns and addresses John, telling him Mary is now his mother. Now does anyone believe that if his mother really was at the crucifixion the other gospels wouldn't mention it? Of course they would."

"But you know there's credulousness in Luke too. Luke is believed to have also written Acts, where he shows himself a big a sucker for Paul. A man every bit as ambitious as John, with the same feigned humility. Paul also goes in for speaking of himself in the third person. He knows of this man (wonder who that could be?) who fourteen years ago was raised up to the 3rd heaven. Not mind you the first or second heaven, where they let in any old prophet or saint. But the 3rd heaven, where only the elect of the elect are admitted. Luke seems convinced that Paul is right - the apostles shouldn't have taken it on themselves to pick a replacement for Judas, to fill out the twelve. It should have been left for Providence. The implication being that obviously Paul was Providence's choice. But Luke never seems to consider the ambivalent ramifications of filling Judas's slot."

Christianity is a concoction of Paul and John. "The Whole may well have agreed with Athanasius to aim lower, this is what is suitable for the bulk of humanity. But it's a lot more barbaric than the revolutionary revelation Jesus wanted to teach and preach. There are two acceptable – defensible positions. We are all the sons and daughters of God. Which is my view. Or no one is. Jesus didn't take himself as the only Son of God, or as some sort of Savior. That was all created afterward. He conceived of himself as the Messiah but a different kind of Messiah. John, and his followers, started the overreach. Then Paul, a man who never met Jesus, no matter what he imagined, solidified the doctrine. Paul had been a Jewish enforcer, persecutor, but the Whole needed an organization man, so he was drafted. The half Judaic half Pagan religion we know is a product of Paul not Jesus."

"Jesus would be surprised and aghast to find himself worshipped as God - and by Gentiles. He thought the world was about to end. He thought the generation he was addressing was the last generation. He specifically instructed his disciples *not* to go to Gentile lands or enter a Samaritan town. Recall what he said to the Gentile woman who wanted him to exorcize her daughter, before he gave in: Is it fair to give the children's bread to the dogs? That's what Jesus thought of non-Jews. It was the Whole who had other – bigger – plans." B thought baptism and the Eucharist were nice rituals but any modern person who believed in them was pitiable. It was part of the reason he dismissed Luther. Yes he was a reformer in that he opposed the selling of indulgences. Catholic corruption. But Luther was actually a puritan reactionary. In his trip to Rome he was incensed that priests didn't take transubstantiation literally. He maintained you had to believe that the congregation was really eating Christ's flesh and drinking his blood. When peasants, inspired by Luther's teaching that

164

everyone was free to make their own decisions, rose up against the princes, Luther turned on them and urged the princes to slaughter them. Because Luther actually followed Paul - obey earthly authorities & faith matters more than good works - not Jesus."

The cosmology that got B in trouble was full of paradoxes. Speaking for myself the hardest one to contemplate was two universes involved in 'mutual creation'. First he posited that the universe we're in now has no real space or time. It's in the Void. The Void, true to its nature, self-cancels. Evacuating from in to out and out to in, creating the Big Bang. An important point was that this was instantaneous. In fact in one way, since this universe exists without real space or real time, in the Void, even though by our reckoning billions of years have passed, in some objective way it all happens at once. Being nothing the Void couldn't resist Being from the next universe prying it open, separating the explosion from the contraction. This first Being was unique. And it became what B referred to as the Whole. Its nature was another contradiction. It was born when the Void became itself, and being nothing, even had to separate from that. The Whole in a way facilitated the 2nd universe and all its beings. Because it was the Void's being it was empty. Nevertheless as the Whole it was the midwife of Creation.

All objects here are made of *maya*. Basically just Void. But since the only material they're ever going to encounter here will also be made of *maya* it doesn't matter (unintentional pun.) However what we take to be time, is really life. The excess of Being from the 2nd universe. What physicists call spacetime is made up of Void space and excess Being from the 2nd universe serving as time: the 4th dimension. But as I said the hardest part was to conceive of the two universes as co-existent. B's mutual creation. Because this universe has no real space or time it exists as a singularity. Separate. Only the beings and what happens are real. Yet this singularity is a blessing in disguise, as our souls get made of an unerasable, unchangeable, immortal fabric. B stipulated that we think of the next universe as in the future. And when we are there we will think of this universe as the past. Yet in reality they are cotemporaneous. At least for as long as it takes to finish the job. That's the process of mutual creation. Each is the origin of the other. But try imagining that.

B tried to help us with his film analogy. Film representing this world as a flat 2 dimensional plane. Opposite the next universe with 4 'real' dimensions. In one way you could imagine film filming; exposed to and capturing the forms of the next reality onto itself. In another way its film projecting those forms into the next world. Through manipulation by the Whole the 'lens' between the universes allows the projection of the souls in this world to go where they are free and independent, consolidated in their being; in a realm where they have power we can't imagine. And in the other direction refracting these very souls, confining them not only in material bodies, but in places that needed filling for the story It was telling; revealing truths of nature and human nature, and covering all qualities and experiences. This was sort of helpful but it still required mental gymnastics. Both are the origin of the other. I had a friend of mine in class who summed up B's predicament I think pretty shrewdly. He said we could appreciate the doomed fate that had come down on him. The community which had expelled him, the physicists, had the minds to conceptualize his theory. But since he had been tagged as a crazed heretic they weren't going to bother. Now he was cast among the free thinkers in the humanities. We would hear him out. We didn't start with any antipathy or a priori convictions. His putting life literally at the center of his cosmology didn't offend us. The problem was that we lacked the sort of minds one would need in order to imagine his conceptions. He could talk, and we could listen politely. But we didn't have the background or the faculty required. I think my friend's summation of B's dilemma hit the nail on the head. Repeating something is not the same thing as understanding it. I could repeat verbatim a zen koan I'd heard, that wouldn't tell you that I 'got it'.

B would say it was easier to see the perfection of the 2nd universe. It had proper order. Liberation from handicaps. Ease of movement and connection. And yes things here are backwards. The Whole is forced to work around not only our deficiencies but also the Void's cancelling. Yet B said we should try to see the perfection that is here. That once that is eternal. When it's over, complete, it never changes. Frozen as is. Since the beings born here will not be hampered by any impairing conditions in the 2nd universe, the shaping and imperishability are what is important.

Inside this first universe there had to be a balance. In the outer cosmos huge numbers, huge quantities. But relatively simple compounds, chemistries, and actions. The scale compensating for the simplicity. In the center (Earth) great complexity. Life: the one-celled; the multi-celled: insects, plants, animals. Culminating in the human brain/mind. And the later the more complexity. As B taught the end was the portal that Being entered from, so it had the greatest magnitude. It came from the 2nd universe in the opposite direction of what we see as the 'flow of time'. From our perspective it came from the end and went towards the beginning. B also said causation was largely illusion. He compared our reality to how a flat painting gives the viewer the illusion of depth. We traveled in the direction of exploding space, collecting being on our way back to its source.

All the forces of this universe, save gravity, belonged to space. That tension between evacuating away-outward and evacuating away-inward created the electro-magnetic and nuclear forces. Gravity belonged to Being, and was the attraction of being to being. Hence its relative weakness to the others in this spatial domain. It would never be possible for physicists to fold it into their models no matter how hard they tried. B said all the distant galaxies were already gone. They didn't exist anymore. And B had zero interest in atom smashing. "Remember Leucippus, 5th century B.C.E., coined the term atom. It wasn't what we call an atom. It meant the final building block. Atom meant uncuttable. I can tell you the composition of the final building block. Reflection. Everything else is built on top of it, out of it." B maintained that reflection was one quality the Void had. The Void was nothing. What was reflection? Bouncing back the image from outside, not showing your self, showing something other than your self.

B's theories on humans dividing into breeds like dogs would have created enough problems. Why he denied that Arthur Jensen was a racist was hard to figure. He thought Jensen had no idea what intelligence was and yet he had the effrontery to set himself up as an expert. To decree his "imbecilic findings" based on IQ tests. Yet he publicly defended Jensen, at least to the extent that he denied that Jensen was a racist. People who didn't know the background then grouped him with Jensen. As far as I could tell B's reasons for believing Jensen wasn't a racist were pretty weak. That Jensen was sincere - he really did believe his ridiculous IQ tests measured intelligence. So what? B was persuaded that Jensen was too cultured to have any conscious bias, it had to be unconscious. He was an aficionado, like B, of classical music. By all accounts apparently a quite competent amateur conductor. To B such a cultured individual could never be a crude racist. This went counter to the general suspicion that Jensen embarked on his testing with a secret agenda. He was going to come up with a rationale for the low numbers of minorities in colleges and universities. A scientific finding that they simply couldn't hack it. No need for guilt. They required their own special schools.

Another feature that raised clouds of suspicion around Baccala was his hatred for the Kennedy clan. It started with the patriarch Joseph. A man he called a Nazi appeaser. All of his children B labeled RSBs, his abbreviation for 'rich spoiled brats'. The 'Joe McCarthy brats' in particular were JFK and RFK. I don't need to reiterate that they're being Irish Catholics stoked the ire. B's disillusionment with Americans measuring up to their destiny seemed to start with Vietnam. He blamed JFK and a general Taylor for the war. For sending the first troops. He didn't blame Eisenhower for reneging on holding an election. He believed there was a secret deal between Kennedy and the Pope to support the minority Catholic ruling class in Vietnam. He was always going on about some Cardinal Spellman, as if we knew or cared who he was. I wondered if it was such a secret deal how did B know it existed? His hatred for the Kennedys wasn't rational. He even thought JFK and RFK arranged for the murder of Marilyn Monroe. They didn't trust that she'd stay quiet so they got 'Daddy's boys' to poison her.

B asserted that ultimate self-consciousness was reached by our immediate pre-Homo sapiens ancestors. Which was uncharacteristically generous and open-minded of him. But as I said his division of ethnicities into breeds was the real hurdle. He believed the Australian Aborigines represented proto-modern man. They left Africa before the races split up. (I think the last, or maybe only, physical anthropology book B read was Baker's "Race".) Unlike the later emigrants he didn't maintain that the Australian Aborigines had been chased out of Eden. They somehow had seagoing boats in order to reach Australia. But once on the island continent they gave up seafaring for good. To B Australia represented a captured time the Whole had preserved. Its isolation exemplified by marsupials filling all the niches.

His views on Africans (defined as sub Saharan) were pretty complicated. They were the 'Real People'. But 'the first shall be last' meant the Africans victory in claiming Eden brought an unhappy consequence. Complacency – why should I change? The swagger. Being superior but not being able to get beyond basking in that knowledge. Who needs to change? The arrested development that comes from 'Look at me. I'm the best.' B said this was primarily a male problem. You can't get very far in a society if everyone is looking out for number one. It left them vulnerable later on to people like the Arabs who weren't that cohesive themselves. But at least Arab clans and tribes were developed enough so they could coordinate to capture or buy African prisoners from other African tribes. B maintained that when African Americans became a majority in a sport the norm changed. Celebrating a touchdown in the end zone. Boasting. Insulting your opponent. Pushing for position to get a rebound. "Its all 8 year-old-forever behavior. 'Look at me! Look at me!' All about self and braggadocio."

He would say things that were problematic on their face. For instance that African nations would go blaming colonialism and developed nations' interference for all their ails. But don't hold your breath on them getting their act together. "They have all the potential. Genetically they're the only ones that contain all variations. If all the narrow Mongoloids and Caucasians were wiped out, it wouldn't matter as long as the Africans survived. But as far as them fulfilling their potential there isn't enough time." He believed there was a reason they were tagged with 'uppity'. It wasn't just the White racist Neanderthals they had to deal with. It derived from their real attitude. He believed most Blacks who could or would 'play the White game' had White blood in them. This included heroes of his like Frederick Douglass and W.E.B Du Bois. The American Administration of Justice & the Prison System were deliberately rigged and unfair to them. As was real estate, banking, employment, and the whole political power structure. Yet he doubted Blacks would obey the laws of a perfect system. Their incarceration numbers would always be higher. Same with broken families. They were above it all. Arrogance. Looking out for number one. (Again this was more Black males - not females. The females had some of the attitude of the winners, but mostly they had to cope with the hand they were dealt.) Then he would say things that seemed to go in the opposite direction. One day there had been a news story about a troubled youth in L.A. murdering his mother. And B announced to the class, "A Black or Brown boy would never do that! You'll never read a story like that about a Black or Brown kid because it's so unnatural."

Being the victors of Eden was a mixed blessing. It wasn't just the humans and the plants that found it ideal. So did the tsetse fly (sleeping sickness) and the mosquitos (malaria). As did the great beasts: elephants, lions, leopards, hippos, crocodiles, hyenas, and cape buffalo. B, who believed in karma, believed there was bad karma in how Africans treated albinos. Of course in Africa's climate the absence of skin pigmentation was a survival disadvantage. He said albino babies would be killed at birth or limbs cut off to perform magic rites. When the Europeans came to sic evil it was karmic payback time.

Balance was always a key underlining principle with B. Of course 'first shall be last' worked with that. And you could see how this could be interpreted as justice. The Africans are the victors of Eden. They drive the inferior people out, sentencing them to mix with more primitive humans, but also to innovate to survive. B said the Chinese had the greatest civilization in human history. Coming in first there. Yet it's also a slave ant organizational order, with minimal spirituality. The Indians on the other hand reach the pinnacle of spirituality. That's their coming in first. But in the process they crystallize an antique polytheism and a criminal caste system. Western Europeans stay barbarians until long after Rome has fallen. That's their coming in last. So they will reach for change, hunger for development, and in the end rule modernity. But their machine minds have disconnected from their souls. And if the Asians take the baton from them it will just be more machine minds disconnected from souls. I could see the balance and justice in such a view. But it also seemed to have an aspect of almost Nordic predestined gloom to it all. As if it didn't matter what one did. It was pay now or pay later but you're going to pay.

I remember he was surprisingly uncritical of Jaspers. Maybe it wasn't surprising as their biases aligned. He would give lip service to the pre-Columbian 'Mongoloid' civilizations in the Americas; to Egypt; and the 'fertile crescent hybridizers' of Mesopotamia. But like Jaspers he elevated the ones he found to have a transcendent understanding. I.e. Persia, China, India, and, of course, the Greeks. He did differ with Jaspers on the Jews. He didn't think they had a distinct civilization at all. I think I should make clear that B was a feminist. He believed that you could judge societies on how they treated women. Not just societies in the past, but in the present day. And he would underline how basic it was. "Don't kid yourself that its all that complicated. As in differing gender perspectives. It derives from male animals being bigger and stronger than females. Its that simple and brutal."

It was never entirely clear to me when B thought modernity began. It seemed to move around. Sometimes the American Civil War, sometimes the 20th century. But whenever it started B held that the Turks were responsible for opening the

Pandora's box of genocide. The idea that you could practice genocide in the modern age. (As if the assumption had been, until they violated it, that you couldn't.) The Turks were doubly cursed because their clerics participated in, even led, the massacres of Armenians. To a lesser extent the Kurds were also cursed for collaborating with the Turks. Their karma would be to be torn apart and have no country. Whereas according to B, the crimes of the Japanese in World War II didn't count against them. They hadn't been civilized, in the modern sense. I couldn't understand his reasoning. Most Germans accept the guilt of the Nazi era crimes. There might be families of the worst killers who make excuses and are privately unrepentant. But as a whole, and certainly officially, they admit what happened. The Japanese are more like the Turks, you get nothing but obfuscation, mitigation, and outright denial.

B, as one who despised Henry Kissinger, shared one aspect of his outlook. Kissinger, rationalizing his interference in Chile, said dismissively history doesn't move through the Southern hemisphere. B never stated anything so crudely but that also seemed his view. Even though the hybrid 'Mestizos' were one of his favorites. His 'New People', a blend of Mongoloid-Indians, Iberians and Africans. As with the 'Real People' there wasn't enough time. And he was dismissive of the islanders: the Polynesians, Filipinos, Malaysians, and Indonesians.

He had this template about slave mentality. Which mixed in with his critique of Marx. Jesus was the real communist. What was Marx? A sharp critic of capitalism, with some halfway good observations about class. A German intellectual who ripped off Hegel, turning all of Hegel's principles on their head. Replacing the evolution of the spirit with the evolution of materialism. Marx as a would-be revolutionary living in England partially supported by Engels, scion of Manchester manufacturing. How do you get more capitalist than that? His first great error was thinking his elite (or any elite) could be trusted with power. His second great error was thinking worker's had nothing to lose. Workers almost always have something to lose. It's the serfs that have nothing to lose. Hence Russia and China. When you combine the ignorance about power with the ignorance about who will rebel, you end up with Stalin and Mao. "Slaves really don't have much to lose. They will revolt. But when they win what do slaves want? A master." While the Chinese had the greatest civilization; the Russians had great composers like Tchaikovsky and Shostakovich; a great playwright and short story writer in Chekhov; and the greatest novelists: Tolstoy and

Dostoevsky. But the Chinese and Russians would always have a slave mentality. B said it was ironic that the most famous slaves were the Jews in ancient Egypt and the Africans in the New World, when they were among the people furthest from slave mentality.

He would refer to the Arab – Israeli conflict as Cain and Abel. Semitic brothers battling it out. Each one sure getting the title of Cain would be a great honor. The Jews had the advantage in being defeated over and over. This drove them to develop their minds. Splitting hairs over the Torah to figure out how the chosen people of God kept getting stomped on. The Arabs, unfortunately for them, never lost. They conquered their conquerors. Instilled their own values and religion into them. As a result they let their minds go. So they were spiritually rich but mentally backward. A combustible mix. Of course as I said he had this whole thing about good Jews going to America, bad Jews to Israel. He said as it stood the most despicable people in history were the Germans. But if the Jews in Israel nuked their Arab neighbors those numbers could come in to a higher total than Nazi Germany. They could pass the people who had premeditatedly shot and gassed them. This is a terrible thing to say but my impression was that the symmetry appealed to him.

When Menachem Begin became Prime Minister, most, if not all of us, were appalled. B was elated. He went rambling on about 'Irgun Jabotinsky fascists'. But it was evident that he wasn't chagrined, but triumphant, that his predictions about Israel had been borne out. He didn't seem concerned at all that this torpedoed peace prospects. The only thing that bothered him was the idea that if the Israelis somehow lost we would be obliged to welcome them in as political refugees. He was always going on about how we now recruited the worst people in the world. "Once we welcomed the talented but oppressed. People who wanted a chance, a freer environment. The truly wretched and persecuted. Now, as a result of the evil we practice around the globe as a hegemon we have to take in our clients. Opportunists willing to oppress their own brethren to get ahead. The Cuban and Vietnamese version of Tories. As if our kind of people are those who serve a foreign power."

People now think that attacking 'political correctness' is a rightwing occupation. But originally it was left-wingers like B who attacked it. No one in those early debates concerned themselves with conservatives. Except maybe as obstacle dummies. The opposition from freedom-of-thought types wasn't about ideals or goals. It was more a reaction against self-righteous prigs creating unthinking herd conformity. More of a pricking of assumptions, tweaking pomposity. I remember B using 'Mongoloid idiot' and 'retarded' long after it had ceased to be acceptable in polite company. And I know he did it on purpose. B refused to excuse Mexican emigrants who sneaked into the country unlawfully. Even though as I said 'Mestizos' were among his favorite people. "They love their children more than your common denominator American does. They love their parents more. But there's no denying their developmental lag. And this isn't the 1700's. We're not their safety release valve." Even the normal appeals of compassion - poor people struggling for their families - that usually worked on him, he rejected. The overriding principle here he said was responsibility for keeping your own numbers within reason. "I have the number of children I can support. But the family next door keeps having children beyond their ability to shelter, feed, clothe and school them. Does it become my responsibility then to care for their children? My wife and I were sensible and prudent, while they were not. Should my children be crowded?"

He would casually assume the 'lack of depth' in Asian art was symptomatic. "No depth in the visual, music, the play or story." He was implying more than not mastering perspective. Until contact with the West B said they stayed on and were satisfied with the surface. A friend of mine asked why Mudrick allowed B to assert such things? Well Mudrick allowed B to teach and say anything he wanted. And to be honest about it, Mudrick was hardly in a position to correct B. My impression was that he regarded all Asian literature as too primitive to even bother with. B loved not only the Sanskrit Scriptures of India but also her traditional music and dance. He revered Lao Tzu and the Tang dynasty poets of China, especially Tu Fu. He revered the Zen sages of both China and Japan – and other countries as well. Japanese poetry from Hitomaro and Akahito to the haiku poets he considered great: Basho, Issa, Chora, Buson and Shiki. He never failed to point out that nothing conveyed the incredible variety of moods and thoughts people experience, often without self-consciousness, as well as haiku. He often said the Chinese and Japanese crafts reached a level of refinement unmatched by any other culture. It's true he did regard them as 'conforming' people - a legacy from Homo erectus. But he never implied that they lacked wisdom or feelings. And even the conforming business had a socially positive side.

B generated an atmosphere of intimidation. Once after class, I don't know the cause, he told me, "You know what your problem is Tenace? Intellectual laziness. Passivity. You're waiting for everything to be given to you. Understanding isn't accumulating facts. It isn't piling up knowledge until you hit some magic level and it all comes together. A person has to *work* to understand. It can't be handed to you. It can't be torn off in bite size pieces like you were a baby bird and all you have to do is open your mouth and swallow. Everyone's makeup is different. Everyone's past and perspective is different. No one's route will be the same as yours. Yet every person has to take it for themselves, if they really want it. Do you understand?" I couldn't say anything I was so surprised and taken aback. All I did was nod meekly. Imagine being told off in such a way out of the blue.

We had a saying that 'there was Ockham's razor and B's dissecting knife'. We believed there wasn't anyone living or dead that he couldn't cut to pieces if he wanted to. In one of our powwows we decided to test this proposition. As much as B esteemed philosophers, poets and writers, and visual artists, he granted a higher perch to composers. Because the medium they had to tame "was a language different from our common ones. The tonal medium of pure emotion." We knew one of his favorites was J.S. Bach. The plan was that the next time he drifted into his topic about the compulsion to worship we'd produce a flurry of hands. Whoever he called on would then ask 'Aren't there exceptions? Artists whose work is so remarkable that they are actually worthy of worship? Like Bach.' We got the expected fusillade. Worship? There were large parts of Bach's work that any unbiased person would have to call boring. All the cantatas for example were yawning torture. Yes there were nuggets scattered here and there in them, but the arid stretches to get to them were hardly worth the wait. Bach ripped off Vivaldi, Frescobaldi and Buxtehude. And if he was pleased with one of his own melodies you could bet he'd recycle it over and over and over again. Without knowing it B had proven our point.

In B's scheme self-consciousness was an important marker as we approached the ultimate magnitude of Being at the end. Yet he maintained the wrong kind of self-consciousness had hamstrung modern art. Not just the visual arts, but poetry, plays, literary novels and classical music. His definition of getting off the track had two large components. 1) Becoming self referential, art playing off art, not the world and people.

174

(The reason he said that great art usually came from precincts separated from cultural centers.) Confined art, dedicated to reflecting only art, no matter how entertaining to a certain inside audience, is insipid and sterile. 2) Intellectual anticipation of where your art will go becoming the artist's guide. Which was death for true art, which should be guided by what the soul felt. "When you follow the intellect unmoored from emotion it is sure to end in nuttiness. It's backwards, a pose, the art a guess, a pretension. Maybe there's nothing wrong in theory with the 12 tone approach. The idea that all sounds are a resource, utilize them all. Ignoring that Western music had evolved where it did for a reason. But you still need to judge the results with integrity. Not lie to yourself and your coreligionists. The only thing its good for is creating the atmosphere of alienation. It does that, quite well, but nothing else. Likewise the modern visual artist can't convince you with their work. They have to persuade you with philosophical explanations. People buy the ideas and accept paltry art."

"Art has traditionally been taught as an excess product possible only if there was wealth and leisure. Only rich societies could afford developed crafts and arts. For example in ancient Greece we know the patrons were a privileged class. They could indulge temples, sculptures, plays. As could the medieval church, the Medici court; European kings and aristocrats in the 17th 18th 19th centuries. Post industrial revolution however, with widespread literacy; machines doing a lot of the work, there was more time for the average person to reflect, think and create. The franchise had broadened. All to the good. But with the study of the history of art, and the biographies of favorite artists, came the game of anticipation. Artists not doing their job. Which is to reflect/capture the world, reflect/capture humanity. Instead they got caught up in art only reflecting other (popular) art and trying to anticipate where their particular art was going based on trends as they read them. Their forecasts weren't good, but the whole approach was wrong. Intellectual guesswork does not suffice and is not a substitute for the deep feeling great art requires."

The best location was to be in touch with a nurturing 'vital' cultural center, but far enough away that you were almost forced to do it your own way. Not sharing the popular - but artificial, an artist could employ the real and authentic. He drew parallels with Russian and American writers. And as much as he revered Chekhov, Dostoevsky and Tolstoy he thought the Americans had the advantage. Dostoevsky's

Russian Orthodox Church certainly had its own mysticism. But its rigid structure would have stifled 'democratic transcendentalism'. America's population was more diverse and so were its spiritual selections. This was plain not only from Jefferson and Emerson, but from Hawthorne and Melville also. (Since he liked Poe and Twain somehow magically they weren't Southerners. Though it's clear that Hannibal Missouri was pro-Confederacy, and Poe was not only a Southerner, but a notorious racist to boot.) He'd ask us where were Russia's Franklin, Washington, Jefferson, Hamilton, and Madison? But this was an unfair question. None of us knew enough Russian history to answer. I would guess there were individuals who tried to change their system, but we didn't know the names. However I bet B did. The Bolsheviks didn't spring up out of a vacuum in 1917. Something similar must have been true in China too. I'm sure he knew who the reformers were there before the Chinese communists. But he wanted to make his points without cluttering our heads with contrary information that might prompt questions and dilute his black and white classifications.

"The gift to each succeeding generation is to know more. However there is a compensating effect. Each time and place has its own uniqueness. So we know things that Emily Dickinson didn't and we can evaluate her lines from angles her world didn't know. But there will be passageways that were open to her – to her feelings, views and experience – that are closed to us because of our bits of knowledge. Whose existence we aren't even be aware of." B taught that the twin peaks of American poetry were Dickinson and Whitman, jelling around the time of the Civil War. Both mystics. But extreme opposite personalities. The outward extrovert Whitman, the introvert Dickinson. It was easier to see Whitman's greatness, harder to gauge hers. Her approach was more subtle and subjective. But B said she was Whitman's equal.

There was one exchange I had in my years as a student of his that stands out. I was working on a paper of contemporary poets and I felt overwhelmed. It turned out that there were far more poets to evaluate than I had anticipated. And their styles were so different I started thinking who am I to judge one as good, as 'authentic', and another as not? So I approached B and admitted I felt I lacked the criteria to do justice to such an assignment. He didn't blow me off, which he could have. He was actually helpful. He said not to worry, whenever we read an appraisal we assume it's through that person's taste. What else could it be? So don't fret about that. If you respond to one and not another accept it. Aware that some time in the future you might react differently. A poet that moves you now may not move you in the future. And one you don't get now may open to you in the future as possessing deep meaning. As far as styles, check to see if it seems organic to its subject. Be suspicious of too clever tactics. They might work to grab you initially, but they don't sustain. Schools and doctrines aren't important. You could have a group with a nutty doctrine yet inside their cohort you might find a substantial poet. Remember exceptional poets usually strike their contemporaries as rough-hewn. Their allegiance to their work makes it impossible for them to conform to whatever format is popular at that moment. Stay clear of poets that strike you as having chosen their form and persona-voice first, and then write poetry that exemplifies that artificial figure. These are poseurs. Not worth the time it takes to read them. It was all very helpful advice. Unique, unlike any conversation I ever had with him before or after. I think what sparked his response was seeing I was struggling, that I had taken the assignment seriously, and he knew it was tricky territory - in a subject he loved.

The superficial conflation of Mudrick's critique of Shakespeare with B's was another lazy mistake. Not as injurious as confusing Jensen's racial rankings with B's 'breeds' but still inaccurate. I took literature classes from both so I think I can speak with some authority. I would characterize Mudrick's discomfort as moral. Closer to Tolstoy's and Shaw's position; a queasy feeling that Shakespeare was this amoral bootlicker. Whereas B held that Shakespeare's lowness, "the type to enjoy bear-baiting and executions", was one of his strengths. It contributed to his ability to manipulate the emotions of his whole audience. He knew how to do this because he felt what they felt. His other strength was in selecting which stories to steal. "If he were alive today he'd be writing soap operas."

Mudrick, for all of his famous defamations, must have deemed him a great poet. He'd do rigorous examinations of his work, line by line, word by word. B would no more parse Shakespeare than he would an anthology of ribald limericks. He would have been much more likely to close read the imperialist Rudyard Kipling. B believed Shakespeare relied on faux drama in his poetry to mask its vacuity, while he relied on the 'façade' of the poetic in his dialogues, to enable his plays to be taken as elevated. His work was all in effects, little substance. "What he learned from his glove-making father was if you attach shiny gewgaws people will fall for anything." He was an entertainer. B would often say one play by Ibsen, Chekhov, O'Neill, Beckett, or Arthur Miller, told you more about humanity than all of the puffed up mimes of Shakespeare combined. Because Elizabethan theater was the beginning of theater in its modern form, a greater freedom was permitted. No one knew how the form would finally congeal. Where the boundaries on representation were: what is thought, what is speech (flowery language?), what is realistic? The Elizabethan audience in their uncertainty allowed liberties. "The plays in time would acquire that lacquered shine that age bestows on the antique. Later generations would grant it any permission. It was 'Elizabethan'. It was 'Shakespeare'. Grand stuff, everyone agrees."

B thought Mudrick was right that Chaucer's people and poetry were superior to Shakespeare's. Yet while it might serve as some comparison example it had ceased to be relevant. B held that Chaucer was no longer accessible. "Young people have trouble with Milton. To them Chaucer's language isn't even English." He preferred pointing to John Donne, a contemporary of Shakespeare's, 'a true poet'. He would say if you couldn't tell the difference between the reality & weight of Donne versus the artificiality & empty air of Shakespeare, you should just keep quiet. B had particular contempt for Jewish scholars who had happily joined the bardolatry. He said Marlowe, who turned against people easily, traveled throughout Europe, and was involved in diplomacy and espionage. He might well have encountered Jewish moneymen and come away with a resentment. Which could have generated "The Jew of Malta". But Shakespeare never left the island, and England had exiled its Jews centuries before. He made up murderous Shylock merely to piggyback on Marlowe's successful formula. To excuse such blatant opportunism so you could keep faith in the idolatry of a false religion showed a lack of even minimal integrity. Another absurdity was scholars searching for a lost play, "What the world needs is one more hack collaboration by the burnt out Shakespeare". Equally farcical to B was debating whether the man was a secret Catholic. "A court flatterer has no steady convictions. He would hedge his bets. Public Protestant and closet Catholic. Figuring, whichever one turns out to be God's preference, I'm covered.

To look in his work for evidence – when such a character is endlessly negotiating, looking for the way out."

We inadvertently got caught up in substantiating B's view. He was carrying on about mankind's need to worship and cited Shakespeare as example. His pretense at being a respectable gentleman, servant of the crown, a good family man, while being a thief and a debauchee, walking around with a 'for sale' sign on his forehead. Someone may have snickered. Or I think B imagined that someone snickered. I didn't know then, and I don't know now. Anyway B stopped, and issued a challenge, "All right, pick a play." We huddled, deciding Hamlet was too predictable, so we chose Lear. It had a reputation for gravitas. I'm not sure any of us were that familiar with it, just that it was a late play regarded as weighty. So we thought if anything could stand up to B's scrutiny Lear might survive. B said our next meeting would take place in the Old Little Theater. He would get play-scripts from the UCSB theater arts department. When we next convened we apportioned the roles.

I wanted to be Kent, a rather straight-forward part. Loyal as a dog. But B insisted for some reason that I play the Fool. The first time we just had a read through to acquaint ourselves with the action and characters. Some of us had to play multiple parts. And then the next class, though we were sitting down, we tried to speak the parts like a performance. I never saw B enjoy himself as much as at that reading. He was animated, walking around yelling "Bastard!" - to punctuate the primitiveness of the plot I think. Or laughing when the obviousness of the plot direction was preposterously simple. I can't remember him, in class anyway, having such a good time. In my opinion anyone who tells you Lear is a great play has drunk the cool-aid. There are moving touches - Lear's reaction to Cordelia's death. But the plot is thin and flimsy. The villainy of the two older sisters, and Gloucester's "Bastard Son", is comic book stuff. The writing is pretty much a mess, and the further it goes the more of a mess it becomes. How it got a reputation for deep and serious I don't know. And it bears out what B always quoted Jonson as observing. That Shakespeare wrote in haste and showed no concern that the resultant language was nonsensical. There were muddled speeches everywhere. Don't even ask me about the Fool. Such inane drivel: the codpiece that will house before the head has any. The writing is so frivolous that Shakespeare has the Fool make a mock Merlin prophecy, then break character to explain "This prophecy Merlin shall make, for I live before his time." And this during the storm scene, the supposed height of the drama, with Lear railing at the elements. It does make you wonder.

It underscored B's thesis that you can turn anything into a 'work of genius' if you have that need. Humans have the ability, and propensity, to project. You can perceive what you want to perceive – create untold dimensions that aren't really there. So it's always doable. But I don't think anyone in that class would ever voluntarily attend a performance of Lear again. B explained that the Gloucester story Shakespeare took from Philip Sidney. But the main story came from Holinshed, as a lot of his plays did. But originally it wasn't a tragedy – Shakespeare turned it into a tragedy. B shared what he believed was Shakespeare's motivation in choosing the story. Shakespeare had achieved worldly success. Money and property. He worried about being taken advantage of in his senescence. His only son had died young. That left three females. The wife he was tired of. The daughter that had disappointed him. And the daughter he thought of as his good daughter. In his will he would leave everything to her. He wouldn't be swayed by mere words. He knew all about mere words. B added that as it happened he drank himself into the fever that would bring on his death at the favored daughter's wedding.

A particular dislike were the 'Modernists' in American poetry. Wallace Stevens, T.S. Eliot, Ezra Pound, Hart Crane, et al. He thought they were not only overrated but basically frauds. Stevens played the anticipation game to perfection, but his work was entirely bogus. Eliot passed off philosophy and references as poetry. And like Yeats he suspected Eliot was more than half fascist. (Yeats' poetry however he respected.) But the one that really got his goat was Pound. He thought Pound's poetry was as daffy as the man, absolutely worthless. Pound had become a tool of the fascists in Mussolini's Italy. Broadcasting propaganda for Italy and Germany; ranting about the pernicious influence of Jews and their usury. Captured after the war, with the help of famous friends like Eliot, he was found insane. B would bemoan, "How such a traitor evaded hanging! What do you have to do?" But the fact was that many literati, including Jews like Allen Ginsberg, had made the pilgrimage to St Elizabeth. (The hospital for the insane, where Pound was confined.) We all knew that Mudrick too had made that pilgrimage - he was very frank about it. And Mudrick was Jewish. B would never criticize Mudrick for anything. And on almost any other issue between the two the students would tend to backup whatever position Mudrick took. Maybe this was a generational thing, but we didn't see in the Modernists what our elders saw. As revolutionary pioneers opening up possibilities. Most of us saw them the way B did. Certainly we saw Pound as he did. Mudrick calling up Pound, to be granted an interview by the great man, was perplexing. Mudrick, with such sharp critical faculties, and high morals.

B's Metaphysics classes were tricky. Sometimes they were in classes labeled Philosophy. Other times in classes labeled Physics. And sometimes inside classes that really were Philosophy or Physics, he'd suddenly go off into metaphysics. B had a high regard for Buddhism. But Indian and Buddhist teaching proclaims that the self is illusion. All our striving, fears, attachment, anxiety, anger, suffering, come from holding onto this illusion. But this whole belief was completely absent from B's theology. Of course he believed attachment to possessions; succumbing to 'control' and 'ego' were low. But he held that the self - identity - was part of Being. So attachments to people, the good, and real quality, were natural and positive. Not anything to overcome. The self was a manifestation of the soul – your independent eternal one. So it was the very opposite of the Eastern concept of the self as illusion. Your individuality was eternal because you were.

Often B asserted that you could have opposites with each being true. For example: each person was responsible for who they became. Balanced by: we are all a construct of our genes, upbringing and environment. Simply a product. So from that perspective not responsible at all. It reminded me of Aquinas, the reconciling of both free will and a predestination known to God. As I said B had this view that as history neared its end, drew nearer to Being, the material world, though still 100% maya, solidified. Became more concrete - harder to move about *deus ex machina*. Who would notice this? "The interesting person is the conscious individual who falls in between science and the spiritual. Who accepts scientific data and doesn't trust religious dogma, yet feels science is missing the heart of existence. There's hope for that person. Too bad there are so few."

He would talk about things that 'had to be'. Even if the space here was deceptive, couldn't we conclude that real space had to have 3 dimensions? That the extensions of width, height and depth were simply logical. You had to allow for side to side, up and down, forward and backward. "Are the axioms of logic true? We will maintain that they are. Are the principles of geometry true? We will maintain that they are. Can a circle have any other qualities than those we know? Can a triangle, square, line or point? No." And on the great clue planted in the dynamics of reflection: "What can we deduce about its mechanics? Look in a mirror. The image is exact. But it's perfectly backwards. Your left side will appear as your right side. Your right side will appear as your left." He was fascinated by water. Including, but going beyond the necessary-for-life aspect. It's 'surface tension'. That water could be a vapor, as in clouds. When flowing it's look and sound. Frozen, becoming a solid. And of course when still its reflective capacity.

There had to be a representation-reflection in Creation of there being two universes. "If I am right about mutual creation there should be an expression of it in the bodies containing higher consciousness. Two parents, two sexes. The bilateralism of all higher animals. They're all two-sided. Pregnancy in mammals reflects the next world being born in this one." The way he made us question the order we assume things happen was unnerving. He posed it as a series of three or four steps. Something happens. The brain/mind takes information from our senses and through electric-chemical signals composes a version of what occurred. Finally that composite story is filed in memory. B asked what if this entire sequence was backwards? That struck me as science fiction. It would have the memory, coming from nowhere (or the 2nd universe), initiating the process. Sending its version to the brain/mind. Which projected and caused the phenomena. I had read something similar to that in a Buddhist book once. And found it then confounding and implausible. I don't know how seriously B meant it, or if it was just a mental exercise.

On the other hand his concept that as we drew nearer to that window or door to the next world & Being, we would see a greater reflection of that world in ours, was intriguing. B said here it would have to be mediated through technologies, but the general powers or abilities were discernable. The ease of movement. The concentration and accessibility of knowledge. Greater and swifter communication. This thinking might have been one of the reasons some people categorized him as a reactionary. He did use the term 'end-time'. And it's true that he regarded these technologies, their proliferation, doubling speed, as signs, even proofs. He didn't know when the end would come, only that it had to be near. So he left himself open

182

to being pegged a 'repent!' evangelist, but the resemblance was only on the surface – and very misleading.

He did use the computer as a metaphor, or more than a metaphor. Yet looking back I have to say in a pretty limited way. More as a centralized power. Closer to what now we would call a supercomputer. I think if he had truly anticipated the ubiquity and power of the personal computer that would have helped his analogy. The fact that with a 'smart phone' one is walking around with a very powerful computer which can keep you in contact with your friends, take pictures, keep you updated on news, guide you on which route to take. Its true we still have to go to some sites for search engines or products. But if he'd foreseen this development he could have stressed how its independence reflected each soul's independence and power in the next world. From the advantage of hindsight it's obvious that this was a branching direction he underestimated. A related idea was a comment B once made about calculations going on in our subconscious that were exactly like the programs as run by computers. (Which was a copy of the other?) He didn't say if this was only for the individual, or for larger problems maybe the Whole might be working on. Or if it related to 'machine mind'. The most remarkable part of this assertion was that the calculating computer language wasn't mathematical or binary. In what seemed like a throwaway line he said it was a pictographic code. "Very like Mayan. It may be Mayan." I assumed this followed the logic that once you started using a specific language, i.e. code, you were stuck, you had to keep using it. But I don't know. It caught us all by surprise, and unfortunately there was never any follow up. Was it only conjecture? Because he held the Mayan heyday as the center of history? - which could be chronologically eccentric, remembering the weight he gave total human population and complexity. Or was it stimulated merely by the name Mayan? Or did he have some vision or revelation?)

He got some resistance that all theologies provoke, from the lives beset by problems. Those to whom bad things had happened, like an accident or a severe disease. Where was the justice? Couldn't this be called injustice? B couldn't understand why everyone couldn't see the bigger picture. The Void had certain demands following its nature. The Whole worked around those demands while checking off its own list. B said no affliction carried over once a soul was released. He often did a radio analogy. With our bodies as the radio, our souls as the program. Sure if the radio was compromised it could alter and affect reception and broadcast. But it wouldn't affect the program. The program in this analogy was perfect. There were no long-term problems. Even bad lives or traumatic experiences would be transcended. The capacity of the soul was greater than we could imagine.

"Pay no attention to our idiot biologists or neurologists. Like all scientists those with the human body as their field are convinced materialists. They can't explain consciousness or life, but don't worry they will tomorrow." What was striking was B's emphasis on location. As if the greatest achievement of the physical body was notching a location for us in this field. I don't think anyone except B understood what he meant. Also curious but a little more understandable were perorations on humanity's energy coming from the once living. Not only food: vegetable or animal; but fuel, especially 'fossil fuel'. By his presentation it was obvious that he thought this significant - as something that had to take place. He never bothered to explain it in detail but I assumed it related to complexity. It wasn't that he opposed cleaner alternative energy sources. He was always for limiting pollution. Yet he believed the majority of the energy in human history had to come from the once living. He also had a funny view of nuclear bombs & energy. He thought it was dangerous to play with either the weapons or the nuclear power plants. Yet as much as he loathed Edward Teller, he believed humans had to invent and had to develop the hydrogen bomb. Because the nuclear fusion process was the one occurring in the Sun. Again I didn't understand why but that's what he held.

Dreams were an inversion product of our imprisonment here. The soul in the next universe is free to create or join any environment it wants. Here it was not only stuck with a given environment but its only release, when we are deeply asleep processing impressions and emotions, was not controlled. At the mercy of stream-of-consciousness memories and feelings, reacting to the reeling out of these fictional conglomerations. To B dreams were like great art - as ultimate expressions of our captured state.

If you were hostile to his thought you'd find his conception of the Whole a contradiction. If you were open to it you'd go along, at least to concede that it fit within his system. He'd say, "You have to understand the double game the Whole is playing. Never forgetting our participation in it all. There's an assuring aspect. The positives of spirituality and the good side of religions. To most modern people the world seems a given, a preexisting set factual reality we have to adapt to. When in a way (an indirect unconscious way) you could say the universe was designed by us to fool us." He also had an arresting thought that maybe the fullest experience of death and dying wasn't from those who knew the spiritual truth. That is those who knew the soul, and intuited the next life. But those who thought this was it. Precisely because they believed that when they died everything would be extinguished they squeezed the maximum out of each moment. Suffering from their ignorance, dreading each step, they milked it for all it was worth.

The idea that the Whole doesn't evolve/learn from events and accumulated knowledge, was another great error. Very importantly the Whole learned what success does to people. The mushrooming ego: 'If Creation is all about me, I'm God's darling...' According to B the Whole moved to counter that. Since it could do pretty much whatever it wanted in the cosmos behind appearances the challenges were doable. In the last 5 or 6 centuries humanity had learned so much, was able to do so much, that the shifts were commensurately dramatic. For instance the blow that the Sun doesn't circle the Earth. The Earth circles the Sun. If we set aside the prehistoric period, when every tribe lived in its own reality, the later in time, the more extreme the counters. Discovering there isn't one galaxy, many of what we thought were stars are actually galaxies, and there are billions of galaxies. Our planet appearing in relation to the cosmos as a tiny speck in the vastness of space. You had to buy in to B's conception of the Whole – that it could do anything it wanted macro and micro. And the rigging wasn't just to combat ego. B believed the test had to be harder to make it fair for earlier people who weren't given all the later compiled knowledge. "What constitutes a more perfect test set-up then when people think they are alone, unobserved?" He did believe that death in every age had always been an equal opportunity challenge. There's the motionless body of a loved one. What do you make of it? Though he was convinced earlier people, and even traditional people today, were more in touch with the spiritual.

With the extremity of all this you couldn't help wondering at times if you were being held hostage by some kind of nut. Were his ideas powerful because he was mad? B's notion of the plasticity of this universe, and all its time being one, coupled with the Whole's complete control of maya, meant it could wait to 'fill in' Creation until the very last minute. So for instance it could wait 'until' Renaissance explorations in anatomy to finalize internal body organs and functions. Even delaying further details for later. The mechanism of the solar system could wait 'until' the invention of the telescope to be filled in. The whole micro cosmos could wait to be filled in 'until' the invention of the microscope. The galaxies could wait 'until' Hubble in 1929 discovered the red shift and the expansion of the universe. (By the way B said scientists were too complacent in accepting the 1:1 correlation between speed and distance. They should have been more suspicious of this too perfect equivalence.) To B none of this was a problem because of his conception of the Whole. Aside from the demand that there be a balance of quantity outside equaling complexity inside (the center), the Whole could manipulate the cosmos any way it wanted. He did stipulate that the number of galaxies and their stars had to approximate 'an infinite number' to the human mind. Likewise microscopic life had to approximate 'an infinite number'; i.e. beyond the human ability to comprehend. Which certainly seems the case.

"Remember the Whole appears at as close to the beginning as you can get. If the beginning is nothing this is the Being of that nothing. So it is Whole, it is One, but its singular. That is it has Being, but its the Void's being, its without identity. A placeholder and facilitator. You could say it lacks the self of the creatures/souls that it helps birth in this universe and exist for eternity in the next one. Or you could say it divides itself up into all these creatures and things so it can return to nothing. My point is the Whole only exists in this universe. There's a lot to doubt in the Old Testament. Not just theology that long ago ceased to have a purchase, but also all the stuff about Egypt and the migration, the Canaanites, et cetera. But one story that rings true for me is Moses's encounter with Yahweh. After he's given his marching orders he asks Yahweh: If the Israelites ask me who sent me, what do I say? And the answer he gets back is: 'I am that I am. Tell them *I am* has sent you.' This I believe is an accurate report because it resonates as true. What is 'I am' but one way of saying being? Yet 'I am that I am' also has a circumspection. It doesn't assert identity." (B was Unitarian. Their liberality allowed all members to have their own beliefs. Whether people regarded him as a Christian depended on their own beliefs and on their definition of a Christian.) "The primary task of the Whole is to use the widest spectrum of souls in the story - human history - and imbue them with the widest range of qualities. The opposite of nothing. Checking off the variety of experiences it wants to cover as it goes. To do this, if it has to, it bends the souls to fit into the story, with slight concern about brevity or distress. Measured against eternity it doesn't seem that unfair. In endless time all traumas dissolve. Another factor in the design that the Whole attends to is concerned with how entities will function together in the next world. I would characterize this priority as a consideration of long term fit and perpetual motion."

On instinct he would say simply study a large flock of birds circling in the sky. Or a film of a school of fish spinning round. Do you think any animal is controlling their part? No. A girl in one class was upset that, if this was true, why had the Whole allowed species to go extinct? It turned out she had in mind specifically species that had never had contact with humans, and thus had no fear and in consequence got slaughtered. B seemed surprised by her reaction. "You misunderstand the relationship. There has to be some equipment in the creature. You can't expect the Whole to send a warning beforehand: 'Be on alert - humans are coming! This is what they look like. This is what their weapons and traps look like, and how they work.' It isn't that sort of relationship. Especially as history escalates. If the animal is an easy target, not very bright, it's too bad. No one's fault though. It doesn't take a Darwinist with blinders on to admit survival is a factor."

Sacrifice was to him some sort of key. I'm not confident I ever grasped exactly how he saw it. But it was clearly very important to him. Its existence in early and traditional religions everywhere was no accident. Nor was it due to some human psychological weakness. It touched a basic truth – Law - of Creation. B believed this knowledge was once universal. The Whole letting humanity – every tribe - know this condition. That sacrifice was part of coming into existence, part of the deal. There was another student, also not a member of our group, who once had an outburst or protest. Exclaiming that B's scheme of Creation was 'unfair'. Instead of cutting him down as we all expected, or dismissing the response as emotional, he tried to widen the perspective. "You have to let go of any fairytale God, and make some concessions to necessity. Especially if we are only one step away from the Void. Are in fact still in its no-space space, no-time time, with maya matter. Take the underlying expectation, which generates your response, and translate it to a demand that existence go directly from the Void to Heaven. And what you're asking is that there be no stop in between. Put that way does it seem reasonable? No trials, but also no history, no origin, and no explanation. Everything implanted as if at a factory making dolls. Let the skeptics and childish fault God, 'Why is there suffering? Why is there evil?' These are unfair and ignorant digs. People make up a fantasy God and then blame this fictional Omnipotent Deity for not making them angels in Heaven. Like spoiled brats complaining, 'Why can't we skip all this difficult business?' It's hard enough to pull the trick off with this universe as the intermediary. To hold onto a straight-to-heaven scenario is something we should only let a child demand. Adults should know the relationship of the complexity of life to creating character. Adults should be aware of how difficult it is to make anything. And how difficult it is to really learn a lesson that will stick with us. We – if we are truly mature - should not be so rash and thoughtless."

There were clues. At least according to B. Sometimes he would refer to them as 'breaks' or 'tears', like a rip in fabric. They allowed a glimpse of the real game being played. But they were all weird occurrences. Like precognition. This included not only classic prophecy, the oracle at Delphi and such, but 'gifted' psychics. He also believed completely normal people could on occasion have a vision - a slice of the future. With precognition he grouped déjà vu, which he believed frequently was exactly as it presented itself. Of course precognition was possible – explainable – through his theory that this universe all happened at once. It was merely getting an opportunity to glimpse a separate location that existed around the corner as it were. He took most such accounts as true and as supportive of his theory.

He also took the life after death experiences as real. You know people who supposedly died, experienced that, and then for whatever reason came back. Often seeing their body. The famous long tunnel with a light at the end. This would usually occasion a rant by B about skeptics in general and scientists in particular. Going on about disconnected souls and group-think. "A neurobiologist could have an out-of-body experience and afterward convince himself it was all a trick of the brain. That's how strong their false religion has become. Even though he saw his own body. Even though the brain could not have an out-of-body experience. Doesn't matter, they know what the answer has to be. Can't fool them. There is no reaching such people."

He believed those who said they remembered past lives. This was another break. When Tibetan lamas went looking for a child there was a basis for this. Yet he didn't believe in the standard Eastern understanding of reincarnation. He would tell us to look at it as Nature (or the Whole) being economical. You don't want to go back to the drawing board for every new person. So the astral bodies were particular types used over and over. But that personality armature was only part of what made up a soul. He would use cut out paper dolls as his example. You fold paper, cut an image, and when you pull them out you have a line of identical figures linked holding hands. But he said having different lives cuts them free. The Indians and Buddhists with an insight jumped to a mistaken conclusion. There is a connection: hence those memories. But at death, while the astral body may get reused, each soul is its own self. Going off perpendicular to that line. "The astral body is only one component. There's the biological genetic inheritance from your two parents. There's the distinct life experiences. These components are as consequential as the astral personality, and together they create a unique soul."

Another 'break' were those rare individuals with total recall – photographic memories. B's explanation involved his conception of how memory would function in the next world. As with everything else it would be superior to our memory now, yet like our memory here it would fade over time. Not a bad thing. But our memories of this life, whether long or short, would stay perfect. Collectively helping humanity catalog all experience. For most of us, while alive, the soul's perfect memory was out of reach. The rare individuals with perfect recall had this ability, according to B, because of a freak rip in the fabric. They were able to tap, while still alive, into their soul's perfect memory. He obviously believed this, but how do you prove that is the explanation? I have to say B was probably the smartest person I ever met. But it never seemed to bother him that for many of us these 'clues' weren't proofs. And with the exception of the memory savants, doubts circled about the reality of these other supposed events. There are fair people, I include myself, who need to be convinced that precognition actually happens, that astral bodies are real, or life after death experiences aren't imagined. Bringing these freak occurrences forward as your evidence only makes skeptics more skeptical. Makes it easier to cast aspersions of dubious probity; if not unsoundness or susceptibility to charlatanism. Yet to B it wasn't a problem that these phenomena all fell into a gray credibility zone. He didn't think it was bad luck or happenstance. The clues couldn't be convincingly solid material. In other words to keep the test fair, and not too easy, the Whole had settled on these phenomena. How do you argue with that?

According to B the Passion of Jesus was more about the Whole using Jesus to tell *its* story. Which, if true, would go a long way in explaining why it was so strange. In B's version the story is that the God of this world (i.e. the Whole) sacrifices itself for our good. 'There is no greater love than this. That a man shall lay down his life for his friends.' It was sacrifice, but it wasn't a man and it had nothing to do with original sin or any other absurd doctrine. In some classes there were some students who were clearly uncomfortable with this interpretation. An identity-less Whole being the real Savior of humanity. B, assuming they had been raised in a church going family, would offer them the consolation that being anointed the surrogate figure was a high honor. B had trouble with the resurrection. Not that he doubted it took place. He believed it did. He said a master at the level of Jesus could come back and reanimate his body if he wanted to. But what was the point? His ministry was all about the superiority of the spirit over the physical. So why make a big deal about transporting a body made of maya to heaven? Beyond the impressive demonstration there was a certain absurdity, and it was contradictory to the whole point of the ministry. If we put to one side the question of did it happen, or did it not happen, B's problem was he couldn't see that the average person needs a miracle demonstration. On this I think Jesus (and the Whole?), Paul and the later church fathers, were right in understanding mass humanity, and B was obtuse.

The mechanics of B's eschatology were bracingly straight forward. The universe we view in the sky disappeared eons ago. The distant galaxies - it was simply their light reaching us after traveling so far. They were long gone. The acceleration, doubling of speed, took them all away, except for our own - the Milky Way. And it would disappear in short order. What was occurring in compensation for all this activity on the periphery was growth in the center (us). This was the fate of the universe at its end - the center becoming all. Reaching the speed of light. Because everything near us was mushrooming at the same speed it wasn't perceptible. This would be the end of the 1st universe, the concluding side of the Big Bang.

"You couldn't be here if you weren't there." When B spoke of his conception of the next world he'd preface his remarks with qualifiers. As this is my speculation or conjecture. Or this is my deduction from my hypothesis, combined with what we do know, or from what I observe here in the contained backwards Looking Glass; and what I extrapolate as constituting both opposite & continuation. For most teachers such qualifiers or admission of personal disposition were routine, but for B they were rare. Usually he'd hit us with flat statements.

B would often use turtle hatchlings as an example of creatures transitioning from this world to the next. Because everyone had seen those nature films of ocean going turtles once a year coming up on a beach to lay their eggs. She departs and some time later they all hatch together. Safety in numbers. Except there are predators waiting. On the beach and in the water. So the survivors are probably a minority. B's point was that it didn't matter. Each existed, that was what mattered. Animals and plants in the next universe would feel-create where they wanted to be. Not conscious control like higher animals or humans, but going with the flow. Relations from this world as a beginning and those connections intersecting outward. Plants that grew by other plants, animals that shared the same habitat. It wasn't exactly the lion lying down with the lamb though. Predators could hunt, and if successful eat. But the prey would escape, making a new body instantly. Because in the next world souls control. The soul makes the body. Animals and plants would transition from young to old as the mood hit them. They would 'inherit' the abilities they received here from the Whole, i.e. from what we label instinct. This would be their 'natural increase', that didn't violate who and what they were. Plants and animals would be subject to human manipulation. (Often when B would talk about how we would manipulate other creatures, even the microscopic creatures, my imagination would go to that Disney film "Cinderella". The part where the fairy godmother turns animals into coachmen and such.)

A key principle was that every creature, including humans, could in the next (conducive) environment, be more, but only 'times' themselves. As I said before this was a boundary set by being. One couldn't extend beyond who you were. Even in a world where the powers were exponentially greater and the medium cooperative/conducive instead of resistant. You were your own limit. By the way there would be sex. No procreation. Birth was the exclusive right of Creation. One student, wanted to know if we were all fated to spend most of our time with those who occupied our time here. B said "Not at all, or not necessarily. This is a special chamber. One way of looking at it is the personnel of the 2nd universe are refracted to fit into the story of the 1st universe. Primary importance – to us anyway – is the person. Who you are. But the Whole is concerned not just with placing all the constituent beings somewhere, but with balancing the story it's writing and directing, to cover all experience and types. The brotherhood & sisterhood of all humanity will be much greater in the next world. The sharing and understanding of each other there will surpass our norms. The galaxy of feelings will be accessible through knowing others. Knowing one who went through a particular experience while knowing them as the particular person they are. Our lives here are brief. You're stuck with a relatively small circle. Must needs be. This doesn't determine who you will chose to associate with when you are totally free. I happen to love my birth family and my own family and maybe this limits my imagination when it comes to those who weren't loved, or were cruelly treated. Not to mention those, and it happens, who simply don't have all that much in common with other family members. Or those who look back on their life and acquaintances and decide they were just too limited – 'I want something more.' Dissatisfied. But it's up to every person. You really will be free. In a way that's very hard for us to imagine."

B would frequently speak of the next world having a reverse order. Or the correct order. This world was backwards. Here we had to deal with all the 'givens'. We were obliged to react, make limited decisions, take limited actions, cope as best we could. Nor could we claim (with the exception of a few stoics, yogis, and Buddhist monks) that we controlled desires and emotions. Whereas on the other side each individual soul was in charge – could command not only what they wanted in their orbit, but internally could control – if so inclined - what they thought and felt. Even to a particular mood they wanted to be in. Here we were dependent on the physical, and vulnerable to the circumstantial. There everything started with the soul. Where you wanted to be, with others; or you could create the surroundings you wanted. Every soul would have the ability to correct any malady. Someone commented that it was a strange reality he was describing. "No, *this* is the strange world, with all its deformities, setbacks and resistance. We've just gotten used to it. Not knowing the alternative we accept it as normal. As how things should be, must be. Error."

Even though B's spiritualism was transcendent, his expectations for how most people in the next world would adjust their views was, in my opinion, pretty cynical. He thought it likely that those to whom religion was important would find a way to rehabilitate their old religion, even their old rituals. Which seemed surprising, when they'd be in a world where they possessed godlike powers. Also they'd see all around them people who believed in other faiths, not to mention people who hadn't believed in anything. "When I was younger I believed attitudes would flip. That ideal of all people traveling different paths converging on the mountaintop, and from there finally seeing how it was all laid out. That wider perspective, concentrated being, and the shock of a different reality would thrust everyone to a higher enlightenment. And I'm sure some of that will happen. But after you observe people long enough you see how stubborn their mentality is. They don't like to change and they find ways – sometimes very convoluted squirming ways – not to change. Or to change as little as possible. They look for reasons, they rationalize, they stretch small things into large things. So I think most of the religious will adopt the Whole as God. We could say they actually did this in life, only mistakenly. God has always had a distance for most people. At least in the West. And in the Earth's major religions, to the vast majority of the believers, the pivotal figures, the revelations, the commencement of their tradition, happened a long time ago. The sacred is mixed up with a special holy period long ago and all the other believers in their community, especially their family, who followed these religious observations. We could guess that the added remove of being in the next world will only make it more holy for those to whom distance was always part of their worship. We can't say that gratitude isn't a spiritual grace – and a correct attitude. Nor could we argue that we don't, in a way, owe our existence to the Whole."

"The atheists for their part will be forced to admit that they were wrong about the soul and the next life. But they will claim to be right about religion. And they will argue that since the Whole lacked identity they were right about God also. Indians can project-create their gods. Buddhists won't have to change much. Of course I will maintain that all souls, constituting a congregation of the whole, of one, will be more enlightened than they were here on Earth. And those that had the light here, that combine a humanistic spirituality and a spiritual humanism, will be inspired to pursue good works in a divine atmosphere with even more brio than they did down here in the vale of tears."

Our little group's most successful stratagem didn't happen during class, but after it. We'd all read Fritjof Capra's "The Tao of Physics" and one of our number said this is the perfect book to use as a wedge on B. Because Capra was not only open to seeing a harmony of Eastern wisdom with the most advanced Western science, but the man had studied under Heisenberg. So his views were right, the subject matter perfect, and his qualification unbelievable. We thought it best to approach B after class, which would allow him to expound if he wanted to. We didn't know in what direction he might go. As it happened it got him into talking about how the pieces of his cosmology came together. Something, oddly, that he never spoke about in class. There he tended to present his system as fully formed. As if it all came together, all the parts, and at the same time. After we brought up our enthusiasm for "The Tao of Physics" he went into kind of a reverie about what he had been meditating on when working on his theory, and how his conception crystallized and evolved. He talked about Bohr's work on understanding quantum, and Heisenberg's Uncertainty Principle.

"The aha moment came after wrestling with the problem of capturing images on a flat finite plane-plate from souls and life that are eternal, that have no end? How can such disparate entities cooperate? I thought 'statistical probability'. Which rings the quantum bell. It couldn't be a coincidence – could it? Then I thought maybe an exposure equal to the 1st universe's duration was 'sufficient'. Another quantum bell. I'd already conceived of the 2 universes and mutual creation. I hadn't yet confidently rolled Being and Time here together as one. They were floating about each other but the idea hadn't congealed. I think if you'd challenged me back then 'was excess Being from the 2nd universe, and what we take for time here one?' I would have tentatively answered yes. But it hadn't become a positive assertion. A definite part of the theory. I knew that Being/time had to come from the evacuating 'in' direction. Any good physicist knows that logically time can flow backwards as easily as forwards. I really think it might have been Hume's insight on causation that helped solve that riddle for me. If our souls *experience* a world moving in the direction of space evacuating 'out', its irrelevant that in an objective sense this universe is static. Parmenides no movement all one. Or that the Being which is used here as time comes from a counter chronological direction. The experience is what is important. What will last? Only the being and the experience."

"And quantum prodded me, not only could I put consciousness and life into the equation – I had to. The different points of Einstein and the other deadheads are simply positions. But having positions without consciousness is meaningless in the real world. The deadheads are devoted to their old notion of science. All their nonsense – a random universe, and measurements that would be accurate if you could only elimianate 'subjective' humans from the process, to get some laboratory pure results." It was startling because he never spoke about the formation of his cosmology. Which I think was a mistake. Hearing this gave it a narrative of discovery. Everyone in class knew what he regarded as important, but this not only made it more interesting – appealing - it let you glimpse how he saw things when it all started to jell. The sequence, the emphasis, how things fit as he conceptualized it. By him looking back, telling us what came first, I believe we had an insight, a way of looking at his cosmology that the other students lacked.

When I became a teacher at the school B's attitude towards me didn't change. Not that I expected it would. Yet he saw an opportunity. Since I'd taken all his classes, most of them more than once, I could sort through the enrolling students. "Simply check whether they'll fit. Find the class suitable." What he really meant was find out if he'd find them suitable. So I would have a little 'talk' with anyone signing up for one of his classes. In the beginning the ethics, not to mention the legality, of this screening didn't bother me too much. I rationalized I was helping both sides avoid unpleasantness. I knew who he liked, who he didn't. Those most likely to be offended. Southerners and those of any rigid religiosity were ruled out. While his favorites, Blacks and Mestizos, still had to be examined to catch any skeptics. This was one of B's little tics. He didn't care about the spiritual skepticism of Caucasians or Asians (not including people from Pakistan or India). He assumed a majority of Caucasians and the far East Asians would be 'spiritual zeros' – disconnected. But Black or Brown kids – if they were spiritually skeptical it was unnatural. They were 'defective', and he told me he wanted all 'ringers' removed before they contaminated his class. There's no way to defend this, but I complied.

This rule on skeptics also would have applied to students from the subcontinent and Arabs. They were expected to be spiritual also. But I don't remember a problem with Pakistanis or Indians, and I would never let an Arab take any class B taught, afraid of what he might say. He believed they hadn't developed their minds and he was quite capable of telling them this to their face. Southerners were a big no go. (What hadn't occurred to me as a student was the carry over mindset of Northern Italians towards Southern Italians. They regard them as criminals and scum. Not as fellow countrymen. As a teacher I realized that inherited template of disdain made it easier, natural in a way, to group American Southerners. I'm sure it wasn't conscious. Most of us carry a notion of good up, bad down. Heaven up, hell down.)

The way I sounded a prospective student out was by asking him or her what their interest was in Metaphysics. It was easy to slide from that to an offhand query about spirituality. If I then detected a disbelief obstacle I'd redirect them with the stunt I used on all the students who I wanted to deflect. "Oh you want real physics." Or "Oh you want real philosophy." Or real Literature – whatever it was. As if B's class was a faux substitute, and it was a good thing we found out before it was too late that they wanted the genuine article. It always worked. I'm not exaggerating. Most of the stubborn difficulties occurred with foreign students. An Israeli refused to take the hint and finally I had to tell him, "Look B believes the good Jews came here, the bad Jews went to Israel. Believing you're the 'chosen people of God' B holds as a conceit certain to lead any people straight to damnation. Any modern person who believes that they are the chosen of God will become evil. He thinks this has infected the Arabs too. The other sons of Abraham. You're a perfect match for each other. Two brothers set on annihilating the other, deluded into thinking becoming Cain will be blessed victory." That did the trick, he backed off. However he did write a complaint to Mudrick; which meant it went nowhere. There were two students from Germany who couldn't be dissuaded from taking the Philosophy class. Again forced to be honest I finally said, "I'm trying to protect you. B believes Germans mixed with Neanderthals. Why Germans got so nuts about race. He thinks you're half Dr. Frankenstein, half the monster." They were incredulous, "Why, because we found the bones?" They still insisted on taking the class. There was nothing I could do. They had the right. Surprisingly they liked it. Of course B loved Leibniz and Hegel. And even with Nietzsche and Heidegger there were insights that he would praise.

The faculty picnic was an eye-opener. My girlfriend was now my wife, and she had listened to my stories about B for years at that point. I would recite monologues and tantrums the class had to endure from 'Herr Professor'. It never occurred to me that in another setting his behavior would change. Or for that matter that he would lower himself to fraternize with his inferiors. Yet on the day of the picnic there he was. With his whole family. The children were younger than I had expected. And his conduct was altered from what students and fellow teachers encountered at school. His children were running around like any other kids. They weren't cowed by discipline, which is what I expected. And clearly the one in charge of keeping the children in line was his wife, who he fondly deferred to. He appeared the most indulgent husband/father. My wife turned to me and asked, "This is the Heidelberg professor you're always going on about?" It was like someone else had been given his body and hired to play him that afternoon, but hadn't studied his character so they were getting it all wrong. I think with his family it must be that his Italian heritage took over. All the grievances were left back at work. He was going to enjoy this time with his family, relaxed and happy. He was even friendly to us. I whispered to my wife to find out from his wife if the kids were getting private tutoring. This is something I took for granted because that had been B's early experience. However Mrs. Baccala told her no. The older ones were enrolled in a Waldorf School, but that wasn't unusual in Santa Barbara.

As a teacher I discovered that some of the teachers had set up a whole gambit designed to taunt B. They would make sure he was in hearing range and then bring up a subject that was one of his pet peeves. But it had to be something on which he and Mudrick differed. They knew that his loyalty to Mudrick would constrain him from making his usual condescending attacks or snide dismissals. So topics would come up as if in a normal conversational way like, "Did you hear Marvin's quote from Pound?" Or "Boy Marvin was raving about the New York Ballet's performance of..." Knowing how much B disdained Pound and ballet. Another favorite they constantly resorted to was the Black comic Richard Pryor, whom Mudrick loved, and B absolutely loathed. B liked Dick Gregory, Godfrey Cambridge, and Bill Cosby; people he thought were doing their race proud. He despised Pryor, calling him the grandson of Stepin Fetchit. Often muttering "*Not* the talented 10th", which was kind of funny in itself. So any quoting of Pryor, ascribing it to Mudrick, whether that was really the case or not - was sure to get a rise out of B. On all these provocations you could see his plugged agitation. He couldn't allow himself to comment, out of fear that it could be taken as a negative swipe at Mudrick.

There was another physicist at the school that Mudrick, very naïvely, thought would hit it off with B. I guess because they shared that background. Of course they detested each other. It was very predictable. I didn't know a whole lot about this other fellow as I was in B's orbit. Since he was in the mainstream his view of B's ideas would lead to what the field had concluded: religious or madman. B's put down of him was that he was a good example of the hero-worshipping Einstein apologist, who grudgingly paid lip service to quantum because they had no choice, but were still mentally retrograde, always searching for a magical explanation that would show quantum only appeared the way it did, inside it was all normal physics. That is how the fellow impressed me, but I could have been prejudiced by B's analysis of him.

Every semester B would alienate a certain percentage of the students. Hardly surprising. They'd enrolled in the school with a list of the open protocols touted and then ran into a teacher who violated all of them. Some would dropout, some would stay but complain to sympathetic teachers. And there were many members of the faculty that B had inadvertently insulted. Like the music composition teacher. For no reason, certainly without being asked, B decided to favor him with some advice. Since Chopin had studied Bach this fellow's students should study Chopin. Which might be good advice – who knows? But when you imply that you know more about another's subject than he does, you're going to create resentment. B didn't stop there. He went on to tell him forget Schoenberg and Stravinsky; emphasize Mahler, Sibelius, and Shostakovich. He did similar things to other teachers. Even those he hadn't insulted had heard from students complaining about his highhanded manner. So a petition got formulated to force Mudrick to terminate B for cause before he could reach tenure. Personally I wasn't convinced tenure was a real concern. There was something not copasetic about B's employment. Not just what he was allowed to get away with, but what exactly his official status was. I don't know this but I think there was something irregular about B's hiring, the classes he was teaching, everything. Later I tried to check the records but I couldn't find the relevant papers. My friends thought that the leverage on Mudrick would come from the worry that news of this rebellion might reach the Santa Barbara authorities. And I believe they were proven correct. Mudrick would let B do anything, violate all the procedures, but he couldn't let him jeopardize CCS - his baby.

I didn't want to sign the petition even though it was my friends who were circulating it on behalf of the students. (It was felt that only teachers should sign. Students shouldn't be asked to stick their necks out.) Because of my identification with B my friends believed the weight of my name was crucial. Mudrick reading my name on the complaint would have to feel the jig was up. I need to say there wasn't one item cited in the petition that wasn't true. B did trample on all the principles of CCS. Finally relenting I said I would only sign it if they changed 'racial stereotyping' into 'insensitive racial generalizations'. I felt that was a softer characterization of B's 'breeds'. They agreed, and then I reluctantly signed. It worked. Mudrick felt he had no choice. I heard that he informed B that this had to be his last semester. But Mudrick promised that he'd do everything he could to secure him another position somewhere else.

I don't know if Mudrick told B I was one of the signatories. It's possible that someone else showed him the petition. One way or the other he found out because I heard he was referring to me as a Judas. Saying, "I couldn't give a class he wouldn't sign up for. He was like a stalker. Now he sees his chance for 30 pieces of silver and it's *sayonara*. I even helped him transition here as a teacher." Which wasn't true. I was the one doing him the favor. Screening registering students. A job, which if it wasn't illegal, could certainly be seen as violating academic norms. After the petition resulted in his termination I wanted to explain to B how reluctant I had been and why I signed it. But when I next ran into him he looked at me with a contemptuous smile that stopped me. It was a smile that said 'You turned out exactly as I would have predicted'. In other words that my becoming a Judas didn't surprise him. So I let it go. I did feel bad. But if I had turned down my friends and their effort had failed after they'd risked their positions, I would have felt bad about that. It was a no win situation. And as I said every particular in the petition was justified because they were all true.

We all assumed this would mark the end of B's teaching career. He was a wrong fit for CCS, but anywhere else he'd still be an awful teacher. Bringing up his father only made him look worse in comparison. We thought he'd end up at some think tank or research foundation. It couldn't be Princeton, the most logical place, because that was Einstein Central. However there were plenty of other places that would fund someone as brilliant as B, so he'd never have to teach again, and could devote all his energy to writing his eccentric books. What we hadn't counted on was that Mudrick, as always, was as good as his word. He composed the perfect reference. It left out B's imperious teaching manner, his alienation of students and fellow teachers, the buildup of resentment that precipitated the petition. No mention of his time with Jensen. Mudrick wrote to his contacts at U.C. Santa Cruz a profile of B the physicist, as some wronged victim of persecution.

I was kind of shocked at his choice of Santa Cruz. To my mind Santa Cruz was one of UC's more politically correct campuses. It wasn't possible to be less politically correct than B, so how was this going to work? What I overlooked was that Santa Cruz was also New Age ground zero. The people there could con themselves into thinking they understood B, bending it to their own beliefs, and then imagine him as the incarnation of the synthesizing prophet/answer-man they had been waiting for. We had carefully studied his thought at CCS, semester after semester, without kidding ourselves that we comprehended it all. In Santa Cruz apparently they accepted his decrees without worrying about the fact that they didn't understand them. And his environmental extremism fit right in. In Santa Barbara, not exactly a backward camp of barbarians, he got 86ed from a store for yelling at customers. He was telling a young couple with children not to buy strawberries. Someone had informed him that these strawberries were coated with pesticides. When the young couple, who didn't know him from Adam, didn't put the strawberries back, he stirred a commotion by denouncing them as negligent parents endangering their children's health. They probably thought he was just some random crazy person. The market told him to never return. In Santa Cruz his views are the ruling majority, and such an incident could never occur because non-organic pesticide sprayed strawberries would never be offered for sale at any market.

As much as we loved Mudrick we could on occasion underestimate him. The story he spun about B was a testament to his ability. Not that it was fictional – only that he omitted so much from it. All the negatives. None of us could remember Mudrick having ever shown any interest in the spiritual. He was the author after all of "Nobody here but us chickens". Yet he portrayed B's career as a tragedy, the unjust expulsion of a man of principle from the field he loved (physics), by a coterie of narrow-minded power mad atheist zealots. Instead of making the UC department the heavies it might have been more accurate to portray the whole field of physics as turning on him. But in Mudrick's melodrama B had dared to have spiritual convictions, and then refused to remain silent after being warned to stay silent or suffer the consequences. He had dared to utter and even publish his beliefs. Thus, in a manner reminiscent of the Star Chamber, Berkeley banned him. B as a martyr for freedom of conscience and freedom of expression. Quite a remarkable role for the man who stared down students rash enough to argue with one of his suppositions. The physics episode was certainly part of B's problems. Yet it was only a part. Like an Act 1, with Acts 2 and 3 to follow. In which acts it will be revealed how B's character flaws contributed to his plight. Only Acts 2 or 3 got scrapped. Mudrick presented to Santa Cruz an Act 1 as the whole story, explaining everything.

The victim of persecution story worked like a charm. To our astonishment he even got embraced as a popular teacher. That was a real head scratcher. He went on to achieve tenure and retire emeritus. As far as I know he still lives in Santa Cruz, and still has a little cult following up there. Quite an amazing twist and denouement. I guess if you are cast as someone the establishment has unfairly condemned and censored, you can get away with anything. Yet except for his little circle his thought never reached a wider audience. That might be the ultimate penalty for his attitude. U.C. has gone on publishing his books over the years, but no one reads them. Which may be unfair to his thought, but is a just fate for the man. If his antagonistic personality eclipsed his ideas whose fault would that be? Though I'm sure he blames individuals like me, and the dullness of the poisoned and dumbed down students. In the end, not counting the amen choir in Santa Cruz, his fate was to be forgotten in both physics and philosophy.

He came out with "Separation" about a year or so after he left. Not surprisingly he dedicated it to Mudrick. It was supposed to be a synthesis of what he taught in his 'Literature' & 'Western Art' classes. But out of some mistaken sensitivity not to displease Mudrick the book was a mutilation of his courses. Anyone who had taken his classes could see the elisions. I guess because he felt Mudrick needed support in his critique of Shakespeare he devoted a long chapter to "Bardolatry". This was entirely disproportionate to anything he ever did in class. He wouldn't even have done the Lear reading except he heard, or imagined he heard, snickering. Normally he only used Shakespeare, "the wily pretender", to make his point about 'elevation' to satisfy humanity's need to worship; and how easy it is to convince people that what they're eating is to their taste. But the book was mangled with distortions throughout. The Modernist poets were as important to B as the 12 tone composers and abstract painters in his argument about how 'intellectual anticipation' derailed modern art. Yet they were never mentioned. No doubt again out of a misplaced consideration for Mudrick. B's critique of artificial inbred art, that only reflects other artificial inbred art and not reality, always ended with the royal/aristocratic-sponsored ballet as its penultimate example. But Ballet too was entirely cut out of the book. This was all wrong. Mudrick wouldn't have been offended. He wasn't thin skinned. He was aware that B had differing tastes from his own. The book was a travesty.

When Mudrick died in 1986 I was involved with the group putting together a brochure for the memorial. Honoring someone we all loved, we hoped to create an elegiac remembrance (that Marvin would have accepted) for those able to attend but also something we could mail to those unable to make it. Of course we had to ask B to contribute. I made sure my name didn't appear on the request. What we got back was so over the top it was unusable. I'm not a lawyer but we were all pretty certain it was libelous. And we knew B was completely serious. He blamed Chancellor Huttenback, and a TV critic, Alexander Woolcott, for Mudrick's death. Yes Huttenback had forced Mudrick out as provost in 1984, and I guess Woolcott must have written something disparaging about Marvin's effrontery in doubting Shakespeare. But B's overreaction was simply nuts. How many school administrators (if you don't count a visionary like Vernon Cheadle) or pop culture critics have the foundational wherewithal to go against groupthink and tolerate an iconoclastic revision of Shakespeare? Let's say zero. Why someone who never stopped complaining about the mental density of the herd would need that explained to him is beyond me. B's spiel reminded me of nothing so much as Shelley's harangue after Keats death, when Shelley blamed the unfeeling critics for doing Keats in. No Percy it was tuberculosis actually. People have poor health and they die. The problem we had was that no one dared edit B's submission. I certainly wasn't going to. The fear that the 'dissecting knife' would come after anyone stupid enough to abridge his tribute stopped us. Which was a pity since it meant we couldn't use the heartfelt parts either. I dictated a regret, made up some phony reason. No one wanted their name on it, so we issued it as a reluctant decision, by a committee running out of time.

At least once in life it's good to have a primal encounter where all your presumptions are challenged. If it happens at all it'll usually happen during your youth. Late teens to mid 20s. Which for most of us does coincide with schooling. There's no denying, even with all his problems, that B was the agent provoking that confrontation for me. The way I saw the world before his classes and the way I saw it after had very little in common. His "atheists are handicapped people, no less than someone deficient in another sense." The way he portrayed scientists as being captured by material knowledge into materialism. A human connection with the universe's overseer: "We are in partnership with the Whole." The universe and human history as something scripted; the calculation and distribution of quantities and qualities. A composition we (unconsciously) participate in. That very unique relationship with the next world: "You couldn't be here if you weren't there." His concept of mutual creation, which from the first time I was introduced to it, I've never been able to shake. As I assume I've made clear, he was an awful teacher and flawed human being, who made zero effort to correct his biases. But if I didn't acknowledge his uniqueness as a thinker, if I didn't confess the impact his thought had on me, I wouldn't be relaying the whole truth. This was a man and an encounter that changed how I looked at everything.

Let me once again express the debt I owe to Art Tenace for allowing me to reprint here his entire chapter on Baccala. His generosity was overwhelming. Personally I think it's an invaluable insight into the late 70s early to early-mid career Baccala. There's nothing else like it, and trust me I've looked. I should add Professor Tenace made no stipulations about how I could use it, nor did he ask to see the context it would be used in before we published it. After such graciousness on his part you might find some of my observations snarky, if not downright churlish. Yet I feel an obligation to note discordant perspectives. The first point is trivial but hard to overlook. Towards the end he explains why Baccala's tribute to Mudrick was unprintable, because it libeled both "Chancellor Huttenback" and a TV critic "Alexander Woolcott". I understand why the name Alexander Woolcott might stick in his mind. He *was* famous. As a critic and member of the Algonquin Round Table. And maybe even more famous for being the inspiration for the central character in both the play and film of "The Man Who Came to Dinner". However as he died during a radio broadcast in 1943, I doubt that he was a TV critic, and I doubt that he was a target for Baccala's ire.

Maybe this is equally trivial but I fail to see the reason Tenace contracted Baccala into 'B'? He's not widely known. On the other hand anyone who ever took a class from him, either at CCS or Santa Cruz, will instantly recognize whose being described. To mention that his father was famous, and at Yale, would clue anyone still in doubt. Its unlikely that Baccala would ever read anything written by Tenace, but if that was the concern the name he needed to obscure was his own. Why use B? Make up an entirely fictitious pseudonym.

While Tenace notes that Baccala frequently referred to Charles Darwin as 'Iceberg Chuck', in a disparaging way, he never explains why. I will presume its because he never pursued the answer. Merely totted it up as another inscrutable quirk of Baccala's; possibly implying carried-by-the-currents, or destined for the Titanic. Of course it does have an explanation. On the famous voyage of the Beagle in South America Darwin came across huge boulders that seemed out of place to the surrounding geology. He hypothesized that icebergs had transported and deposited them where they were. Baccala was mocking him because science subsequently showed that it was glaciers not icebergs that were responsible. It was a cheap shot by Baccala from the advantage of a later age. But you have to keep in mind his low estimation of Darwin as a myopic plodder. He believed he inherited his idea of evolution straight from his grandfather Erasmus Darwin, a man Baccala esteems as in every way superior to his grandson. I only bring this up because I'm old enough to remember when you wanted to research something you had to go to the stacks and request relevant titles – in this case biographies of Darwin. Then you pored over the books looking for the information you were after. However now all Tenace would have had to have done was go to any device and Google 'Charles Darwin & icebergs', and soon enough he would have had his answer. Yet...

I must accept what he writes about "Separation", that it distorts what Baccala taught, since it comes from someone who took his classes. Obviously I wasn't measuring it by that standard. For me the book was the furthest thing from a 'travesty'. And I don't care that the chapter on Shakespeare was manufactured to support Mudrick. To this layman in the arts, even if it was a tangent, it was illuminating. It never occurred to me that you could even question Shakespeare's eminence. I didn't know about the role of Samuel Johnson. His dictionary using Shakespeare quotes. His student and agent in the cause – who just happened to be the most famous actor of the period - David Garrick. Nor did I think about the attraction to actors of opportunities to ham it up. The insight that Shakespeare used drama to rev up his poetry, and the poetic to gloss his plays. How important it was to his legacy that his country would become the greatest power on earth. How over time the fantasy reverence invested in the genius spirit of 'Elizabethan' and 'Shakespeare', treasured antique language and period, encouraged relinquishing any judgment among worshippers. As one ignorant of this mechanism, and the whole history of Shakespeare becoming Holy Writ, I was extremely grateful for that chapter. As it happened it hooked me on Baccala. Accepting that this was written to support Mudrick, it is Tenace who tells us their perspectives, even on Shakespeare, differed. So who cares about the motive, or what he cut out, if the book can stand on its own? For me it stands on its own.

What I find puzzling is Tenace's lack of curiosity. Made more mystifying by the fact that he kept taking Baccala's classes. Let me be concise. I don't find any reason to believe he ever read "2 Universes". First there are no direct quotations from the book. Furthermore points that I believe would have been cleared up for him had he read it persist in a fog. An example that comes to mind is when he quotes Baccala as saying ultimate self-consciousness was first achieved not by Homo sapiens, but by our more primitive ancestors. Tenace finds this unexpectedly generous and open-minded. If he had read "2 Universes" I don't think he would have had that response. There are very few duration equivalents in Baccala's cosmology. The biggest exception being the length of this universe as equal to the sample of eternity - as an exposure time - needed to establish sufficient statistical probability.

Now that is a proper part of his cosmology. However there is another equivalence that isn't integral, which he mentions as speculation. He wonders if the two poles: inflation at what we consider the beginning and ultimate self-consciousness at the end, aren't exact measures of each other? After the Big Bang - not the first fractions of a second - but right after that, came the period physicists call inflation. All the natural laws as we know them were violated in this unimaginably rapid expansion. This period was calculated at 300,000 to 380,000 years. In Baccala's 'speculation' this might match the highest level of self-consciousness. Now at the time he wrote "2 Universes" - and still true at the time he was giving classes at CCS - the thinking among paleoanthropologists was that the furthest you could push Homo sapiens back would be something like 100,000 years. So Baccala wasn't being generous or open-minded. If his speculation was correct he had no choice. Tenace presumably would have grasped this if he had read "2 Universes". I need to mention that in our time the earliest date for Homo sapiens keeps getting pushed further back in time. Its entirely possible that if Baccala was propounding his theory today, with inflation thought to be 377,000 years, he might leave it as inflation = Homo sapiens' ultimate self-consciousness, and hope that paleoanthropologists would go on unearthing even older specimens of our species.

The second serious issue that demonstrates a lack of curiosity concerns Parmenides. Tenace knows that Baccala sees Parmenides as a unique figure in history. Someone he considers a near equal. Tenace reads Plato's book "Parmenides" because it's a class assignment. And he relates how classicists dispute its accuracy. However there survives parts of a long poem we know Parmenides wrote. Its clear to me that Tenace never bothered to look it up. To find a copy of "2 Universes", as I found out, requires some searching. Possibly, if you can't find it in a library, an outlay of money. But there are many translations of Parmenides' poem readily available.

Why do I think the poem is important? Because I believe it is the source for Baccala's warrant (or blank check) to rain his opinions about everything down on us. In the poem the goddess Justice tells Parmenides, a young man when this revelation occurs, that they won't just cover circular motionless Truth. They'll also include the unreliable opinion of mortals. How to study and test the plausible basis of all phenomena. It's easy to imagine Baccala reading that as a quantum reference. And furthermore as a license allowing one to dispense opinions as part of the process of studying and testing what is correct. An experimental exchange of unreliable mortal opinion all to determine what is most plausible. The problem is Baccala seldom labels them as merely 'opinion'. They come out like all his judgments, that is as if laying down the law.

These lapses may not strike you as important. It might rest, after reading his chapter, on how keen an observer you take Tenace to be. I wont judge Tenace's signing the petition, whether that was the correct course or if it constituted personal betrayal. I was not there. I accept that Baccala did not follow CCS protocol. On the other hand Tenace kept taking his classes. Not that an interest in what a teacher expounds obligates you to cover up misconduct. But he volunteers that he's kept the tapes of Baccala while he's discarded the tapes of the teachers he considered superior at the time. And clearly ending up in Santa Cruz was beneficial to Baccala, he found a more favorable environment.

We know Tenace viewed Baccala as the disturbing voice in the wilderness. A personality he found antagonistic and deficient as a teacher but whose intriguing ideas he couldn't tear himself away from. Troubling but unforgettable, or in modern parlance disruptive. I have no idea what sort of teacher Art Tenace is but let's assume he supplies those essentials he listed Baccala as lacking: enthusiasm for the subject and belief in his students – in their ability to learn. Thanks to the honesty of his account we know how Baccala saw him. (Prior to what Baccala viewed as betrayal.) Baccala told him he was passive, a student who expected everything to be given to him. He acted as if he assumed comprehension could come without independent exertion. Which Baccala told him was a delusion. To me this description of Art Tenace, not as a teacher but as one trying to learn, has the ring of truth. He took this diagnosis as an uncalled for attack. But its possible he could have taken it as good advice.

SANTA CRUZ

There is a gap of a few years from when Tenace's account ends to when I began subscribing to "The Banana Slug" in order to read Baccala's column in it, "Prof's Proofs". This of course was after I'd read both Separation and 2 Universes, and had searched to find out where he was. Another aspect to consider to those Art Tenace mentions regards Baccala's reception in Santa Cruz. He describes a New Age cult-like following, composed of people he infers weren't as perspicacious as the students at CCS. But even if your attitude to New Age (should we call it a faith?) is condescending, we have to acknowledge that it does promote the principle of universality; and universality is also at the heart of Baccala's beliefs. So maybe the marriage isn't all that strange. As to the transition that amazed Tenace and his friends back in Santa Barbara, I'm sure the reputation of one persecuted for his beliefs did provide armor, and would excuse a lot. But after reading his column for decades now, and following the letter exchanges (always with friendly readers, he ignores the few hostile responses), I think there's something else at play. No one seems to know when he's kidding. And just as importantly, no one is sure when he's in earnest. Sometimes they assume he's only exaggerating to make a humorous point when I'm convinced he's absolutely serious. Other times they miss that what he wrote was heavily sarcastic. I don't think he misleads intentionally, but with his attitude that 'everyone understands parable truth at the level they exist at', if he notices what is going on, I don't think it bothers him.

I'll excerpt some of his columns to show that in the main his thinking hasn't changed. Most of the trajectories Tenace recorded have continued. There have been ups and downs but his disillusion with the United States has only gotten stronger. I think "Cross of the Christlike President" proves that. Yet his appraisal of other nations to carry the 'lamp of enlightenment' always ends in their disqualification. Foremost China and India, with Brazil as a dark horse. Primarily they're too hopelessly backward and corrupt. While China and India have their own form of diversity they aren't true 'melting pots' of all human races. The 'New People' of Brazil are, but their population lags so far behind in intellectual development that "there isn't enough time". Which is also his judgment of his other favorites, the 'Real People' of Africa; though no African nation qualifies as a melting pot.

Part of the problem is his odd humor mixing with his very complex view of actors and forces. All of it subject to a favoritism he makes no effort to balance. His position on the Afghanistan invasion and the Iraq War exemplified both insight and prejudice. His readers needed to perceive that he cared nothing about bin Ladin or Al-Qaeda. They weren't important. Nor did he care about the Taliban rulers of Afghanistan. Our allies, the Saudis and the Pakistanis, were our true enemies. The Arabs provided the funding, the Pakistanis the schools to brainwash poor Afghan boys. The Afghans were simply victims. "Of course the Pashtuns are keeping women subjugated – they're savage pedophiles." (He's never referred to the ancient Greeks as pedophiles, savage or otherwise.) Baccala told his readers that bin Laden would have no compunction in lying to Mullah Omar about the 9/11 attack, 'We had nothing to do with it.' And Mullah Omar, being simple, would have to take his word. To Baccala bin Laden was just another RSB [rich spoiled brat]. A worthless instrument of history.

It's helpful to know that to him the blame for this terrorism, and the Afghanistan dilemma, went back to Jimmy Carter's administration and his National Security adviser Zbigniew Brzezinski. "If the Russians invade Afghanistan we condemn it, but it's none of our business." To Baccala Poles - like the Irish - are defective Catholics. (Making John Paul II pope was a terrible idea.) Poles do hate Russians, not without reason, and Brzezinski saw his chance to bleed them like we bled in Vietnam. Which short term was a success, long term lead to all our Islamic terror problems. Baccala's ultimate villain in all this, along with the Wahhabi Saudis, is Pakistan's General, President, and dictator Muhammad Zia-ul-Haq. Zia-ul-Haq played us for suckers. Baccala insists on calling him the 'Great Snake', and even today – the man died in 1988 – refers to all Pakistanis as the 'Children of the Great Snake'. "Zia favored the simple-minded and deranged. When Reagan came into office he had an even bigger dunce to manipulate. Besides creating the future quagmire Zia was also zealous about nuclear proliferation. Not just for Pakistan, but exporting it to China, North Korea, Iran and Libya." This is all true, but we shouldn't let it excuse Baccala's prejudice. He later crowed when bin Laden's sanctuary was discovered to be in Pakistan. Yet the average Pakistani is not responsible for what Zia did, or what the ISI is doing now. There's no genetic difference between the 'spiritual Indians' and the populations of Pakistan and Bangladesh. To dismiss them as the 'children of the Great Snake' is in every way - descriptively and ethically, ugly and wrong.

The Iraq War exposed Baccala's partiality in favor of Iran. Baccala considers the Persians not only historically great but artistic. He repeatedly reminds us that they wouldn't have a theocratic state except their elected president was overthrown by the Brits and Americans for planning to nationalize their oil. Installing the Shah set in motion all the unnatural reactions that ended up with backward fundamentalists ruling a superior people. Recently he referred to this as "Our elites were happy with the trade of 25 more years pumping oil in exchange for their hatred; a bunch of nutters running their country for 35 years." Baccala continually denounced American support for Saddam Hussein in the long bloody war between Iraq and Iran. For him a choice between Arabs and Persians isn't even a question. When it came to the Iraq invasion though he was in a tricky position. He did denounce the fraud of connecting Iraq to 9/11, and the phantom weapons of mass destruction. Pointing out 'idiot' Netanyahu and Likud's connection to the neocon 5th column rushing RSB 'Hollow Boy' Bush to diss the inspections and attack. He thought the New York Times' Maureen Dowd captured the appeal to the younger Bush, as an Oedipal twofer. Revenge on behalf of the father who left the dictator in power (the dictator supposedly later trying to assassinate the elder Bush). While showing the father up as he does it. But the father and his advisers understood quagmires, the complexities of foreign societies, and the risks in 'nation building'. 'Hollow Boy' understood nothing.

Yet unlike anyone else on the left, not counting those who were so freaked out by 9/11 that they became tools of the right, Baccala cheered the commencement of the war. Because he correctly saw that its consequences would aid Iran. (Plus he thought this would set in motion the Kurds long march towards reestablishing Kurdistan. Later adding pieces from Iran, Turkey, and Syria.) The majority Shiites in Iraq, once it was a democracy, would soon ally with Iran even though they were Arabs. Baccala knew the outcome of the war would cause more Sunni terrorists to get recruited but he didn't care. He didn't anticipate that we'd use Saddam's prison, humiliate and torture our adversaries, set up a poor system that allowed innocent people to get arrested on false charges by personal or tribal enemies. Or guards taking bizarre pictures of the torture and humiliation. As jaundiced as Baccala's view was of Americans after Vietnam, even he didn't guess we'd sink to that level of depravity and stupidity. However, as always, his reactions were unpredictable. As someone who usually defends the free press everywhere (including Al Jazeera), it was striking that in April 2003 not only did he admit that our forces had deliberately targeted journalists, he defended their doing so. "Their slant, whether on purpose or not, served as propaganda that stirred Arabs to come join the fight and fire on our troops. Its legitimate in war to target those recruiting more fighters to come to try and kill your people." Not only that, later he defended L Paul Bremer's controversial decision to purge Baathists from holding any office in the new Iraq. He said it was comparable to blacklisting Nazis in Germany. "They might be good at their job, but should decades of oppression go unpunished? And who would trust them? Even those who did not perpetrate crimes themselves were at best amoral collaborationists." There weren't that many people in the aftermath saying that Bremer had done the right thing.

His subsequent views, years later when Sunni terrorism was at its peak, were also peculiar. The main judgment he said fell on the parents. "Any brat who can believe murdering people is acceptable if they disagree with your religious views, and somehow God sanctions this, has a mind & soul of no consequence. The serious focus should be on the parents. How did they fail? Why didn't they instill the basic sane values we should expect?" To Baccala the issue was a good lesson, in a dramatic form, not just for Muslims, but all the religious, on the danger of zealotry. "Those with true faith don't feel a need to lash out. They aren't threatened by what others believe, if they believe differently. They aren't threatened by modernity. The Whole has decided that we need to cull a certain number. Brand as damned those who hear and answer the call of negation; who find release in hatred and violence. Infection first needs to be identified before the body sends its antibodies to eliminate them."

Sometimes as I said its impossible to decipher if what he says is serious or its tongue in cheek. Whether he even thinks about or cares how it will be taken by different readers. The example that comes to my mind is his recommendation on how to outlaw assault rifles. This was after the Sandy Hook massacre of very young children and their teachers by a young psychopath. President Obama pushed for a modest proposal with overwhelming popular support but Congress, fearing the NRA, wouldn't pass it. In the wake of that disappointment Baccala wrote, "Learn the history. The NRA was set up by Union veterans appalled at the poor marksmanship of their comrades. Especially those from the cities and not from the country. They emphasized shooting and safety. But in our age the organization was captured first by those controlled by fear. That then made it attractive to the gun merchants to fund. That selling of the soul then made it attractive to the very enemy that had spurred its formation; the children of darkness. This cabal: the fear-centered, the whores for the gun makers, and the native fascists; knew that America was glutted with guns. So they had to stir up the weak-minded to buy more guns than they needed with paranoia about Big Brother coming to get them. 'Better stock up on guns and ammo!' Here's a little secret of commerce polite society never mentions. Sometimes the profit margin of a restaurant is the obese customers. Sometimes a bar's profit comes from the alcoholics. A casino is in the black thanks to the gambling addicts. So the Nazi Rifle Association preyed on the weak-minded, whipping up their paranoid fear. Whenever a nut massacres a bunch of people with an assault rifle they act like it has nothing to do with them. In the age of George III, in the colonies of a few thousand people, you might want to keep a musket handy to fend off the redcoats. Now in our age, in a country of 300 million people, you either believe in and trust your fellow citizens (who are the sovereign not some king), and by extension trust their officers; trust our courts, the rule of law;

democracy; or you are an agent of negation - an enemy of civilization."

"What can we do? Let us learn from our enemies who are adept at devious power maneuvers. I'm thinking in particular here of the anti-abortionists. They couldn't win by democratic popular vote or by an appeal to law to coerce individuals. So how did they get their way, in the backward states where they've gotten their way? By intimidation. They print pictures of doctors who do abortions with targets over their face. They publish their addresses. Periodically one of the nuts in their movement will then kill a doctor. Like the Confederate gun shills they then protest their non-involvement. But the murder not only eliminates that doctor, it frightens others away from the practice. Terrorism that works. We imitate that procedure. We research purchases, websites, subscriptions, to get a pool of probable paranoids. We cast our net wide. We provide pictures and the addresses of all the executive and board members of the Nazi Rifle Association. And the executives and board members of gun manufacturers, domestic and foreign. We inform the paranoid that 'These are the demons who deliberately stirred up your fears only to make money. They don't care that they've driven you crazy and you suffer. What does evil look like? It looks like these people. What does deliberate evil to make a buck deserve? We leave that up to you.' Then when the merchants of death are sprayed with bullets, or a bomb takes out a large assembly, it'll be our turn to act shocked and innocent." I have no idea if Baccala was exaggerating to make a point, or if he was in earnest. I honestly don't think he cares. Its hard to find a trace of the consciousness of 'God in everyone', or loving your enemy, in this.

216

It might help to know how this ex-Catholic has always framed the anti-abortionist, 'right to life' people, as "the very worst hypocrites - the people Jesus despised the most. There's absolutely no scriptural support for their position. It's entirely made up. The original belief was that life began with the first breath. Yet their righteous showboating costs them nothing. They get to pretend to care, pretend to be moral, without obliging themselves in any way to do anything. Hence its appeal – it's cost free. There are always exceptions, but can you imagine the average poseur – especially the men - adopting a minority baby, or one with fetal alcohol syndrome, with its irreversible damage? No, it's all an act. There is nothing that suggests they favor providing shelter, nutrition, health care or education for poor children. At least for those whose parents aren't members of their congregation."

His hatred for Clinton, and all the Democratic Leadership Council elites, "smuggling Republican Lite in, selling it as 'moderation' to the media and the sheep, while getting funding by advertising your availability to Wall Street" carried over onto Gore. A man he condemned for suppressing his real passion - concern for the world's environment - and picking Joe Lieberman, another DLC dolt, and "An agent of Likud". Not that he ignored the travesties of the vote counting in Florida. "Forget the obviously biased brother Bush as governor, or the thugs and lawyers the Republicans sent down there. Simply look at the crooked Secretary of State who designed a ballot that got elderly Jews to vote for Pat Buchanan, a man who defends concentration camp guards. It was predictable that the Opus Dei mafioso Scalia[2]

[2] Besides Southern Italian Scalia a particular dislike was John Paul II. Readers had to endure years of reading about the tie between the Pope

would push his four partisans to stop the recount, award the presidency thereby to the RSB. Only the Stanford grads, O'Connor and Kennedy, have souls and minds, and can be held accountable, judged by history. The other three, like most conservatives, are fascists first with no fixed principles. The fake credo that they're for the Constitution in its original intent, you know back when only White men with property could vote, and slavery was legal, is just a line. They'll do whatever they want to do and make up the rationalization for it afterwards."

Four years later it was a different story. According to Baccala the American people had elected and reelected a senile actor in Reagan, "the Hollow Man". Revealing a lack of perception and intelligence. But the younger Bush "the Hollow Boy", had deceived the American people about the reasons for the Iraq invasion. The occupation was obviously a disaster for our troops and our reputation. Plus his opponent Kerry represented to Baccala the warrior who keeps his integrity and his conscience. Unlike the RSB Bush, whose father pulled strings and got him safely stationed in the Texas National Guard, Kerry fought in Vietnam and realized not only that it was unwinnable, but that for the US to enter into a civil war and declare 'free fire zones' so we could kill anything that moved, was immoral. "Everyone knew the dark secret of Curtis LeMay and Kissinger, that a superpower needn't fear standing trial for war crimes. But that didn't make it right."

---

and his 'favorite', the Mexican Legion of Christ founder Marcial Marciel; sexual abuser, drug addict, embezzler, plagiarist, and father of many children. "His crimes overlooked because of his strict rule and the amount of the donations he funneled to the Roman curia."

A Texas oilman, T. Boone Pickens, paid for ads featuring bloodthirsty rightwing Vietnam vets hurling charges that made Kerry, a decorated hero, look like some sort of traitor. It created a new political term, 'swift-boating' for an effective sliming attack on an opponent. You could say Baccala's bitterness flowed into his disillusion or his disillusion flowed into his bitterness. "How can you go to a place that you don't belong, kill millions of people, poison the land with nerve agents - babies still today being born with birth defects, litter the country with unexploded bombs, and it doesn't count? There's no consequences because you're a superpower, and your people are so stupid or without a conscience that it doesn't bother them. How is your character better than the Germans, Japanese, Russians, Chinese, or Turks? And maybe the modern German is different, maybe they have a soul and a conscience."

In the wake of the 2004 election Baccala had the Banana Slug print a color-coded map of the US. As you would expect the Southern states were red, and labeled "Damned'. Virginia and Florida were labeled "Contested". The middle of the country was a sort of beige color with "Dog People" across it. Below the map Baccala helpfully explained that dog people weren't evil, but they were vulnerable to the appeals of evil. It included Indiana but not Iowa or Ohio for some unknown reason. The upper Midwest along with New England and the West Coast (including Nevada, Colorado and New Mexico) were stamped "Human". In case you were wondering Alaska was "Damned", while Hawaii was "Human". I assume most readers thought this was a trenchant send up of the appalling election results. Yet I'm convinced Baccala was absolutely serious. I think the giveaway was calling the heart-landers Dog People. That's such a Baccalan assessment. And you can bet he didn't have smart breeds in mind.

His readers are used to explanations that his 'terminology' is tricky, usually in response to a friendly letter nudging him not to be so judgmental. Then he'll make a conciliatory gesture to the effect that I'm sorry you took my artful figure the wrong way. As: "Of course what I said was figurative. Everyone has a soul, everyone goes to heaven. Not just humans but all sentient creatures. In fact I've come a long way since I was young, when I was puzzled by traditional people regarding inanimate objects like rivers and mountains as possessing souls. Now I think I was wrong, they were right. Everything that exists, that is manifested, including rocks, planets, et cetera, has being, so has a soul." He comes off not only as non-judgmental but the most open-minded person you'd care to meet. With the above goes his explanation that when he refers to the 'damned' that's only metaphorical. However he can't resist adding the troubling adjunct, "Of course we are unable to appreciate the weight of an inerasable transgression times eternity." But think about it, if that is the case wouldn't it excuse using 'hell'? Yet Baccala never ceases to condemn the churchmen for employing hell to scare the common folk. Though his heavenly 'quarantine', albeit self-generated and sans torture, comes close to eternal punishment: "The initiative comes from narrow people desiring their own narrow 'gated community'. The freedom of association is going to grant them that wish."

I don't want to write this and forget that in 1998 two separate teams determined that the universe's expansion didn't go as expected. Neither continuing at the same speed forever, or slowing on its way to an eventual Big Crunch. To everyone's surprise (with

220

the possible exception of an individual in Santa Cruz California) the two teams found that the universe's expansion at some point had actually accelerated. Now if you remember Baccala had two predictions on future data that would go towards supporting his theory. One was information from the edge of the universe showing that galaxies reaching the speed of light didn't continue harmlessly on their way (the speed of light being only 'relative' to us). Instead we'd find evidence that they had been incinerated/disintegrated. The other confirmative prediction was that at the time of the solar system/Earth's formation & life [Baccala's 'center'] there would be an evident alteration in the universe as a whole, as it compensated for this change. It was clear to me, as one who knew his cosmology, that Baccala seized on the acceleration as that proof. Yet he never said anything explicit to his readers regarding this. He did write that he believed this acceleration occurred at the time of the solar system & Earth's formation; adding he didn't believe it a coincidence. But that alone wouldn't inform them as to why exactly he saw it as significant. (I should tell you that I'm repeating Baccala's assertion that the acceleration occurred at the same time of the Earth's formation, without any independent source corroborating that that is the case. To be clear.)

His view of other scientists unsurprisingly tends to be very critical. There was a funny column concerning the physicist Roger Penrose. Penrose, with someone else, had written a very long book. Baccala begins by listing several of Penrose's achievements, saying each one alone warranted a Nobel Prize. With that beginning you think, aha here at last is a scientist he holds in high regard. Then he tears into the book. "The man presumes he's a thinker, a superior thinker at that. When in actuality he's a stone dense materialist, inferior in intuition to any gum-chewing, junk food eating, football watching fire hydrant."

He should have liked Leonard Susskind's "The Black Hole War"[3] because his antagonist was the late Stephen Hawking, champion of the Einstein view, with Susskind on the quantum side. Yet Baccala, as ever, found reasons to be critical. Deciding that Susskind is "one of the camp that regards mathematics not as a tool that needs to be wielded with skill and care, but as the secret language of the Divine." (Einstein, according to Baccala, was another with that faith.) Susskind is credited as one of the founders of string theory. Baccala isn't opposed to string theory, since he believes the foundation of maya is reflection, the reflection could be vibrating creases in spacetime. One thing that irritates him is Susskind's openness to the multiverse theory. This is a pet peeve of Baccala's because he holds that the only things resembling a multiverse occur in the next universe not here. "The splitting off doesn't start here, it's the next universe. Moreover they're all connected, not an infinite number, each going their infinite separate ways forever. There are multiple links - they aren't wholly independent." But he ignores all that he has in common with Susskind. Susskind, unlike some older physicists, e.g. Steven Weinberg, is not a holdout stubbornly maintaining that quantum can't ultimately be as we presently understand it. A view Baccala mocks: 'This isn't pure science as our grandfathers conceived it. Science uncontaminated by human consciousness!' I think Susskind is on the other side - Baccala's side. He may not conceive of

---

[3] "The Black Hole War" 2008 Little, Brown and Company

Being as this great force Baccala does, but he's open to the 'anthropic principle' – the idea that observations must be compatible with the consciousness that observes them. Baccala of course would be properly placed with an extreme 'strong anthropic principle': that the universe *must* engender conscious life. Believing as he does that conscious life is part of a mutual-creation.

His readers would have no clue why he would say, "Physicists should explore divided reflections in optics if they want to understand the nature of quantum." He finds most atom-smashing a big waste of time. He didn't care a fig about the search for the Higgs boson, the particle/field that yields mass, when most physicists found it exciting. But when the results came out in 2012 he was delighted at the surprisingly weak values registered. Only if you knew his cosmology could you guess the reason he had this response. In his mind it was an indication that mass could be moved over alongside gravity, as a quality that wasn't in space[the Void]'s domain, but belonged instead to Being.

Likewise I can't imagine what his readers could have made of a column in November 2015 attacking the work of Japanese physicist Takaaki Kajita. "If you're the head of something called 'The Institute for Cosmic Ray Research' why don't you do something useful, like researching cosmic rays, instead of wasting your time on some quixotic mission to tweak the goddamn Standard Model?" His readers would have to know (and they don't) that Baccala doesn't want Kajita looking at anything but cosmic rays because 40 odd years ago he decided cosmic rays were the best bet for carrying information about galaxies getting disintegrated at the boundary of the universe. What if he was on the wrong track? I was reading an article in Scientific

American recently about these mysterious fast radio bursts (FRBs)[4], and I thought why couldn't something like this carry the evidence? Maybe a galaxy nearing the speed of light shrinks in size. Because it isn't a cosmic ray Baccala wouldn't pay any attention to it. This is just an example. I truly think he's forgotten that long ago it was a hunch, but it was only a hunch. Even if he's right the evidence could come in a form he didn't anticipate way back when.

There's an inexplicable blank space among all the conjectures that Baccala juggles that he never explores. If we accept that all of the physical reality around us is programmed by the Whole, why isn't the next question to ask could our internal thoughts/feelings/actions also be programmed? If experiences are perfectly divided, why not control responses as well? We may think we're independently taking the initiative, making decisions, when we're following an already written script. The idea flows directly from his cosmology, but he never brings it up. You have to ask why? I don't believe its because it never occurred to him. He's smarter than I am and it occurred to me. If Baccala's mutual-creation turns out to be right, describing this universe and the next, I'm willing to go along with his version of this world as a testing ground where souls prove who they are by the way they react to their specially rigged circumstances. But the possibility that their reactions are also part of the programming and distribution has to be considered.

Yet Baccala presents a Whole manipulating maya, factoring in human values and needs

[4] "Flashes in the Night" by Duncan Lorimer and Maura McLaughlin Scientific American April 2018.

(including the need to have their egos whacked and humbled), before looping it all back to us as this Creation, which contains a good deal of deliberate deception. It would seem natural to then ask could all that we regard as our free will, the exertions and assertions of individuality, also be illusions the Whole has programmed us to believe are our doing? We could still be consolidations of our eternal selves, refracted through the lens of this universe, and yet the independence of our self here could be an illusion. The true counter to the next world, where we really will be free and independent, might be to get 'customized' here with all our attributes and experiences. This would insure that every soul is distinct and all variations are mapped. If everything is being perfectly divided why would the Whole leave our internal character to chance? While I can believe inherited characteristics and differences in life experiences might produce the desired range, isn't it incumbent on Baccala to address this possibility if he wants to be intellectually honest and thorough?

I think he avoids mentioning it because even to entertain the idea, even as a hypothetical, puts a cloud over his credit. In Baccala's own narrative he is the truth seeker & speaker, scorned and snubbed by his Lilliputian contemporaries; heroically slogging on. Confident that one day his assessment of reality will be hailed as the culminating intellectual achievement that it is. That he alone (with a nod to Parmenides) finally solved the great mysteries of existence. When his day comes all the small-minded pompous asses who attacked him will fall into the pit of ignominy & infamy. But it isn't a culminating integrating achievement if he's merely some actor the Whole programmed to play the part of the one who puts the puzzle pieces together. If that is the final truth of the process then there goes any notion of individual credit. Or blame for that matter. What if this falls into that category of the unknowable that he told Tenace and his classes about? Subjects that can never be determined, that will always remain open to interpretation. Even that, as a possibility would rankle him. This is why I think Baccala never brings up the idea of our being programmed. Of course he thought of it. But the implication would detract from his credit, diminish his life's work and thought, and that is just too much for him to bear.

Tenace's supposition that Baccala in Santa Cruz wouldn't be able to control his political incorrectness was on target. (To be fair 'retarded' and 'Mongolian idiot' were quickly dropped from his repertoire. Though he's the only person I know of who still uses 'noble savage', not ironically, but as a compliment to 'traditional people'.) In truth he has never paid any price for being politically incorrect. I will reiterate what Tenace observed, though it's now forgotten, that the original political correctness battle was an internal fight inside the left. There was no thought about conservatives, who were the reason rules needed to be established; as it was presumed they couldn't help but transgress human decency and universal equality. The leftists rebelling against PC, like the late Alexander Cockburn and Camille Paglia, charged that the lawgivers of the new moral standards were Stalinists demanding conformity of speech on the way to conformity of thought. Such permitted speech and thought would end in 'no thought' for individuals. Though Baccala has stubbornly continued on that track he seems immune to suffering any consequences. In my opinion this is a combination of several elements. His supposed past (victim of persecution for his beliefs). The inability to determine if he's serious – or how serious. The deference his partisans give his knowledge in science, logic, metaphysics, philosophy, Eastern and Western theology. Plus his thought is extremely complicated, integrated and idiosyncratic. It would take a lot of bravado, or foolishness, for someone to claim they understood Baccala and could represent him. Even on something political. When everyone was condemning Russian aggression in seizing Crimea he said no big deal, "Crimea didn't belong to Ukraine. It was merely a gesture by Khrushchev to ameliorate Ukrainian sensitivities. He could do it because he could never imagine the Soviet Union breaking up. So what did it matter? The population is two thirds Russian. There's almost as many Tartars there as Ukrainians." Year after year he says whatever enters his head to his attendees in Santa Cruz and they treat it as inside knowledge.

You'd assume anyone with his views would get labeled anti-Semitic. Scoffing at the modern PC move to shift blame for Jesus's crucifixion from the Jews to the Romans: "Not only disregard everything recorded in the Gospels, but disregard reason itself. The last figure the Romans would fear would be an apolitical itinerant rabbi from the boondocks, healing people, calling for a new mindset in Judaism, preaching love, non-violence and spiritual transcendence. Get a grip." Labeling Israel the magnet for 'chosen people' bad Jews. The neocons a Likud 5th column. What spares him is his equal condemnation of the Arabs. "Each wants to be Cain" stops people. As does his theory that the Arabs were never truly defeated, so they didn't develop their minds. Dismissing terrorists as having a worthless faith and possessing worthless souls. Its all so bizarre that it makes it hard – or impossible – to type him. He condemns equally Israel and Saudi Arabia as "two so-called friends that have hurt us far worse than China or Russia." He speaks of a secret alliance Israel has made with Saudi Arabia "taking the place of the one they once had with apartheid South Africa." His readers assume this is based on something he knows that they don't when most probably its just another perception opinion of his.

If we overlook herding conservatives in heaven 'where they huddled of their own volition' in pens (shunned by decent people because they were unable to reach toward 'the different'), a lot of his prejudices run parallel to theirs. Scoffing at multiculturalism. "We can pretend to respect a culture where a man buys another wife for 3 cows. When in fact we find it abhorrent and should find it abhorrent. There are primitive societies and there are advanced societies. Primitives are more connected to their souls than modern people, and primitive values may once have been appropriate. But they are no longer." Unbelievably when AIDS was at its worst Baccala decided it was the perfect time to use the epidemic as a teaching moment to prove his ideas of where you could locate the strongest strains of promiscuity: male gays and male Africans. Attacking San Francisco bathhouses for refusing to shut down. "Choosing sex and death over life"[5]. Of African truck drivers spreading the disease throughout the continent: "Follow their routes on a map and it will exactly track the disease's spread." Hardcore Fundamentalist preachers were the only ones saying anything even remotely approaching this. And it tells you something about Banana Slug readership that the only protests came from gays. None from Blacks.

---

[5] Though his comments were tactless, keeping the bathhouses open as a civil rights issue must have resulted in extra deaths that could have been averted.

The truth is that Santa Cruz, while being a college town, politically and environmentally progressive, demographically is not representative of California. Its 78% White, practically no African-Americans (there are 4 Asians for every Black), and though the Hispanic population is significant, its half of the state mean. California is solidly Democratic and the party has backed protecting undocumented immigrants by becoming a 'sanctuary state'. Supposedly so they can report crimes without fear of deportation. Baccala hasn't veered from his opposition to this. Even though, as Tenace noted, they are part of his New People. Their backwardness, numbers and proximity to Mexico make them poor candidates for assimilation. "The Canadians have always had a merit based screen, requiring wealth or exceptional skills. No one calls the Canadians racists." He claims to have seen a large Mexican flag at the front of some demonstration in L.A. "Illegal immigrants lower wages, and are exploited by unscrupulous employers. The only reason the Democratic Party holds the position it does is opportunistic. Imagine, and as conservative Catholics its easy to imagine, that Hispanics voted like Born Agains. Really it's only the bigotry of right-wingers against Brown skin people that drove them away. Do you really think if they were a reliable Republican bloc, like the Cubans in Florida, that the Democrats would be so zealous in defending them? Don't kid yourself. Democrats see the Hispanic numbers as clinching a lock on a future majority. That's all there is to it." When people write in to Baccala that these immigrants are doing jobs Americans don't want to do, he has a twofold response. Get employers to pony up instead of exploiting illegals. "If you pay good wages people will do the jobs. Look at coal miners. Horrible conditions, hard work, shortens life, but for good pay people will do it." His other response addresses agricultural work. "They are going to come up with self-driving cars. Think of the complications that involves: visual, mechanical, computational. At high speeds with lives at risk. Do you think they can't come up with machines that pick strawberries and peaches?"

How could anyone categorize his views on Black Africans? The victors of Eden, who because of that early success, haven't budged beyond an 8 year old 'look at me!' chest-beating attitude. At the same time he has long embraced Reparations, though he calls it restitution. Anyone with African blood is helped with jobs, free education, healthcare, support with housing, food, and childcare.[6] But as far as Blacks obeying our laws he's skeptical: "Why should the laws of the many impinge on my freedom and independence to do whatever I want to do?!" Especially for the males the potential will stay bottled as potential. With last being first its the losers driven out of Eden who are destined to win; even though they interbred with 'sub-humans'. When a reader writes in asking if he isn't making too big a deal about Caucasians and Asians mating with older species, "After all we're talking about a very small percentage of the gene pool. Some anthropologists guess that this mixing aided our ancestors ability to adapt and survive in the conditions these earlier people had already acclimated to." Baccala dismisses this observation: "Well biologists tell us that we share 96% of our DNA

---

[6] I probably should add that he also favors these programs for all low-income people. So Blacks and Native Americans might be first, but they wouldn't be alone.

with chimpanzees and bonobos. Kind of makes you think that 4% might be pretty important doesn't it?"

President Obama could do no wrong. If we sat down and tried to imagine what would be the perfect make up and background for Baccala's ideal leader, it would look exactly like Barack Obama. Hawaii as separation. An African father whose basically a sperm donor. Who will have zero to do with the child, as either an influence or role model. An idealistic mother who stresses the priority of education and universal equality. And because of – and growing out of her ideals, the child experiences life in a 3rd world country (Indonesia) during his formative years. Later maturation is spent with her parents, the 'greatest generation', inculcating their values: the work ethic, personal and civic responsibility.

Granting Obama's intelligence and decency, and that he took the office seriously, what Baccala has refused to ever acknowledge was that his skimpy political background and apparent distaste for the nitty-gritty of politics compromised his 8 years as president. Nothing even approximating the vaunted 'audacity' ever materialized. Rather caution bordering on timidity. Compare how similar his record actually is to Bill Clinton's, a man Baccala loathes. There was "Clinton's 'premeditated pre-negotiated sellout'. Like a Republican, declaring the age of big government over; the poor found to be responsible for their state; caving in to Wall Street with deregulation, hands out for the payoff."

Well the truth is Obama could have picked two Nobel Prize winning economists for his administration: Joseph Stiglitz and Paul Krugman. Instead he picked acolytes of Robert Rubin, Clinton's man. That's just a fact. And after the financial collapse who got bailed out? The big players. They were deemed just too important for the economy as a whole. The small investors and homeowners were left to fend for themselves and deal with their losses as best they could. As if *they* should have known better. This is no different from what Clinton or any Republican administration would have done. Maybe they didn't "pray to Ayn Rand like Alan Greenspan or Speaker Ryan", but so what? Their actions are what counts, and they followed the same playbook. Obama's Foreign policy ended up no different. After all the excellent ideals expressed in Cairo dissipated into air, 8 years later there were more dictatorships and failed states, and we were still stuck in Afghanistan[7] and Iraq.

Robert L. Borosage dismissed the idea that Obama would rate as a 'transformational' president when he wrote a summation of his administration in 2017. "His signature appeal, he believed, was that he could transcend partisan and ideological divides. He was mentored by Robert Rubin, architect of much of the financial deregulation under Clinton. His leading economic appointees---Tim Geithner, Ben Bernanke, and Larry Summers---were all tribunes of continuity. Consider these hallmarks of the conservative-era consensus: the assault on government, deregulation and financialization of the economy, corporate-defined globalization, and growing inequality. All of them characterized the status quo when Obama was elected president in 2008, and all of them remain in place as he prepares to leave office."[8] How could anyone argue with that?

Baccala likes to throw Thomas Frank's critique at the Clintons. They think they live in a meritocracy. They look across the table and there are their old

---

[7] See "Thieves of State" Sarah Chayes W.W. Norton 2016

[8] Robert L. Borosage The Nation January 2/9, 2017

school chums from the Ivy League working for Wall Street. But Obama could say to himself exactly like Bill Clinton, 'I came from nothing. I worked my way to the top.' Yes the Republicans were obstructionist. And in the light of where they've gone subsequently the suspicion of their underlying bigotry appears confirmed. But let's look not only on what Obama did, but at what he never bothered to try to do. Not just, after all the handwringing, that he ended up staying in both Iraq and Afghanistan. Far more than Bush he relied on killer drones. When Bush did it Baccala spoke of recruiting eight future enemies for every current one we killed. "How would we like it if a foreign state took on itself the right to keep killer drones hovering overhead in our country, deciding who lives and who dies?" Yet Obama increased the practice and he never said a word.

You would think the first Black president would use the 'bully pulpit' to attack all the lives ruined by the drug war and the 'Prison Industrial Complex'. Michelle Alexander's "The New Jim Crow" profiling how the War on Drugs was a ruse used to disguise the continued discrimination and repression of Blacks came out in January 2010. Obama appointed a Black Attorney General and that was it. His effort was feeble. As Michelle Alexander pointed out, Obama was raised by White grandparents in a White neighborhood. His drug experimentation followed the track of suburban youth, occurring at college. No threat of real punishment. It didn't occur in a ghetto where kids are busted, branded with a record, not able to get a job, unable to escape a system set up by racists, not for rehabilitation but for free labor, private profit prisons, and full employment for prison guards until the end of time.

As for his big achievement, The Affordable Care Act, I'm fine with admitting it was a step in the right direction. His heart and his instincts contain decent goals, of course. And in my opinion the conservative scare tactics about made up 'death panels' forfeited one area, along with prescription drugs, where real savings could have been established. The last months of life often see us extending suffering at great cost, while the quality of life disappears. But let's not gloss over where the plan originated. At the rightwing think tank, The Heritage Foundation. And the pilot program was conducted in Massachusetts by "hedge fund RSB Mitt Romney". Thanks to Joe Lieberman The Affordable Care Act didn't even allow a public option. So how was it superior to Hillary Clinton's earlier proposal which Baccala attacked for preserving, depending on, private health insurers? What did Obama's plan do? - the same.

What did Obama do to help the average worker's wages go up? Does anything he said on the topic come to mind? Not to my mind. His trade policies were Bill Clinton's trade policies. What's good for our international corporations is good for America. As much as Baccala praised "Between the World and Me" by Ta-Nehisi Coates, "Finally a Black mind not laundered by middle class Black values or University reeducation", he ignored Coates' criticism of Obama. And as fond as he is of Cornel West he also turned a deaf ear to his criticisms of Obama.

Baccala relishes demolishing the sacred cows of others, while keeping his own. For example his belief that no right thinking person could find fault with any Mediterranean European. He made his mind up early on Barack Obama and there was nothing he did, or failed to do, that was going to alter that idolization. "As close to perfectly balanced as we are likely to see. The temperament and idealistic deep penetration of Lincoln, wedded to Jefferson's mind and eloquence. How the wretched American voters could elect such a paragon twice is a confounding mystery. It must give us hope. Its like a toddler lost in a deep forest somehow finding his way to human habitation. Those with souls see the Providential at work and give thanks."

He was soft on Trump at first. As Shakespeare's lowness gave insight into audience response, so Trump's lowness helped him predict what voters would reaction to. Baccala's hatred of the Clintons was part of this, and his contrarian inclination. Trump was a RSB playboy businessman. Willing to launder money for Russians and mobsters. A huckster who wanted to be a celebrity and succeeded. A hit on TV. "Thinking of running he listened to what people were saying on talk radio, complaining about all the immigrants, and Obama not being born in America, and he thought 'That's what they want? That's what I'll give them'. The proof to Baccala that Trump didn't believe what came out of his mouth was how offended he got when the comic writers for Obama came up with a devastating mockery sendup delivered at a correspondence dinner with Trump in attendance. This decided him on running for the presidency. "If you stand behind the charge that Obama was born in Kenya you don't get offended. But he didn't. It was simply feeding the customers what they asked for. He thought it was bad form for the Obama camp to attack him for making a sale."

Baccala didn't like Trump calling his New People rapists, but he was sure he didn't believe that either. Besides Baccala, who favored Bernie Sanders, doesn't want any more immigration, doesn't like the international trade deals, and is all for restarting American manufacturing. "The grievances are legit. This billionaire is the wrong representative - but they're too stupid to pick up on that." He attacked the left for trying to disrupt Trump rallies. "They have every right to assemble and hear their candidate. How would we like it if rightists came to our rallies to shout down the proceedings? We'd call them Nazi thugs. Beyond counter-productive, which of course it is, its just plain wrong. If you believe in democracy you believe in democracy for everyone, not just your group." During the general election campaign he kept telling his readers that Clinton was a bigger hawk than Trump. Of course in California this is of no consequence. There if George Washington ran as a Republican and Aaron Burr as a Democrat, Burr would take the state.

The proof of his feelings came after Trump's win, which surprised Baccala as much as everyone else. He was obviously elated. Reminiscent of the celebratory reaction Tenace noted when Menachem Begin and Likud were victorious in Israel, as his dark vision of the Israelis got confirmed. The same with the victory of the 'RSB huckster'. The degeneration of the 'Dog People' was now a proven fact. Baccala said that for two elections bigoted Americans, burned by the Iraq war, extended themselves to show they weren't racist. That done they could now go back to the release of bigotry and greed. Under the title Trumped Up Charges he wrote, "This reveals the core principles of conservatives, they have none! They have no fidelity to the Constitution. They are attracted to war but they're not patriotic. The rightwing Christians - they're not Christian. Trump proves they're more political than spiritual. They're Pharisees. Hypocrites. A Christian follows Jesus and what he taught. But if we believe in democracy why shouldn't hypocrites get a representative once in a while? Why shouldn't the stupid? The shallow? The ignorant? – by which I mean those who deliberately chose to stay ill-informed so they can go on believing

236

what they want to believe. That's very American. Maybe human. Why shouldn't liars and salesmen get a representive? Well they've got one now. If you can't see this fellow you can't see anything."

"Forget the Hollow Man and the Hollow Boy, now we have the Empty Balloon. The thinnest veneer, with nothing inside. A narcissist so empty he has to put his name – his 'brand' – on everything. Without substance he can never really hold anything, so there's never satisfaction. He can never be content because he will never possess any contents. Look at the gargoyles he raises up as role models. His Klansman landlord father, stock raider Carl Icahn, and scumbag of all time Roy Cohn. Now you can't blame someone for who their father is. Like Mel Gibson saddled with a Sedevacantism nut job for a papa, anti-Semite holocaust denier. The father's diseases infected the son's mind. Really not his fault. But put Trump's father to the side. You still have two of the vilest people imaginable, individuals without souls, he's proud to say he admires."

"Americans can't tell the difference between fake and real, and if we needed proof the election of a RSB billionaire narcissist provides it.   But the perfection doesn't stop with the elevation of this toad. How he won is equally hilarious. A combination of the Russians and the FBI. Working together at long last! Since Hofstadter[9] in the sixties we've been aware of the strain in our people, the paranoia, susceptibility to conspiracy theories, especially among conservatives and Christian Right types. All people fear the unknown. But Americans in an unknown land, that fear became an innate part of their character. James Comey, the boy scout,

---

[9] "The Paranoid Style in American Politics, and Other Essays" Richard J. Hofstadter (1964) Vintage.

outsmarts himself. Sure Hillary would win he announces a reopening examination of more emails, so afterwards he won't be accused of sitting on important news that could have affected the election. But his announcement affects the election. Trump, anticipating his loss (RSBs don't like to lose) speaks of a 'rigged' system. Then when he wins because he's a pathological-liar salesman he explains losing the popular vote as due to phantom millions of illegals voting for Clinton. His sad voters, suckers for conspiracy theories, believe it. Or at least lack the internal integrity to disbelieve the obvious falsehood." Later when Trump fired Comey for not dropping his investigations, Baccala cackled at the delicious irony.

However Trump ceased to be entertaining after he abrogated American participation in the Iranian nuclear treaty. While taking anything Trump says at face value might be foolhardy, he had repeatedly attacked the deal. Knowing Baccala's partiality towards Iranians; and his dislike of Netanyahu/Likud, the Saudis and Gulf Arabs[10]; his new viciousness was predictable. "Narcissus becomes a demagogue. He continues his rallies. Why? He won the election. He's president. His ego needs the adulation. Yet it can never be enough because he's empty. The Dog People respond to the dog whistles. They taste ever more lies, and decide they really like the taste. The Albinos look at the demographics - they're going to lose their place, which is to say their privileges. The idea of sharing with people of the wrong pigmentation (which is any pigmentation), who actually feel life & have souls,

---

[10] Whether this secret alliance existed when he first proposed it, it now does appear to be true. See "The Enemy Of My Enemy" by Adam Entous The New Yorker June 18, 2018.

means saying goodbye to the world they liked, when those people were second-class. Republicans need to change their name as they're no longer republicans. I suggest 'The Contaminated' as appropriate."

"Look at the people Trump gets along with: strongmen. Beyond Putin and the Saudis and Gulf Arabs, who finance the rascal, the pattern is worldwide. What does he care that Duterte of the Philippines is a murdering psychopath? He books rooms at Trump's DC hotel, and Trump has a luxury hotel in Manila. What does he care that strongman Erdogan in Turkey kept the Jihadist Highway open for years, funneling fighters, arms and money to the Islamic State? Trump has a hotel in Istanbul and interest in a furniture company. We all want negotiations to go well with the North Korean Un, but the poor North Koreans are the embodiment of the *brainwashed*. That Trump is fine with the Chinese scion Xi Jinping moving to dispense with term limits tells you what sort of American values the criminal RSB has."

I need to reiterate Baccala is a fan of the Iranians (Persians), not the totalitarian theocracy. "Since 1981, after Beheshti was assassinated, no one was left except second raters. Maybe we let the geriatric Khomeini get a pass (a man who recommended marrying 11 year olds), and I wouldn't call Rouhani and his circle second raters. But those with real power, Ali Khamenei down, all possess a second rate character, unable to withstand the seduction of power. And remember as corrupting as the power of king, dictator, or hero of a revolution is, it doesn't compare to the insanity of believing you are God's agent on Earth. Remember these nuts have little to do with the Persian people, especially the young and educated. As in Egypt and Turkey tyranny depends on the support of the unwashed and uneducated, the backward and incredibly credulous. The Persians are the people of Cyrus, of a great civilization, the great poets of the past, and the best filmmakers of today. All of what we call Islamic culture and Islamic civilization was taken from the Persians." Again while there's a lot of truth in this, it diminishes other cultures that not only made important contributions to 'Islamic civilization' but to world civilization.

There is no reason for Baccala to ever mention, let alone defend, Arthur Jensen. We know the guilt by association he already carried was unfair since he had lampooned the presumptions, methodology, and extrapolations of Jensen and his team at the time. Baccala speaking generally said, "The conscious or unconscious racist can't resist the temptation to conflate IQ with intelligence." Well who does this describe better than Arthur Jensen? Remember Baccala deprecates 'machine mind', telling us it came from earlier non Homo sapiens ancestors.

One of the few scientists Baccala admired was Stephen Jay Gould[11]. Gould tore apart "The Bell Curve", a book Baccala also condemned as "a rationalization for inequality; pretending to be scientific when it's really a political attack struck by the diabolical neocons at the American Enterprise Institute." Who signed on in support of the "Bell Curve"? Yes, Arthur Jensen. Baccala felt he owed Mudrick loyalty. But he doesn't owe Jensen a thing. He never agreed with him on anything. Yet long after his death he goes on trying to mitigate his stance.

---

[11] Baccala wrote of Gould, "When you hear a scientist declare we should keep separate the spheres of empirical science and that of faith, its best not to trust them. It's a ploy. Gould is the exception. The scientist who not only means it, but even more remarkably, is capable of doing it."

The lame excuse he gives in regard to "The Bell Curve" is that Jensen mistakenly thought the authors were supporting him, so he felt obliged to support them back. It is Baccala who is off here, and Jensen who was, in a narrow way, correct. His work and "The Bell Curve" had the same thrust and the same purpose. (Many people unfortunately have forgotten the controversy. Yet I think inside the conservative citadel, by both its intellectual and the anti-intellectual constituents, the Bell Curve & Jensen's thesis is still thought to be true. Suppressed only because it wasn't PC.)

Beyond that, even if you could excuse it as a desperate search for allies, there's no way you can explain Jensen's relationship with William Shockley. A truly awful eugenics-type racist. But again Baccala concocts excuses. Jensen was under fire, had been called the worst names, so blindly he embraced Shockley. Again because Shockley embraced him. "After all Shockley had won a Nobel for his work on transistors". Does that explain, let alone excuse, the degradation of aligning yourself with such a fiend? Again - *why* is Baccala defending Jensen? He never respected his work. As an associate he mocked it as lunatic. There is the fact that while they didn't agree on what intelligence was, or how you could or couldn't measure it, they both presumed it was around 80% genetic inheritance. So they shared that conviction. It's the personal acquaintance though that I think influences him. While Baccala viewed Jensen's testing project with contempt (and laughs at anyone who would proudly proclaim himself a psychologist); as a 'cultured' individual he did respect him. The idea that anyone who appreciated the artistry of Arturo Toscanini could also be a racist, is to Baccala unimaginable. Racists are uncouth and uneducated thugs. It is history that rebuts this with so many examples of very cultured individuals who in different surroundings acted without restraint or conscience. And in music there's no need to go all the way back to Wagner; we can point to Richard Strauss and Herbert von Karajan.

In the columns he devotes to reviewing books he's hard on scientists. Per Susskind and Penrose. And those he does endorse, with the exception of Freeman Dyson, tend like Gould, to come from disciplines far away from physics. E.O. Wilson the 'ant-man', and Lewis Thomas the 'cell man'.[12] He has a prejudice that strikes me as ill founded, that you can't be 'balanced' if you aren't articulate. When there's no reason that you couldn't be a scientist whose work was penetrating but whose writing was clumsy. That wouldn't take away from the work. Speaking and writing are separate gifts (separate from each other by the way), talents that don't tell you if a person's research is valuable. I think he would have included the astronomer Carl Sagan, who was very articulate, in his group of acceptable scientists, had it not been for Sagan's enthusiasm about capturing extra-terrestrial messages. This was a fool's errand given Baccala's cosmology. Yet to most rational people looking at an endless array of galaxies, hundreds of billions of stars and planets, it only makes sense that out of that huge number there must be some older highly developed societies with advanced technologies.

To Baccala, if you were truly ruled by reason you'd take it one step further. You'd presume these

---

[12] Popular books on science he has praised:

"Complexity" Roger Lewin U Chicago Press 1992

"Guns, Germs, and Steel" Jared Diamond Norton 1997

"Einstein's Clocks, Poincare's Maps" Peter Galison Norton 2003

"The Invention of Air" Steven Johnson Penguin 2008

"Catching Fire" Richard Wrangham Basic Books 2009

other civilizations, since they were older and more advanced, should already have communicated and made contact long ago. It should be a known part of human history from its beginning. "Consider the proposition and ask yourself, if you aren't gullible or don't believe as I do that the phantom UFOs and abductions are as real or unreal as dragons and demons of the past, where are the signals? They shouldn't be hard to detect – they should fill space. But there's nothing. The best rejoinder I've encountered actually comes from Star Trek fans: the 'Prime Directive'. Which is an order of no interference in an alien civilization's development. So the best explanation for no contact comes from an old TV science fiction show. But even if that were plausible, and it isn't, the sky would still be full of communications between advanced civilizations to one another. And there is in fact nothing. The Whole is quite capable of manufacturing phenomena but this is limited to a phantom here and there." I should add, in case I need to, that he never alludes to 2 Universes.

I'll add one snippet from a column related to this that I found interesting. I think of it as a window into his thinking about the plasticity of the world and the relation of isolated consciousness versus greater compounded consciousness. Not exactly dismissing people who swear they've been abducted by aliens and experimented on in their ships. But he 'understands' them in a way that no doubt would infuriate them. "I'm sure the experience of the abduction for them felt real. But this isn't about judging it, or them, its requiring realness to have a larger context. That they are convinced doesn't move it beyond their scope. Our ancestors in China and Europe encountered fire-breathing dragons. I believe this was a manifestation that mixed future elements: loud planes and fiery bombs, with elements from the past: dinosaurs - even flying dinosaurs. But these experiences, which were accepted by less rational societies, still only occurred to isolated individuals in isolated circumstances. Becoming the source for myths in many cultures. We don't grant their reality because they didn't leave physical evidence and they weren't witnessed by masses of people. We correctly require a broader register. It is in that way that these abductions are only real to the isolated individuals in their isolated circumstances. Not real by our normal more stringent definition."

While more positive in economics and politics, it's also the case that he selects authors he agrees with. So along with Stiglitz and Krugman he likes the French economist Thomas Piketty. And the political writers he favors are predictably all on the left. The aforementioned Thomas Frank, with William Greider, Naomi Klein, Chris Hedges and Robert Kuttner. The only possible outlier might be neo-Gonzo journalist Matt Taibbi. For a general introduction to philosophy he points to Arthur C. Danto's "Connections to the World". (He liked Danto on pretty much everything until it came to Andy Warhol.) There's William James' "The Variety of Religious Experience", and whatever scriptures align with a person's inclination. He trusts Bart D. Ehrman on the New Testament, even though Ehrman lost his faith in the process. Those curious about Zen: Shunryu Suzuki's "Zen Mind, Beginner's Mind". For mysticism it was always the work of Walter Terence Stace.

In the popular overview of religion he likes both Karen Armstrong and Reza Aslan (Iranian extraction) though he called Aslan's book on Jesus "idiotic" and "as wrong as possible". Of Armstrong he says, "She invariably finds and emphasizes the good in all the world's faiths." Baccala rarely refers to television but he found a series Aslan did for CNN quite amazing. "From a new cult like Scientology, to older idol worshipping ones in Haiti and Mexico, Aslan, while quite cognizant of the impurities in these low practices, is able to look past them, to genuinely appreciate the pure faith working inside, no matter the intellectual or physical debilitation. It's a marvel. Poets tell us to preserve the child's wonder and joy, a master like Suzuki to keep beginner's mind. But pulling it off is rare. Aslan pulls it off. Its remarkable." Baccala must have qualms about his own judgmental harshness, which can't strike anyone as spiritual. By praising and endorsing those who are more generous and open he seeks to mitigate that impression.

He's also a little more generous when it comes to the arts. Even recommending Tom Wolfe's "The Painted Word", which he also cited in "Separation". Wolfe was not only conservative but a Southerner. Baccala has always appreciated women novelists, ranking George Eliot (Mary Ann Evans) with Tolstoy and Dostoevsky. Giving the Bronte sisters their due, as well as Willa Cather. Agreeing with Mudrick on the greatness of Jane Austen. Now he says we are in a period (of course for him the end period) dominated by female novelists. Probably no need to mention this features 'Elena Ferrante'. But there are several Americans up on this altar: Marilyn Robinson, Barbara Kingsolver, Elizabeth Strout. In poetry he has had two favorites for many years, both American: Jane Hirshfield and Stephen Dunn. He does not stint in their praise. Of Hirshfield he has written, "She does all the things that you'd presume would hobble and disturb a poet of her incredible sensitivity. Traveling, writing essays, doing translations, putting together anthologies. Yet the inspired poetry continues to flow uninterrupted." Of Dunn he recently wrote, "At 75 he is still writing great poetry. And as always with the same heroic honesty."

He continues to struggle with his conclusion that looking back the United States has disqualified itself for the 'Lamp of Enlightenment'. Nixon and Kissinger, unlike Kennedy and Johnson, never believed the war in Vietnam was winnable. Nixon was so evil he sabotaged a peace treaty, an act of treason, and together with Kissinger continued the war only for domestic political reasons. Destabilized Cambodia, creating a vacuum for genocide. "So what about the American people and conscience? They elect the Hollow Man in 1980 who tells them Vietnam was a noble cause. They liked the sound of that. He also tells them there was no blacklist. Despite the fact that it was through the blacklist that he met his wife - his second wife. She came to him to stop having her name confused with another Nancy Davis, who had 'un-American' ideas."

His problem is he can't accept any other nation for the role. Forget the original 'chosen people' of monotheism, the Jews; or the descendants of eldest son 'wild man' Ishmael. "Its hard to imagine two more ghastly people. Jews aren't spiritual, except for the ridiculously narrow superstitious nuts, and what good are they? The Jews sharpened their minds to explain away defeats, exiles, persecution; but they're still the crowd of the golden calf. It doesn't make sense. They weren't obedient. Does it come down to God preferring comedians? The Arabs on the other hand *are* spiritual, but they let their minds atrophy. They peaked 800 years ago. They're among the most backward people on earth now. Look at the 'Arab Spring'. I foolishly had hopes, at least in Egypt. That after decades of persecution, the Muslim

246

Brotherhood would understand there had to be cooperation, compromise, give and take, sharing of power. 'No! Its all us, everything will be the way *we* want it!' So now its back to military dictatorship, no better than when it started. Maybe worse."

He wrote a column about the design of American Evangelicals plotting to use Israeli Jews as their 'burnt offering'. Americans and the Israelis cynically using each other. "Sharon and Netanyahu despised the settlers. They simply used them to grab more land. It's the crazed American Evangelists who push it financially, and are its biggest political supporters in the US. 'Don't worry about bloodshed - there's more to come. We're hoping for millions. Steal their land, steal their water! Didn't God give you this land? Of course He did! He plays favorites. We should know. And when the time comes nuke them! This will bring on the 2nd Coming.'"

"If the Israelis pass the Germans what do these wackos care? They're so stupid they still think the prophesied two thirds incineration of the Jews hasn't occurred yet. No because their idiotic reading of the spurious book of Revelation has it occur after Jesus returns, when only one third of those stubborn people convert. Then fire for the two thirds. Which even for rightwing fundamentalists is an impressive level of stupidity. All witness Jesus coming in the clouds with angels, defeating (a non-existent) Satan, but they still refuse to convert? Its like Paul being knocked down and blinded. He wants credit for changing sides? It's 'born again' without a mind. Revelation is an obvious fabrication made up of bits taken from other books. A collage of Daniel, Isaiah, other prophets, books of the Old Testament, books of the New Testament, with even the apocryphal Book of Enoch and the pagan Sibylline Oracle thrown in. Emperor Nero (666) is the anti-Christ; and

Emperor Domitian, 81-96 C.E., when the book was written, is the persecuting Beast resurrected. There's angels, plagues, catastrophes, 7 this and 7 that, 12 tribes, 7 churches in what is now Turkey. With scary special effects that would fit perfectly into a current blockbuster dystopian movie Hollywood will be making soon. It was the work of an earnest fellow with poor Greek who thought ascribing it to John would guarantee its reach. He was right on that score but it couldn't be more obviously made up. If The Book of Enoch had been ascribed to John, and Revelation to Enoch, would The Book of Enoch now be the Bible's last book? There was nothing about Revelation that qualified as genuine, and Athanasius has a lot to answer for. Possibly more than Sigmund Freud, because Revelation's nightmares have haunted humanity for much longer. The churchmen loved it of course, scares the rabble."

Interestingly when Baccala shifts from the old conception of God to his conception of the Whole, the idea of a favored people also shifts, from subjective error to objective statistics. "Who does the Whole favor? The competition isn't hidden. Who has the most people? Simple total numbers tell you who is favored. There are only two competitors, the Indians and the Chinese. It's easy to imagine the Chinese becoming the world's dominant economic power. Possibly exercising 'soft power' to influence world affairs towards a more peaceful harmonious existence. In other words moving slightly away from their traditional 'Middle Kingdom' attitude. The Han Chinese only caring about Han Chinese - as we see in building phony islands to claim more of the sea as theirs. Yet even if they reformed their self-centeredness you would still have people who don't practice democracy & freedom. They had humanity's greatest civilization. They work cooperatively. They are enterprising, the old adage was 'the Jews of the Orient'. But the syndicate's new boss changes the rules so he can stay in office and the ants applaud. Can you imagine a country ruled by what they call a communist party that provides worse health care to their average citizens than our awful system does to ours? They could call themselves The Chinese Giant Panda Party, get rid of all the images of false idol Emperor Mao, and it wouldn't change a thing. They are about as close to spiritual zeros as you can get. Spiritual zero slaves."

"Now the Indians are spiritual of course. In theory they recognize God in everyone. The people have an independent character. And maybe the one debt they owe the British beyond the railroads: they are a democracy. But you can't ignore the continuing caste system. Or the despicable inequality of women (to give credit where credit is due, the Chinese in contrast have reformed their traditional inequality. Though they did end up with a lot more baby boys). And what about Indian corruption? It's at an African level. You have to pay a policeman or a government official to do their job, otherwise forget it. Better have the money. What sane person would bet on the Indians breaking through the cell walls they built over centuries to imprison themselves?"

Nothing has changed his view of ethnicities as breeds. He's certain that sports, as 'exhibitions', bear out all of his suppositions. The domination of basketball and football (not the quarterback though, that puts a premium on machine mind) was sure to happen once competition was open to Blacks. And just as sure was a change in their ethic, towards the 8 year olds' swagger and show off. His only change is to add baseball, with the influx of Latin players, as a demonstration. "While the Japanese and Korean players outdo the natives in their adherence to correct stoic soldier conduct, the New People let themselves celebrate and strut. They are aware this isn't their country, simply the land of the loot. Keep in mind that the mix isn't just Caucasian and Asian (Mongol), the classic definition of Mestizo. The third ingredient is African."

After one of his columns going on about the "dreadful fratricidal desert Semites", someone wrote in probing: "Professor you're always recommending balance. And of course I agree the Spirit doesn't have a favorite tribe, or a favorite language: Hebrew, Arabic, Greek, Latin, King James English. But however primitive and tribal they may have been, your Whole picked these violent people for the revelation of Oneness. This was given to the West while the East was allowed to continue with polytheism and Buddhist non-theism." Baccala's response was interesting. "I don't think you're looking far enough into the larger balance. I assume you'll agree that there are all kinds of people. And this could lead to emphasizing one truth with one group, emphasizing a different truth with another group. In ancient India it was taught that godness was part of everyone. That's a great truth right? And yes the Whole's oneness is a great truth also. But the consequence in the West hasn't been entirely positive. There's this weird outcome where God is imagined as a personification, and at the same time as a being outside of us. The tradition in the East included practices of meditating into consciousness and direct contact with Being. Now it's true this was pursued by an elite. It wasn't the average person's experience. But common people of these societies carried some approximate idea of the principles and on their own level they honored the priests and monks, and obeyed the religious teachings and rites. I would argue that direct contact with consciousness and Being ends up balancing underplaying the truth of oneness. Your evaluation didn't weigh all the elements fairly."

On another occasion he got worried that his readers were confusing his conception of the Whole with the older idea of an independent Deity playing with mortals in a whimsical offhand fashion. He tried to correct that, "There isn't someone else programming this universe. It is you. By you I mean of course all humanity. It's our input. We are the godhead. With all living creatures, maybe everything, being God. Collectively we not only know what we want, we also know human weaknesses. What constitutes a perfect test. Unconsciously, as an aggregate whole, we manufacture that universe - this universe. As always working with and around the requirements the Void imposes."

Whether its resentment from personal disappointments, or from the world not developing as he had once supposed, the bitterness has grown stronger. Yet I would not want to go so far as to leave the impression that he had abandoned his ideals. He will periodically reiterate them to his readers. Sometimes clinically, like an academic, and sometimes like a minister, with more feeling. "These are truths. Equality, freedom, independence. Eternal truths. As indisputable as a circle is a circle. Has the quality and features of a circle. A square is a square. Has the quality and features of a square. The same with a triangle. There is order and logic. A point. A line. A plane. Then the 4 dimensions we know." Or when he talks of ethical governance, "Set minimum conditions. Minimum shelter – for everyone. They can't fall below. Minimum food. Minimum monthly income. Access to education and healthcare on one level for everyone, not gauged to where you live or how much you earn or your wealth. There would have to be oversight. Especially for big expenditures like housing, cars, appliances and beds. Monies won't be dispersed for gambling, drugs or drink."

"Is this all humanity's capable of coming up with? Capitalism, modified law of the jungle, survival of the fittest, any compassion a separate addition? Or communism, where a group of superior elites make all the decisions and grow corrupted by power? This is it? We're obliged to work with capitalism because its more organic, it evolved over time. You cannot dispense with it altogether. That's like saying we don't like our fumbling language, let's make an ideal one from scratch, with sensible rules, and less confusion. Esperanto. It doesn't work that way. You have to incrementally reform what you're saddled with, which has arisen organically. Unfortunately including a bunch of nuts proclaiming the market is divine. A healthy economy, a healthy society, like a healthy body has good circulation. You eliminate the trap of a bottom. Allow people to make money if that's the reward they respond to, but you tax them heavily and narrow the gap between the classes."

Of course he's still promoting his view of Being. The longest exposition he's ever undertaken in Prof's Proofs came in response to a letter from a woman worried that her memory problems foretold worse things to come, and that this could affect the shape of who she ultimately was. Whether correctly or incorrectly Baccala took it that she feared that her physical affliction could permanently affect the shape of her soul. He was alarmed that any reader of his could entertain such a thought. "You don't understand everything is possible through Being. Its even somewhat true here, but its constrained. But in the next world it isn't. I'm referring to everything - any impairment suffered here. In the next reality all the senses, all the qualities are available to Being. They're simply ingredients there at your command. In a world with real space and real time. Here our consciousness fluctuates from strong to weak. We have a spread out being and iffy control. Physically in this world it's as if we were at the mercy of some hologram we were bottled in. There you will be in control."

"I've written repeatedly, but sometimes wonder if its sunk in, the self-appointed representatives of 'science' and 'reason', disconnected from their souls, but very connected to data about material phenomena, insist there is nothing but the material. We however, connected to our souls, know the most important things – life, consciousness, experience – are not material. Not to mention this universe wouldn't even exist except for Being supplying all the players and the 4th dimension. The proponents of the material, convinced there is nothing else, think it's entirely fair and logical that we produce physical evidence or they win the argument. These champions of reason can't see that this is illogical. Nor are they open to the possibility that they could be wrong. Since we know they are wrong all we can do when they mock us is to shrug. If a blind person insisted that vision was an illusion, or a deaf person insisted that sound was an illusion, you wouldn't get disturbed. You certainly wouldn't ask yourself, 'Hey could they be right, and I've been mistaken all along?' You'd probably feel sorry for them. Though with the pompous condescension the materialists exhibit it seems a just desert that such conceited fools would get the very essence of existence wrong."

"Beyond practical help pay no mind to the medical researchers and scientific 'experts'. They are simply widgets putting on airs without really knowing anything about what is most important. Spiritually they're tree stumps, and that's being unkind to tree stumps. They know they can't assert neuronal activity as consciousness or life. They don't have any evidence and they never will. They don't even have a plausible explanation. So what they do is present a correspondence, and leave it to you to connect the dots and make the leap they've made. But it's all error. The body, including the brain, is just a container. Important in that we couldn't be here, in the Void, except for these containers. And true, if a container is impaired there are effects. All matter by the way is actually made of Void material – maya – spun up from reflection. The important stuff is what flows through these containers. Remember this whole existence is only possible because a field of Being is emanating from the next world. From the excess of Being there[13]. Living creatures are the particles of Being of this field. You couldn't be here if you weren't there. There's a tricky paradox, the animators of the next world are created in this one, which as I said exists because of the excess of Being there. But don't get hung up on that. What you need to know is no physical impairment carries over into the next world." Note how mutual creation, one of the axes of his cosmology, isn't even named now. Referred to only as a tricky paradox. Something not to get hung up on. He obviously still believes it, but has moved it into the background. As if what was a scientific and philosophical enterprise is now something closer to a political, or let's say sociological movement.

---

[13] "Being trumps maya-matter. This truth obtains everywhere. Simply look at the world - the scale level - you live in. Experimental evidence comes when observation/measurement (Consciousness) forces quantum superposition to make a choice of only one state."

The compromise Baccala made after he left CCS and began a new career in Santa Cruz was to pull back from presenting his entire system. This was successful in the limited way a tactic can sometimes work for a single objective. In this case avoiding all the controversies that had dogged him from his Berkeley days. Yet as a long-range strategy it was counterproductive. To only make discrete assertions (by some vague but implied authority), and not to make connections, has worked in helping to create this aura he has. Yet Baccala's thought is systematic (physics, philosophy/theology, metaphysics), but what does that matter if its never presented as a whole? The people who accept everything he says, a piece of physics here, a piece of philosophy there, a judgment out of the blue on something else, take it all on faith. That's not understanding. I don't think it even qualifies as knowing agreement. Art Tenace, like a lot of people, sneers at New Agers, and he seemed to imply that Baccala passed himself off in Santa Cruz, and the naïve people there didn't know any better. The process was more nuanced I believe, and less calculated. I think Baccala *does* identify with New Age beliefs and objectives. It's just given his convictions and lack of self-doubt, over time he has proposed, and as far as I can tell successfully persuaded his audience, that what he believes is what New Age people believe. If you're New Age this is what we believe. Hiding his canon has facilitated this endeavor, but he really believes that his core principles are New Age's, if rightly understood.

Even if Baccala, intentionally or accidentally, pulled off what Tenace considers an intellectual sleight of hand, this might be because there is no agreement on what the New Age principles are. As it's anti-doctrinal with everyone agreeing on equality it follows that everyone's conception of the new final covenant is equally valid. Then who is to say Baccala is wrong? The name itself comes from a consensus that there is a coming destined transcendent age. Something which Baccala has always believed. The realization will be spread by an awakened few at first; but fairly quickly a universal enlightenment will spread. Old religions and old doctrines are treated with respect but their day is done (I observe a lot more bowing to Eastern wisdom than to Western). It's easy to see how these tenets fit with Baccala's eschatology. In fact what did he have to change?

Unfortunately though he does bring additional baggage. As far as I know he still considers himself a Unitarian. It's possible that you can be a Unitarian and a New Ager - they're both decidedly open. But there is a difference in emphasis. Many Unitarian 'good works' occur in the political sphere, and on the progressive side. While New Age stresses compassion, they tend to scorn the political as a dirtying low level of gross power. So you could say they tend to be apolitical or even anti-political. Baccala has worked to erode this aversion to the political. Chiding that if you want to bring 'light' and 'good' into the world you must be humble enough to enter the world where the masses live (Jesus saying 'sinners' are the ones we need to reach). For all its political incorrectness he pushes an agenda that is still 95% leftist. Though he knows a good portion of the left is contemptuous of anything spiritual, regarding it as superstitious, casting themselves as upholding science and reason. Hardly the brethren to help bring universal enlightenment to pass. Need I mention Baccala's cynicism about people, their minds and character; thick as a landslide of mud, which Baccala brings to all appraisals. Neither Unitarians nor New Agers are cynical. Yet concurring with Baccala's judgments means first writing off your countrymen as dimwitted pigs, far too low for redemption; and then viewing the rest of humanity in varying states of corruption that exactly mirrors their 'fallen' souls. Yes he will periodically encourage his readers not to lose heart, saying we're moving towards the light and eventual good; I'm just telling you the truth because we need to keep our eyes open. But if the truthful assessment of the earth's people is that they are so base, "animal small-minded and self-centered", how realistic then is any millennial hope?

"If we were honest we could list all the people who have never contributed to civilization and even today have only put it on as a façade. Start with all the islanders: Indonesia, Malaysia, the Philippines. Throw in all of South America. Throw in Central America including Mexico. Throw in Australia and New Zealand. Add Pakistan and Bangladesh. All of Southeast Asia. It's no one's fault. Its geography, but it's a fact."

"We are rightly appalled at the disregard Caucasians showed in despoiling and poisoning the planet. And the arrogance Africans display in hunting and eating our relatives, monkeys and primates, and calling it 'bush meat'. But don't get too sanguine about the era of Asian stewardship of the world. Yes some of the traits passed down from Homo erectus are positive. Cooperation, being family-centered as opposed to self-centered. But you also have exaggerated conformity. Whereas African and Caucasoid identity and sympathies are programmed and thus can be reprogramed, Mongoloid insularity seems hardwired. The Japanese civilization is extremely refined, possibly the most refined in human history. What did we discover in World War II? That their population actually believed that their ridiculous emperor,

Hirohito, was descended from the Sun. The Chinese torture dogs before cooking and eating them. The Japanese left to their own devices would hunt to extinction all the dolphins and whales in the ocean - that's why everyone keeps an eye on them."

"To contemplate universal enlightenment led by the Mongoloids (not the Southeast Asians or Tibetans; but the Chinese, Japanese and Koreans) realistically requires that we swap secular ethics for the spiritual. Yes there was greatness, Chinese Taoism and Japanese Zen. But all past tense, and always a small elite. Today these people make the French look spiritual. Remember centuries ago the French were devout believers - the whole population." You know this all goes back decades when he thought the divine plan was clear: all the world's races coming together in America and flourishing under Jefferson's Freedom of Religion. Yet talk about small elites, how many Transcendentalists were there? Even the 18th century dissenters he admires, the Methodists, Quakers, and the original Baptists in Great Britain and America, were always a minority. You want numbers look at the 'tent revival' people. Same today, in regards of believers, it would be weighted towards Evangelicals (Southern Baptists the largest denomination), and Catholics.

What I find amazing is how long he has held onto the 'lamp of enlightenment' idea, finding it so hard, even now, to let go of America's destined role. The same man who says Americans are part ignorant, part stupid, and part crazy. Who asks his readers (rhetorically): "What hegemon would divide the world up into 5 'Commands'? Well we know the answer: the self-appointed policeman of the world[14]. What

---

[14] Combat High: America's addiction to war. A forum in June

does it mean if a nuclear superpower in the 21st century spends more on its military than the next 7 countries combined? How would you view any other nation arming up like that? What does it say about our people that they never reflect on this, simply go along? We incarcerate more of our population per capita. Don't kid yourself that there's equal justice. Those that get arrested, how they are charged, who gets bail and who doesn't? Who is forced to plead? Who gets adequate representation, who doesn't? There's no fairness in our 'administration of justice'. And as far as classes, the gap between rich and poor now exceeds the Gilded Age."

Baccala was enthusiastic for the 'occupy' movement during its brief heyday. "Democratic equality, the understanding that there should be no leaders and no dogma." What he hoped was a turning point was just another utopian bubble. A justifiable response to what had occurred: the financial scam, with the perpetrators bailed out, while the innocent had to struggle through the ensuing recession. But while the ideals and spirit may have been wonderful, a movement must be sustainable if it wants to effect changes.[15] I need to reiterate that the 'occupy' people were predominantly political, while those in Santa Cruz, who accept all of Baccala's pronouncements, are apolitical or even anti-political. They have his priority, which is the spiritual, but he follows spiritual values into their political consequences in the world, and they don't. They have plenty of empathy but its not channeled into the political, which they disdain.

2018 Harper's Magazine.
   [15] See the interview of Daniel Cohn-Bendit by Claus Leggewie in New York Review May 10, 2018.

My encounters with New Age types occurs at my natural food store. While it is a 'coop' its still what we would call a commercial enterprise. It's interesting to me that it serves as a center of activities, while being neither a religious building or a political hall. Judging by the posters and notices put up the range is Yoga, Tai chi, Meditation (mostly Hindu origin), some occult, Bahai, Sufi, and self-identifying New Age. With the books and music you'd expect. Only extremely local political concerns ever receive any attention. Yes they're against Monsanto and fracking. And they regard Trump as a beast. But that's only because they heard he pulled out of the climate accord and promised more coal mining, he shovels fast food and soft drinks down his gullet and is a cartoon of a rich smarmy pig. But Baccala's concept of a nation state embodying the 'Lamp of Enlightenment' would have no traction with these dropouts. (And if you told them the agents you had in mind were Americans most likely they'd look at you like you'd lost your mind.) They would be open to individual-to-individual influence that could cross boundaries. New Age belief does have a universal component. But I don't think they'd subscribe to the idea of any political unit - any country - or religion for that matter, being put in charge of carrying out such a program of spreading the spiritual light. It's too doctrinaire. Their concept of the realization of the truth (a 'dawning') would be more like something that when the time's right there's no resistance - no contention. It just happens, becoming an obvious fact, universally apparent to all.

Lately Baccala's gotten into judging societies based on their treatment of women. Which of course is a totally legitimate standard, but you must forgive me for suspecting that it's being wielded to knock down societies he's prejudiced against, as he gets to pick which surveys to highlight. One he uses comes from the International Women's Travel Center. Their list of the "Most Dangerous Countries for Women Travelers". 1) Turkey 2) Russia 3) Venezuela 4) Egypt 5) India 6) Mexico 7) Saudi Arabia 8) Kenya 9) Columbia 10) Brazil. This allows Baccala to get on his soapbox, "I'm for multiculturalism when speaking of tolerance and respect. But what do countries as diverse as Mexico and India have in common? Traditions that allow the males to be strutting brutes, no better than animals. We all know about the primitiveness of India, but Mexico City had to dedicate commuter buses strictly for women due to the incorrigible harassment from macho males."

He also uses the "Women, Peace, and Security Index" from the Institute of Oslo, with this introduction: "There's no surprise, the worst are Muslim and African nations. Syria, Afghanistan, Yemen, Pakistan, Central African Republic, Congo, Iraq, Mali, Sudan, Niger, Lebanon, Cameroon and Chad." The best are European countries with Singapore and Canada mixed in. He doesn't mention it, but even though American women rank high on 'inclusion' and 'justice', the US falls to 22nd out of 153 because they 'aren't safe from their intimate partners'. But alternatively the same year this came out (2017) the World Economic Forum came out with their list of "The Best Countries for Women" which carried some surprises. Included in the 10 best were Rwanda, Nicaragua and the Philippines. Israel only comes in at 44. The US at 49. Other notables are Mexico at 81; Indonesia at 84; Brazil 90; China 100; India 108; and Turkey 131. Now it is true that the very worst again roughly correspond to Baccala's rogues gallery: Egypt, Jordan, Morocco, Lebanon, Saudi Arabia, Mali, Iran, Chad, Syria,

Pakistan, Yemen. I think he avoids this list not only because Rwanda, Nicaragua, and the Philippines rate among the best, but because in their 10 worst Iran comes in fifth from the bottom.

When terrorism was at its most virulent Baccala's observations were always interesting because they were so unpredictable. I mentioned how delighted he was when bin Laden was discovered in Pakistan, 'in the pit of the Great Snake'. But long before that he had argued that any contemplation of capturing bin Laden alive was absurd. There was nothing in his mind or soul to be discovered. No conscience. The same for Khalid Sheikh Mohammed. The only thing our prolonged torture of him by water-boarding accomplished, like our shipping prisoners off to 'black sites' to be tortured by despotic allies, was to besmirch our reputation. However when it comes to Ayman al-Zawahiri, supposed #2, but according to Baccala really always #1, his capture was a different story. He had a mind, and a soul and a conscience buried beneath all the hate. Baccala speculated that it was possible the hate came after Egyptian guards used dogs to rape him - one of their practices. Zawahiri knew deep down that murder was wrong. Moreover he was well aware that by sponsoring Abu Musab al-Zarqawi, the godfather of the Islamic State, they had licensed a criminal psychopath. And unlike bin Laden that would eat at him.

While I might agree with him if we were simply talking about the distinction between individuals, with Baccala there's the uncomfortable inference that this isn't individual, but an ethnic judgment. He can say "the country dirt poor, unwashed, uneducated, with the lowest religious understanding, can be counted on in Iran, Turkey, Pakistan and Egypt to vote for tyranny." Of course bin Laden was educated. It doesn't matter because he was a Arab. Khalid Sheikh Mohammed doesn't matter because he's a Balochistan Pakistani. Whereas Zawahiri does matter because he wasn't just an eye doctor, he's Egyptian. It all comes down to 'breeds'.

When I first began contemplating the direction of my graduate studies, before I decided to narrow it to American history, I read a lot of European history. And one day I was reading Helen Waddell on some early church controversy. It pitted St. Jerome against some poor fellow I'm afraid I've forgotten. It was over some question of doctrine, and these were the days when the canon was being ironed out. It was point and counter argument, citation and counter citation. Jerome's line and logic were always strong, and he ended up eviscerating this opponent. Waddell duly reported the particulars and the result. But then she slipped in an added observation after Jerome's coup de grace. She said the mask slipped, and we could behold the unmistakable grin of hate. I was shocked, and impressed, that she would dare add this. It is what she saw, but there was nothing to gain by mentioning it, and a lot to risk. Jerome was a saint. The man who gave Western civilization the Vulgate[16]. Jerome's views were to become the church's doctrine while his opponents got dismissed in history as heretics. Yet Waddell felt an obligation to go beyond the forensic facts. I remember thinking that's the kind of historian I want to be. Not the careful coward, always aware how any controversial comment might negatively affect his career.

---

[16] Whose Latin, as Baccala puts it, "Would be the *magic language* that the priests know and the people don't. That the churchmen could use for over 1,000 years to further their 'We know God's truth, and rites. You can't. You must obey.' The division of priests and people."

As a student of American history what fascinates me about Baccala are the times he choses to be discriminating, and the other times when he decides he's not going to bother. If, as seemed the case, the election of Trump at first pleased him, as Tenace told us the election of Menachem Begin in Israel did, we presume its because the result confirms his supposition that given the choice a people rotting chose rot. Greed for 'mine', hate for the 'other'. But even if we granted that Begin and Likud were evil, and this was understood in Israel before the vote, which I doubt, it's still a failed parallel to what happened in America. Which we could evaluate by reviewing Baccala's own categorizations of Reagan, the younger Bush, and Trump. Aka Hollow Man, Hollow Boy, and the Empty Balloon. By his definition, these three wouldn't qualify as evil. They barely exist. Referendums won by phantoms amid blinding ignorance can't be used as evidence that the 'Dog People' now hunger for evil. We don't blame specters for being specters, and a population that votes for empty specters may need aid, but they don't need an exorcist. The modern president Baccala assays as evil, Nixon, was devious. So if Nixon deceived the electorate with his posturings & slogans that may say something about our credulousness or shallowness, but that's a different test than a population consciously choosing evil.

The fact that you're smarter than everyone else doesn't mean you're always going to be right. But I think Baccala has given into the temptation of that assumption. He couldn't accept my criticism of his book, sure I was just another historian protecting my turf from an outsider. But it would dawn on most people reading his book that he started with scapegoats and intended that the story he told would prove all his contentions correct. To write real history you have to be willing to look at everything. Even those things that undercut your thesis. If in pursuit of your preconceptions you disregard discordant facts, and reserve to yourself all prerogatives, it's not the fault of groupthink or negative critics that your argument got stranded. You never addressed the opposing factors - and they weren't hidden.

Let me be blunt. I accept as true what Baccala asserts, that most Americans don't want to think about the Vietnam War. This doesn't mean they're covering up, or rationalizing war crimes and mass murder. It's a natural response that falls into the normal range of avoiding things that are complicated and unpleasant. Something similar applies to the 'Dog People' who voted for Trump, including the ones staying with him through thick and thin. Maybe they can't see through him; maybe they do see his flaws but are willing to put up with them as long as he sticks it to the liberals. None of this tells you "everything you need to know". If a performer is empty and corrupt, that doesn't mean, much less prove, that those who mistakenly applaud him are empty and corrupt. But that is Baccala's implication. Baccala speaks of 'arrogant error', well that is an arrogant error. You'd have to examine, individual by individual, their lives, their interactions with others, to hazard any guess about their character. You may be disappointed with the direction the country has taken - "inviting the looters in" - I certainly am. That doesn't allow you to condemn and dismiss millions of your fellow citizens "as beguiled by the satanic siren song extolling the inhuman and predaceous".

The world is full of complicated subjects: botany, hydrology, chemistry, geology, structural engineering, chess, weather systems; that have exegetes coming forward to explain these disciplines to non experts. There was nothing stopping Baccala but he quit. If a subject can be made interesting, presented with clarity and insight, intelligent people will flock, curious to know more about it, and they will enjoy the process of learning. Instead of sulking Baccala could have gone that way, even exploiting videos and/or podcasts to reach people. The universe we live in is naturally interesting. What is more involving than a theory about life and existence? He could have added to his *signs* the movies' computerized special effects, video games with players around the world, trading of photos, and the promise of virtual reality. But with Baccala it all had to be on his terms. He pulled back, falling into self-pity and bitterness.

He laments that the 'New World' had all the portents to be the staging area on the way to the real new world, but the people succumbed to many of the character problems of the Old. (Maybe because they were human?) He finds something seriously wrong with our people; then something seriously wrong - in different ways - with everyone else. He writes off the young, he writes off the old. Whatever his teaching limitations are there is nothing wrong with his writing. Yet after he had moved to Santa Cruz he essentially stopped trying. With the exception/exclusion of that very narrow bandwidth of followers in a town of 64,000. Even counting them, all it brings to mind is 'settling for less'; of one satisfied to be 'a big fish in a small pond.'

Recently I was given this beautifully illustrated book about Gregor Mendel[17], father of genetics. Here was an individual who didn't start life with two

---

[17] "Gregor Mendel" by Simon Mawer Abrams 2006

elite teachers as parents. Or have the best tutors in the world coming to his home to instruct him. As the son of a poor farmer the only way he could get any education at all was to be contracted over to the Dominican order, even though he lacked a religious aptitude. By every account he was a wonderful teacher, but because he stressed out whenever it came time for him to pass his own teacher exams (he had nervous breakdowns), he was never able to get credentialed. His whole life he labored under the title of substitute teacher. As a scientist he never received any recognition. All of Mendel's meticulous work, his list of incredible discoveries, were brushed aside during his lifetime. If you know his biography you might interpose that he too became bitter in the last decade of his life. But that had nothing to do with the scientific community failing to grasp his breakthroughs. Though he lacked ambition the other friars had elected him abbot. What brought him low were official duties, most notably endlessly protracted battles over taxes with the Austrian government. Not simmering resentment at being overlooked. He didn't lash out at colleagues or students, much less at all of mankind.

Mendel was aware of the significance of his work, its implications, of what he had proved. At his own expense (or more accurately at the abbey's), he printed up copies of his findings and sent them out to all the leading scientists of his day. The man had figured out the whole system of inheritance. Including the ratio of hybrids – for several generations. The concept of dominant and recessive traits - that was his discovery. That traits exist independently. Inheritance is exactly equal from mother or father. That Darwin was wrong when he contended that you couldn't fertilize a plant with a single grain of pollen – Mendel did it. The whole concept of a controlled experiment, so essential to the modern scientific approach, came from Mendel. He died completely unrecognized, his work ignored. My point is that he never stopped reaching out to inform others. He never quit.

You'd think with all his pontificating about different nationalities Baccala would want to check things out for himself, not rely on "prefab reports of biased and arrogant journalists". If for no other reason than to see if his caricatures resemble the real thing. The Russians are slaves. Has he ever been to Russia? Not as far as I can determine. The Chinese too are slaves. Has he ever been to China? No. He might well say I don't speak Russian or Chinese so there's no point. You get a translator. Someone you trust. You walk around get a sense of life, of the people. Maybe find an intellectual, even a dissident on your wavelength, and hear their insights. What about 'Catholic-Oligarchic-Death-Squad Latin America'? Has he ever ventured there? No. He hasn't even been to Mexico. How hard would that have been?

I've been lucky. I've been able to do a good deal of traveling. Some teaching related, some simply following my curiosity. While it is true, as Baccala says, that Americans are 'hard-working', they are not alone. Among the many things I've learned is that foreign people, often those Baccala deprecates, work extremely hard. They may not end up with a lot to show for it, materially/economically, but that doesn't take away from the effort they put in. The countries he visits, going by his columns, are all Western European (Eastern Europeans are like Southern Italians: 'innate fascists'). There is more to the world. It's easier to say Arabs have no minds and Israelis are vile racists if you never bother to visit and meet the people. The same with Africa, Asia, Southeast Asia, Pakistan & India.

Even though he characterizes colonialism as a PC whipping boy, "South Sudan is finally free, so whose fault is it that they can't stop killing each other?" he will speak of its horrors in the past. Working African slaves to death in the Americas. What the British did in Bengal. Or how they deliberately addicted the Chinese to opium so they could offload their crops from Turkey. Or the French behavior in Algeria. But its curious that the same man who asks why Israelis & Palestinians are front page news while millions die in the Congo unnoticed, never refers back to the crimes Belgium committed in the Congo a hundred years ago. A death toll estimated at between 8 to 10 million[18]. Now I guess you could argue that the King Leopold II privately owned the Congo, so it wasn't a state crime but a personal one. But he never visited the Congo, and the campaign of atrocities carried out in that Hieronymus Bosch hellscape relied on many other Belgians, primarily soldiers. Why doesn't he bring this up? If we're going to condemn Germans, Turks and Americans for murdering others; Russians, Chinese and Indonesians for murdering their own; why isn't a slaughter of 8 to 10 million worth noting? The argument can't be that Belgians were like the Imperial Japanese, 'part noble savage', hence partly excused. I presume the reason is no more complicated then that he likes Belgians. So let's act like these great crimes never occurred. As Spain being fascist for 35 years or Italy meddling in the Balkans, Turkey and North Africa; oddly escapes notice and is never deemed relevant. We know his blatant favoritism goes back to the CCS

---

[18] "King Leopold's Ghost" by Adam Hochschild Houghton Mifflin Co. 1998

years, and probably before. Baccala faults others for lacking 'considered reflection' yet never examines his own partialities. A challenge on any particular is discounted with a shrug. It's only a personal opinion. ('Opinion', that convenient Parmenides double-edged sword: defensively a lesser level of reality; but assertively an essential part of finalizing Creation.)

I remember studying the McCarthy period, late 1940s to early 1950s. How smugly some of my classmates looked down on those individuals who 'named names'. As if there were no circumstances that could ever get them to 'rat' out former friends. Easy to say in a free academic environment, but when your career – your livelihood – hangs in the balance, not so easy. Factor in the human ability to rationalize any conduct that serves our interests. The same lesson applies to Nazi Germany, when everyone in a safe place distanced by decades from the terror imagines that they would naturally belong with Dietrich Bonhoeffer, risking martyrdom. When the majority of us actually confronting such a situation, asked to chose 'Eastern Front or the concentration camp' would chose the Eastern Front. Not because we're Americans - or Germans - but because we want to live. A similar rule applies to the American South. To think if you were born into a White family in the age of slavery or Jim Crow, that you would see through the prejudice, and chart an independent course, is fantasy. Again the vast majority of us, raised in a family to see racial and class differences a certain way, would see them that way. Not because we were genetically wicked Southerners, but because indoctrination works, and we're human.

Luigi Baccala has never reconciled two personal axioms that he's held from the beginning, and that he still holds today. His categorization of all ethnic groups into breeds, with behavioral programming from birth that a few individuals might escape, but the group as a whole can't overcome. The second axiom concerns his conviction that history (and this universe) must end with a worldwide enlightenment. The 'New Age' transcendence. To a simple person like myself these propositions collide. They can't both be right. One has to be wrong, and I'd prefer that it was the unbending breed behavior.

I am forced to stand by my review. You can't use American history as a prop to work out personal grievances. The reason the United States didn't turn out the way Baccala wanted isn't because soulless villains were waved back into the house to release poison into the innocent and dumb. Nor that the elect, who should have been vigilant, turned out to be pathetic suckers (with Lincoln as a saintly sap).

To his credit Baccala did attempt to communicate with his first two books, and they were scorned. To me they're (unread) classics whose value is yet to be determined. But with "The Draw of the Future", supposedly on metaphysics, he altered his approach. He had said a lot of existential and post-modern (mostly French) 'texts' hadn't served a rational function, but an atmospheric one. That might serve as a precedent I suppose, but I think a more plausible explanation would be that it was a twisted petulant strike at all readers for missing the importance of his earlier efforts. Guess what, readers resent indecipherable incoherent verbiage, terms thrown about in play only to have their applications and meanings withdrawn. Even by low academic expectations this was (deservedly) a bomb from which he's never recovered. He hasn't repeated that stunt, but everything afterwards has been polemical. Whatever its putative subject: education, environment, culture or sociology; they're simply a framework within which to rant. (I would even include the novel, "Lesson Plan for the Manikins". The worst passage there has his alter ego professor at a concert disturbed that there are 'too many Asians in the string section'. Exactly like Wagner perturbed at Jewish musicians: 'this isn't *their* music.') All are excuses to harangue from slightly different angles. Likewise "Cross of the Christlike President" was not written to correct a misunderstanding about the past. The motivation to write it came from present circumstances. It's one more attempt to force us to see ourselves the way Baccala sees us. The only thing that would satisfy him now is if we condemned ourselves, threw ashes on our heads, and repented our unworthiness.

As I said I take my responsibility to NNQR readers seriously. Stating that Baccala's propositions are not substantiated doesn't make me an apologist for whatever mistakes Lincoln might have made; for quitting Reconstruction too soon; for the onset of the Gilded Age; Wilson's racism or unconstitutional measures; anything Southerners or Conservatives do; or people still defending what we did in Vietnam. I had to confine my focus to reviewing the arguments in his book. Finding many of the selections and connections to be slanted and misleading. Done with an obvious premeditated purpose. That was my honest (and yes professional) response. Intemperate scapegoating is simply not acceptable in a work trying to pass itself off as history. I would have been negligent not to call it out. On the other hand I hope this profile of Luigi Baccala fulfills my original intent, which had been to introduce his thought to readers.

www.ingramcontent.com/pod-product-compliance
Lightning Source LLC
Chambersburg PA
CBHW030410030726
47497CB00002B/557